Mules, Knaves, and Close Shaves

Mathew W. Weaver

This book is a work of fiction. Names, characters, places, and incidents are the product of the
author's imagination or are used fictitiously. Any resemblance to actual events, locales, or persons, living or dead, is coincidental.

Change comes in one way or another to the life of every man. However, when Alan Daele, a rut-stuck travel agent, finds himself whisked away to another world seconds after what's probably the last shower he'll take for a long while, he's about to find out that change just might be a tad overrated.

Dragged into a world so bizarre, it's almost normal; having only his towel as his garb and a razor his weapon, he's forced on a Quest to – of course – defeat an evil Tyrant. After all, for what other reason could he be here in the first place?

With uncanny companions to guide the way, he's also supposed to defeat said tyrant by unleashing the powers of Rock, Paper or Scissors… just because that's apparently how things are done here.

With no one he can trust and a price on his head... come what may, all Alan can do is keep moving forward.

For all he knows, that's his only ticket home.

Chapter 1

When there's a story you want to tell, how do you choose at what point to start it? Sure, you launch at the beginning, obviously, but that's just the problem now, isn't it? Where is the beginning? Figuring out which event set off the chain of reactions in question isn't always that easy.

For me, though, for this particular story, well... it's not that hard at all. I know exactly when this whole thing began, because none of it was my fault at all.

It all began on a day like any other, when the god-awful alarm jarred me to consciousness that morning with all the subtlety of a landmine to the ear. I wasn't in the best of moods, as one never really is, seconds after being forcibly yanked back to harsh reality at six in the morning with a full day of paperwork ahead of them.

"Honey."
"Unghrrwr."
Oh, mornings. Always barging in too soon, unwanted, uncalled for. And then there was the

dastardly herald, the clock still chirping with sadistic glee, the cheerful tone a drum in my ears.

"Honey."

"Gonswerfive more minish," I insisted. I squeezed my eyes shut and sank deeper into the covers.

Of course, it didn't help. The clock kept chirping, as it always did. And likewise did my wife's encore.

"Honey,"

"Alright, alright," I moaned.

I propped myself up on one elbow and blinked. There it was, the fiend, buzzing on the dresser conveniently, of course, out of reach. I grunted, stretched and yanked it towards me. Up close and personal, the infuriating tone hammered home the nail already halfway through my skull.

"Honey," Mona whispered again.

"I'm doing it, I'm doing it," I mumbled. I raised my fist and let it hover as I groggily took bearings. I released. I felt impact.

There was Silence.

Blessed, beautiful Silence.

I closed my eyes tighter and stuffed my face deeper into the warm, soft pillow. The sheets were cozier than I had ever known them and the pillow... oh the pillow. In all its nights of faithful service, it had never felt this good.

I cut the anchor and began to drift off again. The dream was around the corner, somewhere... I couldn't remember it, I knew I wouldn't, but I was going to try and see…

"Honey."

My eyes scraped open. There was pain. There was agony.

"*Now,*" I whimpered, "WHAT?"

"You don't want to be late again. Remember yesterday."

I sighed and turned around to stuff my face into my soft, warm pillow.

"Scrooyeshtideh."

"Honey."

"Five moh minish."

"Honey."

It was gone. Over. Not coming back.

"Alright, alright, I'm GOING."

Hands balled into fists, I pushed myself up and balanced on my arms, prepared to roll over the side.

"Hey, Alan," she added, turning over, "Don't forget the dry cleaners."

My suit. The wedding anniversary. The dinner we'd planned months ago and forgotten till just that moment, halfway out of bed on a bleak Wednesday morning. There's nothing like a ray of sunshine at the end of a dreary day to convince one to get out of bed in the morning, and with that to boost me up, I quite agreeably pushed off and toppled over the edge of the bed.

I couldn't be blamed for not wanting to go to work; I was twenty-five, with four years of my career as a travel agent stuck tighter in the rut than the stick up my boss's rear. To be honest, the prospect of getting fired didn't bother me anymore. Heck, I'd even welcome the vacation.

The freezing water went to great lengths to ruin my mood again, and the pile of paperwork on my desk since the evening before returned to haunt me as I chased the soap around the inside of the tub.

Still, I had to count my blessings. For instance, it was a blessing there was actual running water in the apartment so far; and from the state of the rest of the building, it was a blessing we didn't fall through the floor on the way to the kitchen.

Funny I should put it that way.

Roughly twenty minutes since I'd hit the floor groaning, I stepped out of the shower with towel wrapped around my waist and dripped my way over to the sink. Of course, I was fully aware of how Mona would give me an earful for it when I returned, but I couldn't be bothered with my mood the way it was. Besides, it gave me dark satisfaction after her atrocious behavior this morning to see the vision of her mopping it up in my mind's eye.

That image still in mind, I wiped the steam off the mirror and stared into a more depressing one: my bloodshot eyes. Horns blared and tires screeched, the sounds shoving their way through the tiny window to entertain me with their tidings. Another day of crowded streets and sardine packed subway trains, claustrophobic office cubicle and stacks of paper no one ever looked at.

Today was not one of those days, though. Today was different. Tomorrow may be back to the grind, but today was going to end with just Mona and me, a romantic and yet affordable incandescent bulb lit dinner at that place three blocks away. Today, I could get away from the monotony, and go back to when it all used to have meaning… for at least a couple of hours. It was something.

And today, I noticed, I needed a shave.

Shaving cream lathered over my face and my razor dripping and ready for the slash, I felt the need to yawn and stretch. Why, I probably will never know. Perhaps my body somehow sensed what was going to occur next and tried to get a last yawn out before too late. It probably also saved my facial muscles the wear and tear of having to open my mouth all over again to scream later on.

See, I'm not sure how exactly it happened. But looking back on it, what I remember was one second I was standing on slippery wet tile… and the next, I wasn't. The reason why was because, simply put, there was no tile anymore. Or floor either, for that matter.

I was, purely stated, standing on air. It was the moment when I was still in mid yawn with my arms stretched and the towel straining around my midsection when the epiphany finally hit.

Today was definitely going to end different, and something else told me things were about to go downhill very fast.

Quite literally, and very fast. In fact, I wasn't standing anymore. Gravity had shown up, and now I was falling.

Hence the scream.

And then, I landed.

Hard.

If I'd spun around and done a few twirls on the way down, I didn't remember; all I was processing was pain. I was on my back, spread eagled, feeling like I had just fallen off a three story building. I blinked, and my vision slowly came into focus just in time to notice a great big pink bat fluttering above me.

My towel.

Which wasn't around my waist, where it was supposed to have been. Which also meant there was nothing around my waist anymore.

I groaned and slowly sat up, my spine screaming bloody murder and my head throbbing in agony. Above and to the left, my towel gave a final flap and fell gracefully in a crumpled heap a couple of feet away, conveniently out of reach.

So there I was, sitting in my birthday suit in an immense dark room at the foundations of our ratty apartment building. That towel was needed.

I tried to stand, but my left elbow buckled and threw me sideways onto my face. It was when I involuntarily jerked my head up and spat feathers out of my mouth that I realized something wasn't quite right.

Feathers.

It was a pile of feathers I was on, a hundred tiny poking points on my bare flesh that I hadn't noticed amidst the other, more immediate pain taking dominance. I picked up a handful and let them fall slowly.

The heap wasn't even more than four inches high. In all fairness, I should have had multiple fractures or be dead, whichever was more painful. Not that I was complaining, but… physics.

I managed to clamber to my feet the second time. My limbs seemed to be more or less in working order, I noticed. I took a tentative step, and a gust of wind down under reminded me of how my first priority was still the towel.

Falling goodness knows how far down to land in some forgotten basement was appalling enough; doing it naked was asking for trouble. After all, there could be eyes on me that very minute, and I hadn't been hitting the gym as often as I'd have liked for the last few months. Many months.

I limped and shuffled through the feathers, and when my bare foot touched cold stone, I shivered violently. I bent down to pick up the towel and missed. Standing again, I breathed in and steadied myself. On the third try, I managed to grab it, and with a groan of triumphant agony, I pulled it up and draped it back around myself as quickly as my stiff fingers allowed.

The battle won, I finally steadied myself for a look around.

It wasn't dark, but it wasn't very bright either. I couldn't see where the light was coming from; it was as if it was being faintly reflected off the walls or something of the sort. I could make out the color of my hands and the floor for about ten feet ahead, but beyond was all gloom. The walls could have been just beyond there or miles away and I wouldn't know the difference.

I craned my head backwards to look up at the hole I'd fallen through.

Or rather, I tried to. There was no hole where there should have been a hole, which did not make sense, since even in that murky darkness, I should have been able to have seen at the very least a pinprick sized glimpse of our bathroom's stained ceiling.

Instead, it was just gloom and darkness extending out for as far as I could see. Excuse the irony there. Wherever I was, it could have been the size of a broom closet or a football stadium and there was no way to know which. Till now, my brain had been too busy running system checks after the fall to be bothered about being afraid; but then it was at this point when I remembered Mona and I lived on the third floor.

My sluggish, confused mind finally got around to shifting to panic gear.

If my woozy calculations were correct, I should have fallen right through the lousy apartments beneath our lousy one to land in the one-could-only-imagine-how-lousy basement.

Except that this didn't feel like any basement I had ever been in, lousy or otherwise.

I raised my hand to my head and swayed slightly. I didn't remember hitting anything on the way down, which was odd, since there had to have been the floors of the apartments beneath ours. A busted floor just in front of our sink wasn't all that unbelievable, to be totally honest; but a direct link to the foundations of the building? Some things aren't supposed to happen, and as far as I could tell, this was one of them.

My mind snapped to that very frightening fact like a rubber band: I had fallen three floors. It had certainly seemed like three floors on the way down, of which I was faintly certain. I was still more or less alive, with bones only *feeling* like they had been broken, especially after the only thing to break my fall was a heap of feathers barely four inches thick.

My mind raced to put together the variables and come up with a coherent answer, and with a few seconds of pain which might have been either a headache or signs of a fractured skull, it did.

I was dreaming.

I breathed a sigh of relief. This was a dream, and a rather lucid one, considering.

I shrugged and cracked my fingers. I knew just what to do. Squaring my shoulders, I spread my arms, bounded forward and then leaped high, striking my best Superman pose.

If I did fly, it didn't last very long. I landed hard on my elbows, and it was far, far too painful to have been a dream.

"YOWCH!"

"Welcome, Champion. Verily, thy arrival beith fortuitous indeed."

The voice was deep, awe inspiring, and had come from directly behind me. Prone on the ground with my bare chest freezing against the stone, I froze, very aware of just how undignified a position it is to present oneself butt-first to someone else.

"'Fortuitous'? You zapped him here, you pompous goat."

The second wheezy voice couldn't have been more of a contrast to the former Morgan Freeman version without having been female. As it was, it prodded me to scramble to my feet and spin around, which I very much needed right then.

As it happened, I hadn't been alone after all. Standing before me were the Grim Reaper and an old, rheumatic Ebenezer Scrooge.

"YAAAAH!!"

"Hello to you, too." Scrooge… whatever his name was… replied, rolling his eyes. Short and balding, the only bits of hair on his otherwise shiny bald dome were the tufts over his ears, which might have explained the scowl I had a feeling was his expression when relaxed. He wore what looked like a flowery purple dressing gown, and leaned on a thick piece of wood with no distinguishing features other than the fact it looked thick enough to clobber one over the back of the head with and not leave a mark.

On the stick, that is.

Hunched, scowling, bald… he looked like… well, an old, wheezy Scrooge.

And next to him: the Grim Reaper, minus the scythe and in Halloween costume. Assuming Death swapped black robes for green on Halloween and wore classy deep green gloves that looked sinister yet so… cool. Death was eight feet tall, and both terrifying and stylish.

My heart pounding in my ears, I took a couple of steps backward, just to keep some distance between me and the stick and those gloves. My bare heel landed on something hard and sharp, and I hopped forward again with a second involuntary yell.

"Excitable, aren't we?" Scrooge observed.

"Who," I asked, choosing my words with care, as I balanced precariously on one foot, "the… *hell*… are you?"

There was a shallow gash on my heel. I'd stepped on the blade of my razor, the same one I'd been holding just when I'd fallen. Shaving cream dripped off my chin and onto my cold, bare chest.

"I'm the translator," Scrooge said, with an impatient shrug, "And this here," he waved a hand at his significantly taller companion, "is Eduud, Summoner of Champions and the Granter of Choices and blah, blah, blah-betty blah. There we go, meet and greet done. Let's just get this over with."

"That made absolutely NO sense," I said, putting my foot down and gingerly taking another step back, "What are you doing, squatting in the basement? Seriously, there had to be better dumps than this out there."

"You're not home anymore, kid," the translator said, scratching at one wobbly jowl, "And we're certainly not squatters."

"What do you mean I'm…?"

Words failed me, and all I could do was swallow. For want of some kind of action, I lunged at the ground, grabbed the razor and brandished it at them. As fierce as I hoped my expression was, inside I cringed. As if there was any possible way I could have harmed them with it.

"Where am I?" I demanded, pointing the razor at the old man, and determinedly keeping my eyes away from Death.

"You're going to find out soon enough," the translator said, clicking his tongue impatiently, "Can we begin, already?"

"Who *the hell* are you?" I repeated, panicking freely, "And this time, English would be nice."

The old man closed his eyes and shook his head.

"You're up, Eduud," he waved a hand.

The Green Reaper spread his arms, his emerald robes rippling like water.

"Welcome, Champion," he boomed.

The sinister cowl stood fixed, like it had been carved out of rock, and I probably wouldn't have been able to catch a glimpse of the face underneath in full daylight, let alone this darkness.

And speaking of darkness… with a jolt that yanked my stomach down to my knees, I realized the faint light in the room was coming out of *him*. His… its… robes glowed a soft, warm green which somehow lit up a little ten foot circle around him.

Where had he been when I first landed? Invisible?

Before I could say a word, the robe pulsed and the color lightened. Maybe I was hallucinating, the fall probably having knocked me silly. Or maybe I was dead, and was about to go to hell for sending that couple to France and their luggage to Korea last month.

But Eduud was definitely glowing.

"Thine arrival beith at the most opportune of moments," he boomed, the bright green waxing and waning as he spoke, "For nigh cometh the time whence thine people wouldst calleth upon thine talents for the good of all."

"Nice of you to drop by, good timing, we've got a job for you," the translator interrupted in a dull drone. He leaned forward on his stick, the expression none too happy on his face. From the looks of things, he was expecting to be standing there for a while and didn't seem too pleased with the prospect.

Neither was I.

"Evil hath returneth," Eduud continued, "and into peril plungeth the realm."

"A bad guy showed up, and we're, as you would probably put it, screwed."

"'Evil'?" I echoed. "He said evil. Evil is never good."

"Nice to know you're familiar with the basics, son."

"Wilt thou, Champion, taketh up arms and defend thy people from tyranny?"

Arms spread wide, Eduud's cowl finally shifted. He was looking right at me, and I felt goosebumps spread like wildfire.

"This," Scrooge said, "is the part where you say yes, and we move on."

He inclined his head at me.

"Say yes to what, exactly?" I asked, uncomfortably.

"Wilt thou, Champion, taketh up arms and defend thy people from tyranny?"

"Say yes to *that*," Scrooge jerked his head.

I brandished the razor at them again.

"Alright, wait, hang on, now…"

"Wilt thou, Champion, taketh up arms and defend thy peoples from tyranny?"

Eduud's voice had grown perceptively louder. My heart was jackhammering in my chest. Bad enough tension was building, worse was I still didn't have a clue what in the world was happening.

And to top it off, I was still sleepy, darn it.

"Hurry along, kid," Scrooge snapped, "we're on schedule."

"I… no… look," I said, pointing at him, "I have no idea what in the…"

"Wilt thou, Champion, taketh up arms and defend thy peoples from tyranny?"

I wasn't imagining it; the color was brightening.

Scrooge sighed and shook his head.

"Look kid, there are no two ways about it. The only answer you have is 'yes'. Eduud has a nasty habit of fixating on things till he's satisfied."

"Wilt thou, Champion, taketh up arms and defend thy peoples from tyranny?"

Scrooge nodded at him, "See?"

"Alright, STOP!" I threw up my hands and took a step away, wincing as my cut heel stung. I glared at Scrooge with as much ferocity as I could muster, and at that moment, I had plenty to spare.

"Look, I don't know who you are or what this is, but I'm late for work already and if I…"

"Wilt thou, Champion, taketh up…"

"Enough already!' I said, raising my voice, "I want to know…"

"Wilt THOU, CHAMPION," Eduud bellowed, his form literally swelling, ballooning up to terrifying proportions as Scrooge took a casual sidestep away, "taketh up ARMS and DEFEND THINE PEOPLE from TYRANNY?"

The voice slammed into me like a thunderclap, the power so palpable I almost sat on the cold tiles again, bare skin and all.

"Sir, yes, sir," I squeaked, all the fight drained out of me, just like that.

Scrooge chuckled, "Warned you, didn't I?"

"Then, Champion," Eduud said, thankfully shrinking to his originally eight feet, which was already intimidating to begin with, "I now charge thee to seeketh out the Armament and defeat the Tyrant that hath arisen."

"You have to find the weapon and defeat the bad guy," Scrooge intoned, "Preferably before he defeats you. Any questions?"

I swallowed, "What just…?"

"To aid thee in thy Quest, Champion," Eduud interrupted, "I offer thy Choice of the Powers Three. Choose, as thou wouldst…"

"Sorry, son." Scrooge said. The end of his walking stick began to tap on the ground, soft, fast beats that could have betrayed anxiety, " We're pressed for time. Questions later,"

He hastily limped aside, making way between the three of us as Eduud spread his arms again. The man… it… had a taste for the dramatic.

"Behold!" Eddud proclaimed, "The Strength of Boulders!"

In the space between us, a foot tall flickering projection of Dwayne Johnson's long lost brother popped into life. The thing gave me a dirty look, and then started to strut and flex muscles which would have flipped a car over without breaking a sweat.

A similarly proportioned car, of course.

Dazed as I was, it took me a few minutes to process what I was seeing. There was a bodybuilder no taller than my knee sauntering in the midst of us where there had definitely not been a knee high bodybuilder sauntering before.

"How did...?!"

"The Wisdom of Pages!" Eduud boomed.

With a soft pop, a second figure appeared. This one wore white robes and had a sagely beard dangling down to his waist. There was a second pop, and with it came a pile of tiny pieces of wood and other debris settling at his feet.

"W-what are those?" I stammered, "H-holograms?"

Scrooge gave me a smile.

"Watch," he said.

The tiny bearded person threw a look of utter condescension at the tiny bulked person. The latter smirked and flexed his beefy bicep, and in reply the former crouched at the pile of rubbish at his feet.

A few heartbeats later he stood, and trundling along at his feet was an even smaller miniature medieval catapult-thing, with the throwing arm and all.

I was dreaming. I had to be still in bed. Any moment now, the alarm would ring….

The barbarian noticed the tiny contraption and bent over to have a better look as it rolled right up to his feet. Nothing happened, and he began to guffaw, his voice hilariously high pitched and wheezy.

Then the arm snapped forward, and a stone the size of a marble sailed up and caught him right between the legs.

My own hands moved instinctively to my crotch as he doubled over in minuscule agony. The lethal little arm swung again, and this time the marble hit him between the eyes. He went out like a light, falling comically and landing with a crash which made the tiny images shudder.

"Harsh," Scrooge commented.

My heart went out to the little guy.

"The Skill of Blades!" Eduud proclaimed.

This time, I wasn't as surprised when a third figure appeared. This one drew a thin sword out of a sheath at its side and commenced twirling it around like ninja. The scholar/engineer/old smart guy bent down again, but before he could even begin, the other thrust his sword through him and drew it out again in the blink of an eye.

"Harsher," Scrooge said, conversationally.

The scholar clutched at his wound and fell with theatrical slowness. He began to vanish slowly, disappearing to nothing by the time he'd landed on his back. The little catapult collapsed and vanished with him.

Triumphant, the swordsman started twisting and flipping his sword again, in the most pure and satisfied manner imaginable. He didn't notice as the barbarian behind him sat up, shook his head, and climbed back onto is feet.

The swordsman turned just as the barbarian crossed over to him in two steps. A beefy fist connected with smug face and smug face flew backwards and right out of the image.

The barbarian raised his arms in celebration, and without further warning, he vanished.

The show was over, and my jaw was dangling a few inches off the floor.

"What…" I whispered, "Was THAT?"

"Visual aid," Scrooge replied.

"Choose well, and heed this warning," Eduud boomed, "Only once shalt thou recieveth this choice. Should thou Chooseth unwisely, swiftly shalt thine doom follow."

"Choice?" I sputtered, "Now I have a choice? Great, I choose to *get the hell out of here and back to bed!*"

"All the trouble we go to and you don't even pay attention," Scrooge snapped, annoyed, "Kids these days will be the death of me. You have to pick one of those three to use to complete the Quest with. Come on, it wasn't so hard to figure out."

"But… but…" my knees started to wobble and I racked my brains, searching for something to say.

There was a sign hanging on the door of my creative department which read 'Out to lunch'.

"What Quest?" I finished, lamely.

Scrooge sighed in exasperation and passed a hand over his forehead.

"A real winner you picked this time, Eduud," he groaned, then pointed a gnarled finger at me.

"Look, kid," he said, "This isn't fun and games. You've been Chosen, you have a Quest to complete, and there are things out there ready to rip you limb from limb. You get to pick one of these three, though a fat lot of help any would do a buffoon like you. You might as well ask Eduud to kill you now and save them the trouble."

Later on, several choice replies came to mind. For example, there was the "I just fell down a hole with no explanation. You don't get to threaten me!" and the "If you don't let me get back up there, I'll have you arrested for manhandling."; also, brought to you by the part of me still believing this to be a dream: "You think you're tough, Eduud? Come at me, bro!!"

Right then, though, like it always happens, all I could think of to say was, "Uh. Okay."

Scrooge shrugged and spread his arms, "Go on. Choose."

"Uh… um…"

"It's not so hard," Scrooge waved his hand. "Only life or death."

"What happens if I choose wrong?" I demanded.

"Well, you fail the quest," Scrooge shrugged, "And usually when that happens, you die. And... not going to lie to you, kid, but it's not going to be pretty either."

I swallowed.

"Choose!" Eduud boomed.

I ran a dry tongue over my dry lips.

"Uh... um... I choose..."

I didn't.

The floor shuddered, and an explosion somewhere off to my left sent a wave of force which knocked me off my feet. My head slammed against stone.

"Oh crud," Scrooge said, his voice unsettled, "They found us,"

"WHO DARES...?" Eduud demanded, turning to face the disturbance, his size expanding again.

"Who found us?!" I moaned.

The ground was shuddering under my ear, trembling and bouncing in a rhythm somehow oddly familiar. Light, golden yellow light was pooling into the chamber, and it was coming from a large hole in a wall probably fifty feet away.

I squinted, but the light blinded me, and I couldn't see anything beyond the jagged aperture. What I could see, though, were three columns of shadowy figures marching toward us.

I understood why the vibrations under my ear were so familiar. I'd heard it on TV countless times: the sound of a marching army. And this army was starting to form up in two lines, a corridor from the hole to us. More kept pouring out through the hole, and the lines kept getting longer.

And closer to us.

"Who are they?" I yelped.

"They don't matter," Scrooge muttered, "*He's* here."

"Who?!"

Scrooge turned, and his eyes disappeared under his bushy eyebrows in a scowl so full of ferocity, it made Eduud look normal.

"THIS is why we told you to choose!" he barked.

"I'll choose!" I exclaimed, scrambling to my feet, "I'll choose!"

"Too late," he snapped, "Stand behind me and keep quiet."

The lines of soldiers reached us, and I finally had a good look at them. To my half blinded eyes, they were all identical, and they were all bizarrely dressed in what had to be armor from a King Arthur movie, with metal helmets, swords in belts and small, extremely lethal looking crossbows held at attention in covered in metal pieces.

My mind optimistically chose that moment to suggest for the umpteenth time how this had to be a dream. After all, I had just taken a shower in my own bathroom barely half an hour ago and I had the towel, the razor, and a few patches of shaving cream left to prove it.

The last soldier marched into place, both lines ending ten feet away from us. Without a word, they all spun to face the narrow lane that the two columns had formed.

The sounds were too loud, and the pictures were too distinct to be a dream. But…

The soldiers shifted and stood at attention. And out there, the blinding light began to dim, like something big was getting in its way.

"Yep," Scrooge muttered. "It's him."

"Courage, Bass," Eduud said, his deep voice still sounding powerful enough to send tremors down my spine. But even so, his voice was lowered.

If Eduud, the Summoner of Whassis and Conjurer of Tricks was afraid of whomever it was now stomping towards the hole from the other side…

The ground shuddered again, and then a large shadow completely blocked out the light. I heard Scrooge… Bass… breathe in sharply.

"Behold, Champion, the lackey of thine enemy," Eduud said, "I shalt gather for thee the time thou shalt need to seek the Armament and join thine allies."

With the light behind it, all I could make out was the silhouette of whatever it was now climbing through the hole. No one needed twenty-twenty vision to know that it was stomping toward us, though. More importantly, stomping towards *me*.

"What?" I demanded, reasonably distracted.

"He's going to sacrifice himself to save your sorry behind," Bass said, cracking his knuckles.

"What?!"

The silhouette looked human; at least, it had two arms and two legs. But this thing was nine feet tall, and as it trudged towards us, it looked thrice my size around the middle. And it was getting closer.

"Take a good look, kid," Bass said, now shrugging his shoulders, "There's who you're going to have to kill soon enough. And he's just the lap dog."

"Are we going to f-fight?!" I stammered, crouching behind the old man.

Bass turned around to look at me.

"You?" he scoffed, "Like that? Why don't you just hand yourself over and be done with it? No." He looked at Eduud. The Summoner's robes had changed color; bizarrely, they weren't green anymore, but purple.

The lap dog was three quarters down the human corridor. As I watched him stride towards us, dominating the room with his sheer presence, I felt pretty darned lucky I'd emptied my bladder not too long ago.

"Hail, Summoner," he rumbled, his voice as deep as Eduud's and much, much nastier, "I see you've managed to find your Champion."

"Prepare thyself, Bass." Eduud murmured, crossing his arms.

With the light from the hole blinding me, I still couldn't see more than the immense size and the dark outline of the person who I had to kill, but it was enough to tell me I'd bitten off more than I could chew at an all-night buffet with me the only guest of honor. Which was ironic, since all I wanted to do that morning was sign another stack of forms and send another couple to somewhere they would probably regret hours after landing.

Maybe it wasn't irony, after all. It was probably just deserts. And here I was, on the brink of death, making food puns.

"Come out here, Champion, so I can take a good look at you," the guy boomed.

"Thou shalt not set eyes upon the Champion this day," Eduud said, "But I promise thee, When his sword pierceth thine black'nd heart, fiend, thou shalt look upon the face of the Champion thou seekest."

"I did not come here to fight you, Summoner, but I will if I have to," the shadow replied, "So step aside. I have a Champion to maim."

Eduud spread his arms, and the magenta exploded outwards in a dazzling halo. The soldiers at the front of the two rows buckled and fell, and the immense lap dog yelled in pain and stepped back with a log sized arm across his face.

"FLY, BASS!" Eduud's voice bellowed.

"Come ON!" Bass yelled, spinning around and sprinting past me, faster than you would have expected a geezer like him to have run. His fingers closed on my wrist, and before I could react, I was being dragged behind him, away from the others.

"AFTER THEM!" I heard the voice roar, "DON'T LET THEM MAKE THE JUMP!"

"What jump?!" I yelled.

"Jump!" Bass bawled.

And, just like that, I was falling again

Chapter 2

"Wake up, kid."

I jerked awake, and the first thing that made sense was my right cheek was stinging. I blinked, and then realized a pair of thick, ugly, gray caterpillars hovered inches in front of me. I blinked again and watched them transform into eyebrows.

Not an improvement.

Memory returned, and I recognized those eyebrows, and the sunken eyes, creased face and the jowls that went with it. My bowels spontaneously flushed themselves down to somewhere near my ankles.

"Finally," the old man grumbled, letting go of my shoulder, "A minute more and I'd have conked you on the head and seen if it would have helped any. Tom's good at waking 'em up *and* putting 'em to sleep."

All hopes of it having been a dream turned to dust.

I tenderly raised my hand to a cheek now starting to grow numb.

"Did you just slap me?" I demanded, the injustice of it doing away with the remains of my stupor.

"Repeatedly. And here I thought 'having thick skin' was just an expression."

He turned and limped away, completely ignoring my look of bristled, righteous anger. I sat up and drew breath, but I forgot about composing my cutting retort when what he had said finally caught up and prodded me from behind.

"What's 'Tom'?" I demanded.

His back still to me, he raised his walking stick and gave it a wave as if in reply.

My head presented me with a tremendous throb, and I touched cloth wrapped around the top half of my skull. My chest was still bare, and the towel was now muddied heavily at the bottom.

"What's your name?" he called.

"Now you decide to ask?" I muttered, "Alan."

He shrugged, "Can't keep calling you 'kid' all the time. At my age, everyone's a kid."

I sat up and looked around. I was on a makeshift bed with a frame looking like it had been nailed together out of thick, uneven branches, and a moldy mattress stuffed with something prickly which sent a shudder of revulsion ran down my bare back.

That, and a very piercing itch up and down my body.

Also in the small wooden room was a DIY fireplace and what looked like an old boiler stove, along with a crude chair and a small table at which Bass stood tinkering with his back to me.

That was about all the furniture in there with us, but the room was far from empty. Wherever I looked, I saw bags and bundles and boxes of all sorts of things stuffed anywhere there was space. Nets of potatoes and onions and other bulging, colored fruit hung from the rafters low enough to just brush the top of Bass's head. Boxes and sacks of bits of scrap metal were piled haphazardly against the corners.

Bass wasn't in his dressing gown anymore. Now he wore some brown robe sort of thing, the sort Friar Tuck would love to have in his collection.

"Where are we?" I asked, scratching my shoulder.

"Safe house," Bass replied.

"How… where…" I jabbed the heel of my palm into my forehead, trying to remember.

"The robed guy…" I said, "That room…"

Bass froze and turned around to give me a look of contempt.

"'Robed guy'?" he repeated, incredulous, "He saved your life and that's your expression of gratitude?"

Something in his voice told me I'd committed the most grievous wrong a man could afflict a fellow, never mind I'd just been kidnapped out of my own bathroom before breakfast without warning by the said fellow and just woken up in a shanty with no idea where in the world I was.

The same something also told me I had better apologize for whatever it was I'd committed. After all, the last thing you wanted to do when waking up in a stranger's bed in that stranger's house and seeing the same stranger standing a few feet away with a stout walking stick was to insult him.

"I…" I cleared my throat, "I… didn't really mean…"

"Doesn't matter," Bass said briskly, "Eduud conjured up a portal and sent us here. He stayed behind to stop them from following you, to buy you the time you needed to prepare yourself. We're doomed, that's what we are," he muttered.

Things seemed as good as they were ever going to get, and time seemed to have slowed down enough to stand around and talk. I recalled the last thing I remembered before I had woken up here.

"I remember falling," I said, "Is that what you mean by…?"

"Yeah, that's what Eduud's portals do," Bass said, reaching up for one of the nets by his head. He poked his hand inside, rummaged for a moment, and then drew out two slimy purple things which he dropped into whatever was in front of him. I heard a soft splash.

"Then… then…my bathroom… the hole…"

My eyes widened and understood, even as I scratched at a burning spot on my side.

"There we go."

"The hole I fell through? That was a… a *portal*?"

He turned around, his exasperation plain.

"Now, do I really need to answer?"

"But... why?"

He shrugged and turned to the table.

"Look, old timer," I said, jabbing a finger at him, while the others dealt with an itch on the back of my neck, "You don't get to be rude. This portal thing's as crazy enough to handle on its own as it is. You dragged me here without a moment's consideration and you've been insulting me ever since and... and... look, it's not been a nice morning for me, alright?"

Bass turned around and raised an eyebrow.

"And?" he prompted.

"And..." I blinked, thrown off, "And... I want to go back. Right now. I have nothing to do with whatever it is you have going on here, and if I'm pretty sure I just got fired, thanks to you. So help me, I've had enough. And while we're at it, why you brought me here in the first place would be nice to know."

"Didn't take long, did it?" Bass chuckled. He leaned against the edge of the table and crossed his arms.

"First things first," he said, with the air of a teacher laying the rules in an unruly class, "We didn't want *you*. But you're what we got, and so now we're stuck with each other. This would be one of those times where you make do, as they say. If it's any consolation, we're not particularly jubilant with the whole deal ourselves, so there's how it stands."

His words cut like barbs.

"Second. You accepted Eduud's call, and..."

"Whoa, wait," I interrupted, raising my hand, "I did *what* now?"

"You answered yes to the question," he said irritably, "So…"

My head throbbed again and I struggled to remember. A vision came to me: a hood, a loud booming voice, a mantra as annoying as the tone on my alarm clock: "Will THOU, CHAMPION…"

"I only said yes because the two of you *forced* me to!" I exclaimed, "That doesn't count as anything!"

"You still said it," Bass replied curtly, "And as far as anyone is considered, it's as good as a deal signed in blood. Don't blame you, kid, there really wasn't anything else you could have done. Once you're brought in, there's no returning till you've finished the Quest. It's the reason you're here."

"And where is here?"

"In relation to where you're from, I haven't the faintest clue."

He turned around and started messing with what it was on the table again.

"Yours is another world, I would imagine," he said over his shoulder, "Only Eduud has the power to open a portal there. He never talks about how he does it."

"How do I get back?" I demanded, scratching my chest.

"Once you finish the Quest. Once Mugatu is dead and we're all normal again… or at least as normal as it can get here these days. You need Eduud before you can have a portal, kid. And they managed to capture him. The only way you're going home is by letting him go, and the only way to do that is to defeat Mugatu. The math's simple."

"There has to be someone el…"

"There isn't," Bass turned around and limped over to me, a wooden bowl in his claw-like grasp. He shoved it into my hands and walked past to the opposite wall, opening the door to a cabinet I hadn't noticed among all the bundles.

"Eat," he ordered, rummaging inside.

I examined the bowl with a healthy amount of skepticism. A thick, brown sludge filled it three quarters of the way, and the spoon he had stuck in the center pointed straight up. I pulled it out with a faint pop and poked tentatively, uncovering a lump of something which gave a faint wiggle before descending into the glutinous depths.

"What is this?" I asked warily, using the bowl to scratch the back of my hand.

"Tastes better when you don't know," Bass replied.

My stomach rumbled in need even as I felt something acidic rise in the back of my throat. The smell wafting up out of the bowl wasn't far too appetizing, either.

"Haven't you anything else? Like… bread, or something… you know… edible?"

"That's all we have here and probably all you'll have for the rest of the day. Don't knock it till you've tried it."

My stomach spoke up again in his favor. I looked down at the brown sludge and, shuddering, I plunged the spoon in and drew out a thick lump of whatever it was. I closed my eyes and opened wide.

"As they say," Bass said a few moments later, limping past me as I retched on the floor, "It's an acquired taste."

I wiped my mouth and scowled up at him through watery eyes.

"You… you tried to *poison* me…?" I demanded.

He chuckled in amusement and bent down. Even though he held the bowl sideways as he picked it up, his vile concoction was viscid enough to not spill a drop.

"Can't see why you're complaining," he said. He grinned at me and took a long slurp out of the side, then wiped his mouth and held it out.

"It's delightful."

I looked away, "I'll pass. Thanks."

"Suit yourself," he said, tossing it onto the table, "Mind you, you'll be hungry enough on the road. Meat and eggs aren't what they used to be since Mugatu's men started looting around the countryside."

"The road? Where are we going?"

I climbed back shakily to my feet.

"You want to go home. We want to get rid of Mugatu," Bass said, "The sooner we complete the Quest, the sooner you can leave."

"And how long is this going to take?"

Bass paused and sighed.

"A few weeks. A month." He shrugged, "Not going to lie to you, kid, but…"

"A MONTH?" I bellowed, "You can't keep me here for a MONTH!"

"A month, or six, or a year, it doesn't matter," Bass replied dispassionately, "You're not going anywhere till Mugatu's been done with. It's out of anyone's hands, kid."

"Tonight's our anniversary!" I yelled, "I have to… I have to…"

A bucket of ice water couldn't have had a stronger effect on me. My mind went numb, my knees banged against each other, and I fell onto the bed.

"You can't do this to me," I moaned, "I have to go back. She was looking forward to it."

Bass didn't reply.

You know all those flowery descriptive phrases which go somewhere along the lines of 'wave after wave of emotion crashed through him' or something similar to describe that certain kind of reaction? Well, right then I figured out firsthand what exactly it meant. Countless feelings rose up and began to fight for dominance inside me, and all I could do was just sit there and let them, too weak to offer up my own opinion.

There was shock, enough to turn my arms and legs to jelly, there was anger, enough to make me want to tear frail old Bass Scrooge apart limb from limb, there was despair that made me want to lie down, hug myself and cry for a long, long time… and more than anything else, there was fear.

Mona… *my* Mona. She stuck with me through all the debts and all the damp, dirty apartments, all the lost jobs and all the disappointments. She probably still didn't know I was missing. To her, I'd be at work right about now. But then the weeks would go by, and then the months… and then the police would probably give up…

And it's times like these when your mind starts churning out the worst possible scenarios in your head. For instance, police arresting her for the murder of her missing husband. Fast forward to a judge banging a gavel going "Guilty!" and a freeze frame of her with her hands gripping the bars of…

"Isn't easy, kid," Bass said, and it was the change in his tone which forced me to look up at him. For once, he didn't seem like cranky old Scrooge anymore. If I didn't know better, I'd have said it was sadness I was looking at in his eyes; regret, even.

"I… I'm sorry. It's not your fault you were dragged into this. But if there was anyone anywhere who could do what had to be done to save us now, it's you. That's why you were picked."

"But why me?" I asked, and even to my ears as I spoke, it sounded incredibly corny.

"Because only you can finish it," Bass replied, either not noticing the cliché or ignoring it. If he even knew it was a cliché in the first place.

He looked at me keenly, and supplied me with a cliché of his own.

"You're their beacon now, kid, whether you want to be or not. You're their hope."

I closed my eyes and twisted a knuckle into my temple

"Some hope," I muttered. I shook my head and looked up at him again.

"If I finish this, do I go home?"

Bass paused.

"If you survive," he said, tentatively, "Yes."

"Hold on right there," I stood up, "What do you mean, 'if I survive'? Why does that sound like there's no guarantee? Didn't you say I was the only one anywhere who could finish this?"

"You are the only one who can finish it," Bass replied, "If you don't, no one else will. We'll all be doomed for a while. It could happen."

"You're saying I could die?"

To his credit, he didn't flinch or look away.

"Yes."

"And I have to do this anyway if I want to get back to Mona?"

"Yes. Whoever that is."

"She's my wife," I said, torn between anger and raging despair, "There's nothing else that can be done?"

Bass rolled his eyes with a sigh, "No, there isn't."

I felt the fury boil and simmer in me. I didn't try to stop it.

"Screw you, old man," I growled, "Just… screw you."

"Whatever that means, I probably deserve it," Bass said. He tossed a bundle of cloth at me.

"I left your razor at the table," he said, "Bring it along with the thing you're wearing once you've changed. You'll need them."

"Wait… how do you know what a razor is?" I demanded.

Bass smiled an old man's crafty smile, "I know quite a few things, kid."

He turned around, and I had a feeling it was the only answer I was going to get. I wasn't happy, and I didn't think I would ever be at that point. But there was nothing else I could do but get it over with, and fast.

I straightened out the bundle and held out one of the three pieces. It was a sort of sleeveless vest, made of rough, scratchy cloth with a simple hole to stick my head through. Another was a pair of pants, of the same, muddy brown material, with a thin rope threaded through loops on the waistline like a belt.

And the third was a dirtied cloak, identical to the one he was wearing.

"Made these yourself, did you?" I commented sourly.

"While you were dozing. They should fit. Probably."

He didn't seem to be joking, that much was certain.

"There's a lot you need to know, and the plan's been messed up more than any of us expected it to get," he said, I pulled the vest over my head, "And we weren't all optimistic to begin with. At the very least, we'd hoped you'd have Chosen by now. With Eduud gone, that's a slim chance. Mugatu planned well."

"About the choice thing…" I began, scratching at my arm.

"We can talk about that on the way," he said, rummaging in one of the bundles in a corner, "Doesn't matter now, you didn't Choose. Makes the whole thing much more difficult, I admit."

"You said Eduud was captured," I said, starting on the pants, "How do we know he isn't dead?"

"Eduud isn't dead," Bass replied confidently, "He's a Base Spirit or something of the sort, part of the Old Commands. Been here since near the beginning. Still lots to him I don't know, and I doubt I'll ever find out. Base Spirits keep to themselves, and you'd be lucky if one ever decided to speak to you, let alone call you a friend."

He noticed my vacant expression and sighed.

"What anyone needs to know is you can't kill him," he said, jamming a random tool into a sack for emphasis, "You can hurt him, imprison him, drain him off his powers, maybe. But you can't kill him. And they don't need to."

He looked at me, "All they have to do is to keep him away from you till Mugatu finds you. Once he does, and if you're not ready by then...'

He sighed again and shook his head.

"Who am I kidding," he muttered. He gave me a look as I stood there, feeling like a monkey in a cage full of ants as I scratched at every part of myself I could reach.

"We need to leave here as soon as we can," he said, turning away, "His spies would track us here sooner than later. I was never meant to come with you, kid. You're supposed to do this on your own. But we have no choice. You're unarmed, you didn't make the Choice, and you're weak and stupid... to send you alone would doom us all."

It's always nice to know how random strangers have so much faith in your abilities.

"Hey, watch it," I warned, even as I strained to reach a spot on my back.

"Since I'm coming with you, I can tell you all you need to know as we go along," he continued, lugging a second full sack to the door, "But we need to go. We spent enough time here already. Take that sack, and bring the cloth and the razor with you. Keep that razor in your pocket at all times, kid. Never leave it out of arm's reach."

I held it up for inspection. It was a new, slightly worn, double bladed disposable razor. There was absolutely nothing remarkable about the thing.

"Why?" I asked.

"Explain later," Bass called over his shoulder, "Just never leave it behind. Ever."

I shrugged and slipped it into my pocket, and then realized something else.

"Hey," I called, "You don't expect me to walk out barefoot, do you?"

Bass jerked his thumb. I followed his gaze to a pair of large, brown leather boots on the floor by the wall.

"You serious?" I demanded.

He rolled his eyes and left.

I swore under my breath as I grabbed and tugged them on, and then with my towel rolled up under my arm, I followed him out.

We stepped into what could have been the setting of an old farmyard tale; there stood the little paddock, with the dirt track leading from the front door into the distance, the plains stretching out with trees sprinkled here and there. The skies were blue and the clouds were fluffy, and I still couldn't believe how this was all not a dream.

And the noise.

There wasn't any. At all.

No bustling pedestrians, no honking cars, no ringing cellphones, no smoke... I could go on and on. I took a step out, feeling dirt crunch under my boot, a sound I couldn't remember when I'd heard last. It looked all homely and sleepy, and not at all the kind of place that had to do with portals and Choices and what not, but definitely nowhere near what a rundown apartment complex in the dirty city would look like.

For the first time since I'd landed on the pile of feathers, I felt like maybe the whole deal may not be so bad after all.

Ahead of me, Bass was striding purposefully, the walking stick in his hand. He reached the paddock fence and turned to me.

"Behold, Champion," he said, turning and waving an arm, "Your noble steed."

I looked. The steed looked at me. Clearly, it felt just about as impressed with me as I was with it; which was to say, not even a little bit.

"That…" I pointed, "That's a donkey."

Apparently taking offense at my observation, it responded by snorting, pointing its rear in my general direction and letting loose in a trumpet of flatulence.

It took a few milliseconds for the aroma to drift over, but when it hit, it hit strong.

"Aye, and there's another acquired taste," he commented, knowingly, "The first time is always the hardest. And, well, the second. And the few dozen times after, to be honest. You'll probably never get used to it, I suppose."

Eyes watering and nose on fire, it took me a while to recover fully enough to stand again. I gripped the railing and hauled myself to my feet.

"Look, old timer, I'm no expert," I said, cautiously watching the animal aimlessly saunter away, "But that is not in any way a steed."

"Nor is it a donkey," Bass chided me, "It's a mule."

It passed another toot to punctuate the clarification.

"That's an improvement?"

"Look at the bright side. It's white."

This much was true. Apart from being about as high as my shoulders, extremely well fed and as fragrant as a fetid dumpster, the creature was pure white.

"It's an albino. How is that a good thing?"

He held up his hand in reply. Dangling on a long loop of string was a small, wooden tube. I recognized it as a whistle after a couple of seconds.

"Carve that yourself, too?"

"He comes when called," Bass said, "And believe me, that will come in handy."

"Why would I ever want that thing to come near me, anyway?"

The mule pricked its ears, and snorted.

Bass sighed.

"Look, son, the Quest budget's been dwindling over the years. The King just had to have a new palace aqueduct built last year, and a few months ago the Queen just *had* to have it branch off into a sauna…"

"This time, you're definitely joking."

"Mugatu had been scheming and building power for a while now, but none of us knew it was going to be him. We didn't prepare like we should have. What you see before you is the best we have."

"Knew it was going to be him? Prepare? Hang on… did you say quest *budget*?"

To say I was incredulous would have been akin to stating the mule was at the peak of equestrian manners.

"Is there… are you saying that… there was some sort of *prophecy* about him and me?"

"Err… in a manner of speaking," Bass said guardedly, avoiding my look, "Anyway. Mugatu didn't openly start razing the villages till after the budgets were approved. And you know how it can be after that… the paperwork and all."

I stared hard into the left side of his creased, grayed face as he pointedly ogled hard at something conveniently far way, but I couldn't make out if he was joking or dead serious.

"Paperwork? And there's a King now?"

"There's been one for a while. And there definitely won't be if Mugatu has his way. Trust me. If you think it's bad now, you haven't a clue what it could be like if he's in charge."

I eyed the mule with considerably justifiable apprehension. I'd never seen one in the flesh before, much less ridden one. A horse would have been brutal enough, but this… this was just embarrassing.

Either it was psychic or its bowels had incredible timing, but it let rip again just as I had that last thought.

"I'm not going to have to ride that gas tank, am I?" I asked, eyeing it apprehensively.

Bass chuckled, "Consider yourself lucky the gas tank doesn't trust you yet."

"Oh, it's mutual."

"We'll be walking for a while. He'll be pulling the wagon."

"We have a wagon?"

"One of the few things we do have, count your blessings."

I scratched unconsciously at a burning patch on my shoulder.

"Alright, so where are we going?" I asked.

Bass smiled, "You'll see, kid. Let's move."

Chapter 3

That had been three days ago.

The road seemed to stretch out forever, not unlike narrow corridors do in old horror movies, and the heat waves rising off the ground everywhere I looked made it seem like we were underwater. In water nearing the boiling point, I might add, if it hadn't already reached there already.

It had been two nights of sleeping on the wagon out in the cold with bugs as lousy company, and we still seemed to be in the middle of nowhere. We'd stopped in only one small town since we'd left, and Bass had kept me under the hood of my hot, heavy cloak all the time we'd been there.

I'd never have admitted it to Bass, but maybe I'd been enjoying myself just a little bit. I'd been waiting for a change, and fate had delivered, and in no small way, either. Maybe this was fate's way of giving me a one-off for all the crap I'd had to deal with over the years.

Bass and I traveled for hours at a time in silence, which was perfect for me, since all I wanted to do was listen. The wind, the hooves, and the *nothing*. It was beautiful.

As long as I didn't think about Mona waiting for me back home, that is. Wondering where I'd gone, why I hadn't come back, if I'd been hurt or kidnapped. And then my job; I was as good as fired now, and when I got back, I'd have to hit the streets for a new one.

But till then, I could relax and enjoy the moment as best as I could.

The mule plodded on, meandering about from one side of the road to the other, but generally keeping to the path and moving more or less forward. I'd learned the malodorously hard way that there wasn't any use trying to coax it into going faster. The term 'stubborn as a mule' was not to be taken lightly.

The damn thing was strong, though, I had to grant it that. When in the right mood, it pulled the wagon along like it weighed a little less than the average bale of hay. The trouble, I found, was getting it into the right mood in the first place.

And then there was the wagon itself. A more uncomfortable mode of transport I had never encountered, and mind you, this was coming from someone who took the subway to work and back at rush hour every day.

There were two ways open to me as to how I wanted to travel. The first was, of course, the wagon, and not only did it come with bumps, shakes and permanent earthquakes while trying to sleep at night, it also meant I would be at the mercy of the mule and its personalized air conditioning every so often.

The other way was to walk. And there was only so much of that I was able to do at a stretch.

For all the urgency Bass had displayed at the safe house, you'd have thought he'd be spiriting us across the countryside in no little hurry; but here, as I plodded on alongside the wagon with the ridiculously enormous and extremely foul smelling straw hat pulled low over my head, I could hear one of his snores reach its highest crescendo yet.

For three days now we had been trudging to where probably only the mule had the slightest inkling to. The weather was all Bass spoke about when he did speak at all, in between naps lasting hours and puffs of whatever he used in that aggravating pipe of his.

If his training solely included my feet fighting off sores, he was failing miserably.

Under the horrible hat, in those itchy, smelly clothes, with my parched mouth and rumbling stomach, I wasn't in the best of moods when Bass finally yawned and stretched somewhere in the afternoon.

"We reesh taow yet?" he mumbled.

"What?"

"Town. We there yet?"

"Is that it?" I pointed at a hazy lump in the distance.

"Aye, that'd be it."

Bass dug in one of the bags and brought out his old, cracked pipe again. I fumed silently as he struck a match and stuck the pipe between his teeth.

"You should be enjoying yourself," he noted, sitting down and leaning comfortably against the side of the wagon, "I doubt the rest of the way would be as enjoyable as this."

"Enjoyable?" I sputtered, "You made me miss my anniversary!"

"Oh, this is enjoyable. You'll see in a couple of weeks," he drew in on his pipe and blew out, "when things start getting rough. This? This is nothing."

He burst into an explosive fit of coughs.

"You mentioned I needed 'training'," I said irritably, "These last three days been an example of that?"

"Do I look like a trainer to you?" he wheezed, "You were supposed to have Chosen. That would have given you everything you needed."

"Again with the Chosen thing," I complained, "Are you ever going to stop blaming me for missing it and tell me what in hell it *is* in the first place?"

"You'd know if you'd Chosen," Bass said. He coughed once more and cleared his throat.

"There are three… powers, for want of a word… a Champion can choose from. There's the Strength of Boulders, the Wisdom of Pages and the Skill of Blades. You saw them in action."

"I don't know what I saw."

He shrugged.

"Each one is better against one and weaker against the other," he said, "You saw Wisdom beat

Strength, the Blade beat Wisdom and Strength beat Blade."

"Like rock, paper and scissor, except it doesn't make sense," I pointed out.

"It would if you paid attention," Bass reached out and rapped me on the head with the bowl of his pipe. Even through the hat, it hurt.

"Hey!" I exclaimed.

"If you'd chosen Strength, you wouldn't look the same," he continued, "You'd still be just as stupid as you are now, but at least you'd be able to do *something* in a fight. Muscles and so on popping out all over you."

He looked me over and shook his head in disapproval.

"If you weren't an old man," I growled, "I'd show you just how much of a fight I could put up."

"First you couldn't wait to find out what the Choices are, and now you don't stop interrupting,"

"Then maybe if *you'd* stop insulting…"

"If you'd Chosen Wisdom," he plunged on, ignoring me, "You'd be… wiser." He chuckled, "Imagine that."

"How does wisdom beat strength in a fight?" I sighed, "That doesn't…"

"If you had any, you'd know," Bass inhaled, and broke into another fit of coughs.

"If *you* had any, you'd stop smoking before you drop dead halfway through this journey."

"Strength is brute force. Wisdom lets you plan your attack with whatever tools you have, any child could figure that out. Doesn't mean Wisdom always beats Strength, no. But there's an advantage, aye."

"Wonderful."

"The Blade beats Wisdom most of the time. Skill is usually faster, and you need time to think, don't you? Well, in your case…" he paused, and I saw what was coming.

"Don't even…" I warned.

"Strength beats the Blade," he continued, opting to pass over the insult for once, "If you'd chosen Blade, you would be able to use any and all weapons you laid hands on, provided you get a few minutes to hold onto it first. You'd be gifted, not the clumsy oaf you are now."

… and he dropped it in, anyway. I opened my mouth, sighed, and decided to let it go.

"Skill isn't strong enough to beat Strength, though. Not always." His brow furrowed.

"How many people have these… these 'powers', anyway?"

Bass looked into the distance, "A few."

Boulder, Page and Blade. As I scuffed aside a pebble and watched it sail into the grass by the side of the dusty track, it all clicked together in my head.

"It's a lot more like rock, paper and scissors than one-being-better-than-the-other-but-weaker-than-the-next, isn't it?" I commented, "Boulder is rock…

loses to paper - that's Wisdom – and crushes scissors, which here is the Skill of the Blade…"

Bass took his time answering, puffing slowly on the pipe.

"Whatever you say, kid," he said.

I contemplated this for a few minutes more. The sound of the wooden wheels crunching stones started to prick at me, and the fly which had been buzzing around me took another dive at my nose.

"So what now?" I asked.

Bass puffed on his pipe.

"Like you said. You need training," he said gruffly, "And we need help. On your own, we're both doomed."

"Great," I replied, "I'm going to assume that's my fault, too."

"There's no need to assume anything, kid. It is your fault," Bass said, as caustic as ever. "There's someone who might help us. He said he'd stand by if Eduud or I needed it. We most certainly need it now, so we're meeting him."

"Great," I said, the news lifting me up, "Finally. Someone I can actually have a decent conversation with. Where is this guy?"

"There," he pointed his pipe at the growing bulge of roofs, "Where he was supposed to wait for the next few days. Hope he's still here, though."

Bass fell silent, chewing on the stem of his pipe. I glanced at him and noticed the creases on his forehead seemed to have sunk deeper than they usually were.

"What's wrong?"

"He might have left when he heard how sour things turned," Bass said, eyes on the approaching buildings, "And even if he hasn't, I don't know if he'll join us. Not now."

"What?" I demanded, confused, "I thought you said…?"

"I said he promised to stand by," Bass replied irritably, "That was before he knew Eduud would be captured and…"

"…and I would miss the Choosing, continue."

"So you have been paying attention. Once he hears how you missed the Choosing…"

"You like to keep rubbing it in, don't you?"

"… he'd be smart enough to stay away. Only fools would want come with us now."

"And what does that make us?" I asked, knowing full well what he'd say, but not being able to help myself anyway.

Bass chuckled, and surprisingly didn't reply.

The mule finally meandered its way into the town, but this time I wasn't as happy as I had been the first time to get into the shade. Unlike at the settlement before, here I spotted flashes of steel in between the patches of coarse blue cloth, and shiny helmets I recognized from the last morning I'd woken up at home.

"Bass," I hissed, "Soldiers."

"I see them," he muttered, "No need to yell,"

He ducked his head as the wagon rolled in and glowered at one of the shiny helmets.

"This complicates things," he murmured darkly, "But can't say it wasn't expected. Keep your hood down and your face hidden. They don't know what you look like. Let's not give that to them."

"If I try hiding, they'd probably want to know why, anyway," I pointed out.

"Aye," Bass agreed, "But all they need is a look at your face and we're done."

The mule sauntered over to a water trough and dipped its head in. Bass nimbly jumped off the wagon and began to tie its halter to a nearby post.

"What's wrong with my face?" I demanded.

"Anyone searching for you would know to watch out for your eyes. Yours don't look like ours'."

"How not?"

"Do you really want to stand here and discuss this here, boy?" Bass asked, exasperated. He stumped off across the wide, muddy street, leaning on Tom as he went.

I followed him, my cowl pulled low over my face. I was wrong to think I'd stand out with my hood lowered; unlike in the last town, either a lot of people here had bad haircuts or had an uncanny aversion to sunlight. Cloaks and hoods roamed galore, and no one batted an eye at me.

And if they did, they batted them under hoods of their own.

The whole feel of this town was all wrong. The soldiers paced in twos on every corner, and the men outside glowered at them when they weren't looking. The tension was heavy in the air. The soldiers obviously weren't welcome.

And I had a feeling that from the soldiers' point of view, neither were we.

Bass stopped at the opposite side of the street and waited for me to catch up.

"He'd be in here," he said softly, jerking a thumb at the barely imposing structure behind him.

I gazed up at the cracked wooden beams, the broken windows and the chipped sign on the front with a crude, plain depiction of a mug painted on it. While probably every other place in this town was silent and dreary, bawdy laughter roared out through these windows, punctuated by what was unmistakably the sound of splintering wood.

Right next to the wide open door stood a burly, bare chested bouncer with the proportions of a full grown grizzly, his arms crossed and eyes fixed on a couple of cloaked figures just ahead of us.

"A tavern?" I laughed, "You have to be joking,"

He looked at me in genuine astonishment, which for Bass is a rare thing.

"What's the matter with it?"

I gestured, "It's... it's a tavern. This whole mess to me has been a role play of Dungeons and Dragons since the start. Rolled a three, and now our contact is in a tavern?"

Bass shook his head and stumped forward, pushing past the doorkeeper, who ignored him completely.

I shrugged, pulled my hood lower over my face, and stepped after him, only to bang nose first into a smelly wall with a thick coat of chest hair.

I tilted my head back and saw two chins and a frown hovering mere inches from my nose. The small beady eyes narrowed even further, and just as I thought I was going to get a can sized fist hammer me into the ground like a loose nail, the medieval bouncer stepped aside with a grunt and gave me just enough space to squeeze in.

I faintly squeaked and fairly ran into the establishment, which, frankly, it wasn't one of my better ideas. I banged face first into my second figurative wall, this one built up by bricks of stench: sweat, alcohol, blood, and with a mortar of that brand of acidity so often recognizable near poorly maintained public sanitation sites.

I was missing the mule already.

Like any old tavern you might have in your head or have seen in movies, this one was dim, reeking, stale and had tables and chairs placed in what might have been planned patterns when the proprietors laid them out early in the morning; hours since then, they now lived in a perpetual state of motion as the clientele constantly bumped them around in their frolics and used them very so often and quite efficiently to prove points. Wood chips and splinters were as abundant as drink.

The patrons were plenty, most of whom were considerably intoxicated, putting it mildly. No one person looked quite like another; there were all kinds of cloaks, armor and leather and bare skin as well as glints of steel wherever the eye fell. And even in here, quite a few still wore their hoods low and kept to themselves in the darker corners of an establishment murky enough to begin with.

Bass headed straight to the bar at the far end, and just as I thought he was going to order something we'd both regret far too soon, he turned and did a quick scan of the floor.

He apparently found what he was looking for and limped away way between tables as I reached him. Looking at his general sense of direction, I calculated him to be making a beeline for one of the tables in a corner, where sat another man with a hood drawn low over his face, a fact that hardly fazed me by this point. Like almost everyone else I'd come across, this one wore a patched and frayed brown cloak, which was all I could make of him in the bad light.

I pushed and slid through the tavern behind Bass, who seemed to make the crowds part around him like a curtain and close on me like a drunken bear hug. As I shoved through, taking an elbow to the head with a silent curse, something about the whole picture seemed out of balance in my head, as if there was a really important piece missing.

Before I could try to put my finger on it, a loud yell and a thud heralded the start of a bar fight right in front of me. The fists flew, the weapons were drawn and the men jumped in like an all you can eat buffet; and just like that, the portrait was complete.

After all, what's a good medieval bar without a good medieval fight, anyway?

I ducked a flying tankard, dodged a flying fist and just barely escaped being knocked over by a flying would-be participant as I hurried the heck out of there. Bass seemed to have forgotten I was supposed to be with him. He clumsily fell onto one of the stools, drew it closer to the table and leaned his head towards one of the girls who sidled over.

By the time I finally managed to join them, Bass was staring pointedly into space at right angles to where the other guy sat. He couldn't have been more obvious in trying to hide the fact he knew him than if he'd been holding up a sign.

I opened my mouth with a fresh complaint, but Bass cleared his throat pointedly and shook his head. I rolled my eyes and leaned back to let this little scene play out in its own time.

The three of us sat in silence. The girl came over with two tankards, slid one over to Bass and myself and sauntered away. Bass didn't touch his, and I wasn't about to lay a finger on mine. The stranger sat still, his tankard half empty but now untouched.

A full ten minutes later, he finally shifted.

"This him, then?" he asked, his voice low. Fully expecting another cranky old wheezer, I did a double take at the sound of his smooth, mellow tone. He couldn't have been older than I was, and that voice could definitely have not fit into that tavern right then with the ruckus still going on behind me.

"This him," Bass clarified to the wall.

Neither spoke for another five minutes, and by this time I was starting to doze off, even over the curses and yells I didn't fully understand, the latter of which was probably for the best. Just as I was considering whether or not to twiddle my thumbs, stranger spoke again.

"Doesn't look like much, does he?"

I decided right then that the time for pretense was over. With a scowl, I straightened up and pointed at him.

"Don't *you* start, now."

"Not the best selection we've had, no," Bass sighed.

"He's done worse before," the stranger mused, "Still, though. Even an idiot wouldn't point like that, knowing the stakes and the need for secrecy."

I glowered, but lowered my finger. The stranger nodded slightly, and reached for his tankard.

"You haven't heard the worst of it," Bass grumbled, "He didn't even Choose."

Halfway through a healthy chug, the stranger choked and spat out his liquor in a spray of fine yet foul mist.

"Here we go," I muttered.

"He didn't WHAT?"

And that seemed to be the end of the charade right then. But with the sounds of what was unmistakably heavy wood bludgeoning cracking bone over the screams behind us, I doubt anyone else heard his outburst, or was even looking over at us right about then.

The stranger slammed the tankard on the table and the hood turned to me. I couldn't his face except for the tip of a pointed nose, but intuition told me he wasn't smiling.

"He took so long trying to figure out where he was, he let the Dog catch up to us and break into the chamber," Bass said, rubbing it in like only he knew how to.

"Look, before we go through this again," I interrupted, raising my hands, "And God knows I've had up to my fill going through this... I know I messed up, alright? I didn't Choose, and now I'm doomed. Since there's nothing we can do about it, could we at least focus on what we *can* do? Please?"

Bass and the stranger exchanged their first glance since we had arrived.

"He doesn't realize it, does he?"

"I think he does understand... a bit," Bass said, "He just doesn't know how bad it could get."

"Very bad," the stranger said, looking at me.

"He's also right," Bass continued, proving again that he was just full of surprises, "We have to move on with what we have. Dwelling on the past won't help."

"What we have isn't much," the stranger mused, reaching for his tankard again.

"Which is also why we need you," Bass said, "More than ever."

The stranger had the tankard tipped over, and didn't reply till he'd drained it and wiped his mouth. He gave me another wordless, searching glance.

"You do know, Bass" he said, "that you're asking me to die?"

"What's the alternative?"

The hood shifted.

"What's the plan?"

"You're coming?" I asked, relieved.

"I never said I was," he replied, "I want to know what you're planning to do about it now that the Champion is… useless."

I opened my mouth to retort, but by then, I had had enough. My dignity was in shreds. Bearing Bass's blunt thuds was one thing, but this guy's insults cut deeper than Bass's words ever did.

I sat back and crossed my arms.

"Mugatu knows nothing of what he looks like," Bass said, "So there won't be a description of him out just yet. He also doesn't know the Champion hasn't

Chosen. Expecting the power, he would probably be cautious."

"So…" the stranger gave me his searching glance again, "We're going to train him?"

"If we can survive long enough."

"I have a name, you know," I interjected.

They ignored me. Sadly, I was expecting them to.

The stranger lowered his head and seemed lost in thought.

"I am Laehn , Champion," he said, looking up at me again, "And for the sake of the vows I made, I'll come with you and I will defend you… for as long as I am willing to. Beyond that, I promise nothing."

I don't know what I was supposed to feel, pride, confidence, or like a king with a knight swearing fealty to him for the first time. All I knew was I was too depressed to say more than, "Great."

"Just hope this idiot doesn't get me killed before I have to," Laehn sighed, effectively and unequivocally killing whatever moment there might have been.

"You and me both," Bass muttered.

We left Laehn behind and forced our way out of the tavern.

"He'll meet us outside town," Bass said, "We've done what we came for. Now let's get out of here as…"

"You, there! Halt!"

Bass froze in mid step, closed his eyes and sighed.

"Yes, you!"

I heard the sound of running feet and the jangle of metal that could have only been armor. The people ahead of us abruptly turned and walked away. No matter how much the locals resented the guards, we obviously weren't getting any help out of them right then.

My heart jumped to my throat and my legs started to tremble.

"Keep your hood down," Bass said, "Even if they ask you to take it off. They mustn't see your face. Let me do the talking and we'll get out of here."

He turned as two soldiers jogged up to us. I tugged my hood lower and peered out from under it as they reached us and stood stoically in our way.

One resembled a large, beefy upright pig with his armor straining at the seams, and his helmet bore a gold plume. This had to be a Sergeant or some sort of ranking official, because the other, who couldn't have been older than eighteen, looked sickly pale under his oversized helmet and kept trembling violently.

The trembles I assumed were probably directly attributable to the effort he was putting into holding up the hefty crossbow, the end of which was pointed nowhere in our general direction.

"Yeah, what do you want?!" Bass demanded.

"We've orders to look out for an old man and a companion," the older one replied, far less than cordially, "And the two of you fit the description. Drop the stick, old man, and you, put up the hood."

"Old man?!" Bass exclaimed, his voice taking on an edge of eccentricity I'd never heard before. He lifted Tom and waved it in a feeble display of outrage, and out of the corner of my eye, I could see a few people stopping and staring at us.

"Who are you calling old?" he demanded, "Accosting us in the light of day and insulting us to our faces?!"

The younger one blanched visibly under his large plumed helmet, but the older soldier either had a hardcore steadfastness to his cause or was far too used to frisking cranky old men in the light of day to care about making a scene.

"Take off the hood," he repeated, pointed at me, "And you, the stick."

"I… I have a condition," I moaned. I coughed into my fist for effect.

"Inherited. Off his mother's side," Bass agreed, "Very nasty, you'd rather not see…"

"Hood. Off. Now."

He drew his sword, and the younger one agonizingly leaned backwards, managing to bring up the tip of the crossbow in line with our knees.

"What would your mother say if she saw you now?!" Bass demanded, his voice so high, it almost went beyond cracking and smashed to smithereens. His ruse, if it even could have been called as such, was failing. People were losing interest and were moving away again, and it appeared to me like random old men acting up in the middle of the road was probably not as uncommon as all that in this day and age.

I didn't have time to feel depressed over that fact, though; the tip of that bright, gleaming sword was hovering inches away from my eyeballs, and it seemed prudent to remember I had other issues to worry about right then.

"Don't know. Roll in her grave, probably," the soldier answered. His eyes bored into mine, trying to see my face under my hood. I could have been mistaken, but right then, though, I could have sworn I saw a hint of worry in them.

"Lower the hood, or we will take you," he snapped, "Boy, sound the bugle."

The kid looked in shock at his officer and then at me, horrorstruck at the command. His already deathly pale face took on a hue of green; torn between holding the crossbow steady and reaching for the bugle at his hips, he stood vibrating in terror.

"What are you waiting for, boy?!" the man roared, "Sound the…"

Far too quickly for anyone to react, Bass swung his stick. It smashed into the fingers closed around the sword hilt, and the unfortunate owner of said fingers was quick to let his displeasure be known. His companion, already wound up tighter than a spring, yelped in shock as his superior bellowed, and released a crossbow bolt with a resounding thrum that sent up a shower of mud at the ground between his feet.

Bass swung again, this time at the man's face. Wood crunched against steel, and the soldier reeled away.

"What happened to secrecy?!" I cried.

"A little too late for that," Bass replied, grimly, "Run!"

Shaking like a leaf in a gale, the boy dropped the crossbow with what had to be colossal relief, drew his sword and then realized that he had jumped out of the metaphorical frying pan and into the metaphorical fire. Eyes skipping from Bass to me and back again, he stood there with it half raised, apparently not sure what came next.

I looked around to see everyone else getting the heck away from us. If anything right then could have made me feel worse than standing in the middle of the street in a town full of soldiers with one of their number lying at my feet, it was standing there with no one else close enough to blame it on.

Bass gave the boy an approving look.

"See?" he said to me, jerking his thumb, "Now if we had *that* kind of dedication from *certain* people we know…"

The downed soldier lunged for his dropped sword, and with a curse I hadn't a clue as to the meaning, he dove at Bass.

"NO!" I yelled.

I needn't have bothered, really. Faster than I thought he could ever possibly move, Bass parried the stroke and sidestepped. The soldier roared and swung again. Wood chips flew as stick and sword met again and again. Bass ducked low as the sword passed over his head, and slammed Tom onto one mail clad foot. Before the soldier could recover, he spun around, gathering force to swing it right into the side of his head again. I heard a wince inducing clunk, and the man crumpled.

The kid evidently decided on a plausible course of action. He dropped his sword, ignored his crossbow, dove under the nearest wagon and put the bugle to his lips.

Bass froze.

I stood there, stunned, knowing all figurative hell was about to quite literally blow loose.

He puffed up his cheeks… and blew.

The bugle warbled faintly, blown out with what sounded like his last, dying breath. If anyone had heard that, they had either pretty sharp ears or we were extremely unlucky.

A heartbeat later, an answering note fired off from just around the corner.

"Damn," I muttered, "are we unlucky."

More bugles were blown one after another, and over them I heard the sound of hoof beats. I'm no expert, but you didn't need to be a genius to know there had to have been more than a couple dozen horses right there.

"RUUUUN!!!" Bass bellowed.

Like I wasn't already.

The whole settlement was in uproar as we sprinted across the muddy road for the wagon. What the mule had over against horses I couldn't guess, but Bass seemed to have some idea of what he was doing, and with me as clueless as I was, following him was all l could do.

Loud clanking of metal armor echoed as blue trimmed soldiers spun around the corner and crashed into each other. The few citizens still out there in the streets ducked to find cover as the party roared and stampeded in pursuit, a cloud of dust rising behind them like in an old cartoon.

"We're not going to make it, are we?" I asked.

Bass untied the rope and climbed into the wagon with the agility of an ape. He looked at me in exasperation.

"Get in!" he cried.

There was nothing to it. I obeyed.

The mule took a couple of steps and then turned to glance at the soldiers, now less than twenty feet away, plumes bobbing, crossbows raised.

"Bass," I said, "There is no way…"

"We're not done just yet," Bass said as crossbow bolt flew wide over his head.

They were lining up now, all with crossbows raised, and there we were, the mule ambling along like it didn't have a care in the world. For all I knew, it probably didn't.

"We're doomed," I said.

One of the soldiers barked a command. The ones in the lead row dropped on their knees, and the others spaced out so the ones behind would have gaps to shoot through. It was all like a well-oiled machine; efficient, fast and professional.

It would have been pretty awesome to stand by and watch if it wasn't us they were aiming at.

The man yelled again, and the crossbows were raised up to shoulders.

This was literally the moment where one would leap up with sword raised and yell "Today is a GOOD day to die!"

Personally, no day was a good day to die, but there you go.

I drew in a shuddering breath, but before I could so much as let it out again, five arrows shot into the phalanx within seconds of each other, knocking down the leader and four others.

A black horse galloped out into the street, the rider drawing half a dozen arrows at once from a quiver at his hips. He steadied his horse, and with the arrows still in his drawing hand, he drew on the string and took aim.

He fired. And fired. And fired again.

I counted three arrows in five seconds.

Like a machine, he drew, aimed, let loose and drew again, and with each arrow he let fly, another man fell dropped like a sack of flour.

I felt the bile rise up to the back of my throat as the blood spurted and the bodies landed with sickening thuds. The soldiers were in disarray; crossbows fired wild, and the horse nimbly leaped away from them. Laehn drew another bunch of arrows, and by that time, the soldiers had had enough.

They scattered, leaving crossbows stranded in the dust and ducking behind any form of conceivable cover available.

The wagon was rolling away at saunter pace, but the soldiers were broken, defeated. The rider paused and watched them flee, bow and arrows in hand. But, of course, just when I thought it was over and we had won, the steady drum of hoof beats began again.

And with that fanfare, round the corner came the cavalry.

Literally.

"They're coming!" I yelled.

The rider decided to call it a day and leave while the going was good, and I had to agree it was pretty smart of him. He was already on his way out, and his horse galloped past us before I could think up a suitable adjective to sum up the moment.

We, on the other hand, were still on the right way to lose a race against a tortoise.

Thankfully, Bass noticed. He lashed the reins with gusto.

"YAH!"

The mule snorted, reared on its hind legs and gave out one terrific, almighty battle bray. It fell on its hooves with an explosion of noxious fumes, and the next thing I knew was hard wood jolting under me and a throb in the back of my head as we raced out of that little town at what may have as well been the speed of sound.

Chapter 4

It wasn't until a few hours later when we were well away from the scene of the crime when Laehn finally decided to join us. Bass and I hadn't spoken since the incident, and now we both sat in silence, him at the front of the wagon with his pipe and me at the back, hugging my knees to my chest.

The mule had returned to its dopey saunter, meandering lazily from one side of the road to the other. All the proof I had that this this creature had the capacity to clock over what had to have been sixty miles an hour in a pinch was the fact that my throat was still raw from all the screaming I'd the faint recollection of performing for much of the run.

The sound of hooves announced a horse drawing up, but since neither Bass nor the mule decided to take evasive action, I elected to stay where I was and let them handle it.

"I scouted the route out ahead and backtracked the way you came," I heard Laehn say, "It would seem you're in the clear for now."

There was silence, and the clopping of hooves,

"That meeting there," Laehn continued, "I assume, was our Champion's doing?"

"For once, no," Bass blew out a lazy smoke ring, "That was me."

"You must have had good reason, then. Did they see his face?"

"They didn't need to, now did they?" Bass grumbled, "We underestimated Mugatu. They weren't looking for *him*. They were looking for *me*. Didn't see that coming, did we?"

Laehn hesitated before replying.

"That was unexpected, yes."

"How'd they know I'd be with him?"

"A lucky guess, I would assume."

I sat up straighter and glanced over the side of the wagon. The black horse was keeping easy pace with the mule, and Laehn had finally decided to lower his hood, letting his surprisingly long blonde hair reach halfway down his back.

I couldn't help but do a double take at that hair. This wasn't the scraggly long kind you'd expect from someone around here; this was of the sleek and shiny variety, hair looking like it belonged on a shampoo commercial rather than on the head of a guy who had just killed a dozen or so people with a bow and seemed quite unperturbed about it.

And as far as being perturbed went, I had made it up for the three of us. The memory of those arrows hitting flesh and the sound of those screams made the bile rise up again, and I choked.

They turned.

"You're still here," Bass grumbled, "I was sort of hoping you'd been hit and died quietly there. So much for luck."

I was too preoccupied with gawking at Laehn's face to reply, and Bass raised a perplexed eyebrow at me.

"Now what's the matter with you?"

I swallowed and raised a finger.

"You… you're…"

I'm not a gaper by nature. But if any time deserved a gape, it was this.

See, of all the weird things I'd been witness to so far, you'd have expected me to have taken this one for granted by now; but when I saw the pointed chin, the smooth, pale cheeks, the bright green eyes and most of all, the large, pointed ears… well, if I'd convinced myself a while ago things were about as weird as they could get, this smashed that hope to fragments

To top it all off, the bow and arrow act earlier was all the confirmation I needed.

"You're an *elf*?"

Bass's face screwed up in confusion, and the look Laehn gave me was the one people usually reserve for the guy that stands up in a moving train and starts delivering a very off-key opera.

"I'm a *what*?" he demanded.

"You… you…"

I couldn't help myself. If I'd been keeping my cool during all the other crazy stuff I'd heard or witnessed till now, this revelation broke whatever shred of composure I had had.

See, if elves were real, then the whole world as I knew it was tumbling upside down. *Anything* could happen. I couldn't explain what I was feeling right then. Joy, shock, happiness and hope, maybe, to name a few. Whatever it was, it probably didn't look too good to either of them, being on the receiving end to the kaleidoscope of expressions I was exhibiting.

They exchanged a glance.

"Is it too late to tell you about that contract I have up East?" Laehn asked.

"Yes, it is," Bass said, dourly.

I took a deep breath, and pointed again.

"Him," I said, "You didn't… you never thought about mentioning the fact he's an elf? It would have been nice to know elves even existed! Come on! This has to mean it isn't so hopeless after all!"

Watching Bass's countenance change from mild exasperation to almost genuine worry didn't do much good in calming me down.

"Perhaps he hit his head rather hard in your flight," Laehn offered.

"Probably, but no, he's usually like this," Bass muttered. He passed a hand over his forehead, "What in the blazes are you talking about?"

I looked from one of them to the other.

"The bow," I said, gesturing weakly, "His hair… reflexes… and those ears…"

The said ears blazed scarlet. Laehn's eyes widened, and then narrowed.

"I will scout out ahead and double back to see if we were followed," he said curtly

"Wait, didn't you do that alre..." I began, but his horse had already cantered off, leaving me hanging with a finger still in the air and feeling like an idiot.

I looked to Bass for explanation, but he was staring up at the sky, eyes closed. The expression on his face was the very picture of mental anguish.

"What?" I demanded.

Bass looked at me, closed his eyes and shook his head.

"Why did you have to mention the ears?" he demanded, a tone of very real anger in his voice, one I'd never heard before.

"But... but..."

"Boy, you don't go insulting a person's appearance when you've just met them!" he exclaimed, "I knew you were stupid, but this was..."

"What did I say?!" I asked, now thoroughly terrified.

"His ears, boy, his ears!" Bass snapped, leaning over before I could dodge and rapping Tom on my head, "Why did you have to go mention his ears like that?!"

"But... he's an elf, isn't he?"

"What in blazes is an elf?!" Bass yelled.

"Wait, you probably don't call them elves here," I said, the notion dawning on me a tad too late, "But, see, from where I come from, we have tales of people like him. They have superior reflexes, they're pretty darn excellent with a bow, and they have ears and hair like..." I trailed off into mumbles as Bass's face twisted into an expression of incredulity so potent, it sucked the talk out of me.

"Oh, you fool," Bass shook his head, "Elves? That's the stupidest thing I've ever heard."

"On top of a farting donkey that can break the sound barrier and a guy who has a monopoly on interworldly transport?" I demanded, "*Elves* are where you draw the line?"

Bass raised his hand.

"Stop," he said, almost pleading, "Just stop. Don't mention his ears… or… or *elves*… ever again."

"Um… fine," I said. I shrugged, "But I don't get what the fuss is all about."

"The fuss?" Bass said, "Here's what the fuss is about. Imagine you were an assassin who was the best at what you do. Hard to imagine even when drunk, I admit, but let it stand for example. Imagine your profession counted on your anonymity, and being able to blend into a crowd. And now imagine you had prominent ears which could be used to identify you wherever you went."

He paused to let it sink in. It sank in pretty deep, alright.

"And forget the occupational hazards," he continued, "It's the principle of the thing. He's not like anyone else anymore, and it pricks at his pride to be reminded of it."

I swallowed.

"I'm sorry," I said.

"Don't do something else stupid and go apologizing to him," Bass snapped, "Forget this ever happened. And forget he has those ears."

I nodded.

"How did…?" I began, but broke off. For some reason, Bass didn't lash out again.

"It's a skin condition," he said, gruffly, "And… it happened because of an accident. That, his hair and his eyes. That's all you need to know."

And that was the end of that pleasant conversation.

Laehn returned while we made camp in a grassy meadow as the evening fell. He wordlessly accepted the bowl of sludge Bass offered him and sat on the other side of the fire, the light dancing off the tips of those conspicuous ears.

The mule let out a toot to remind us it was still out there, somewhere off grazing in the dark. I couldn't see a thing outside the little circle of light the fire threw, and that sound was strangely reassuring, as bizarre as it sounds.

"What word from your end?" Bass asked, settling against a wagon wheel, bowl in hand and pipe clenched between his teeth.

"Kernine's men have been in town since the day before," Laehn responded, "I have no news of where he is, but his people litter the roads everywhere around here."

"Kernine?" I echoed.

"Mugatu's right hand," Bass replied, "You've met him, briefly."

"That guy you called the Dog?" I asked, in a flash of recollection, "The one who broke in and captured Eduud?"

"That's the one."

"Wait a second. A dog... called Kernine?"

Bass raised an eyebrow and Laehn put down his bowl to look at me. I hurriedly raised my own bowl and slurped a mouthful. An appalling first impression was one thing, but from the looks of things, I wasn't going anywhere near making this guy like me. As far as team motivation went, we were going downhill faster than an avalanche.

The thick, lumpy brew in the bowl gave me shudders, but I forced it down all the same and followed it up with another gulp. The taste hadn't improved any since the first time I'd tried the vile stuff, but it filled me up for a while, which had to count for something.

Mona's cooking, though... for a few moments, I was with her in the kitchen, stabbing at her with a spatula in one of our silly kitchen sword fights. I saw her laugh, and I reached out to wipe the smear of sauce on her cheek.

And then I was there again, sitting there cross legged in the lumpy grass, the wooden bowl of foulness still in my hands. They hadn't noticed my lapse in concentration, busy plotting as they were. I straightened up and began to listen, which I probably should have had been doing from the start.

"What of the King?" Bass asked.

"The castle still stands free," Laehn replied, "But the last I heard, they were preparing for siege. Kernine is gathering his forces, and I believe that their next assault will be there."

"And we should be there and out before then," Bass mused.

"Wait, did you just say what I think…" I began.

"Don't worry about it," Bass interrupted, "We'll handle that when the time comes."

"And we should focus on the more pressing problems at hand," Laehn pointed out. "For instance, the fact he has not Chosen yet."

He cast a glance at me. "Might I assume he at the very least knows about the Items?"

"What items?" I demanded.

"It just keeps getting worse, doesn't it," Laehn sighed.

"He has them," Bass replied, "I told him to keep them on him at all times. Didn't get a chance to explain yet, what with one thing and another."

"Explain what?"

Bass yawned and stretched.

"Alright, kid," he said, leaning back, "The thing about being the Champion… it's that you aren't like the rest of us."

"Again with the eyes thing?" I sighed, "Look, a break now and again would be nice. Just saying."

"Would be nice, aye. Too bad none of us get any," Bass grunted, "And aye, it's like the eyes. The long and short of it: you don't belong here. For that, you'll need to be constantly anchored, or you'll drift."

"Whoa, hang on here," I raised a hand, "Anchor? What do you mean anchor?"

"Anything that came with you when you were Summoned will be what anchors you to the realm," Laehn said, "The blade from the forges of your land shall be your weapon, and the cloth your armor."

The fire crackled and crickets chirped.

"Come again?" I asked, forcefully polite.

"What he said," Bass sighed, "You brought with you a razor and a piece of cloth. That razor is your sword, kid. And the cloth… at least now you'd get why I'm upset."

I reached up to pop my jaw in again.

"Alright. This time, you ARE joking."

"You think he knows how to crack a joke?" Bass jerked a thumb at Laehn, now examining an arrow in the light of the fire.

"So you're saying my *towel* is my armor?" I demanded, "And what, I swing my *razor* like a sword?"

"That would be the gist of it, aye. And not 'like' a sword. It will be your sword. Or something like one when it's Bound."

"And how the hell do you expect that to happen?!" I demanded, slightly more than a little irked.

"The Armament," Bass replied, "Once you touch your razor to it, they will fuse, and then hopefully you can use it to stab someone. That's the only way you can... if we're all so incredibly lucky... defeat Mugatu."

"You do realize this task you put me on gets more difficult every time you keep adding things to the checklist, don't you?" I snapped, "Would you mind springing them all on me at once so I can, you know, have some semblance of peace of mind?"

"Hang on to your towel, we're doing it now, aren't we?" Bass retorted. He hacked up and spat over his shoulder.

"What if I don't use them?" I demanded, "What if I just use something else, and not look like a total moron?"

"Too late for that last one," Bass pointed out.

"If you do not use the Items that were Summoned with you, then you will not be anchored," Laehn said.

"And...?"

"And without Eduud around to keep you here, you'll be pulled out of this world again," Bass interjected, "I thought it was obvious."

Hope flared in me.

"I get pulled back home?"

Bass chuckled and shook his head.

"Oh, you're cute. You wish. No, you don't go home. Especially not without Eduud here to sort of guide you, or whatever it is that he does. You'll get trapped in the middle of here and there, or something of the sort. Don't ask me, I didn't make any of this. Either way, it's not pleasant, I can promise you."

The implications hit me like a hammer to the head, and I scrabbled wildly at my pocket. There were the customary few seconds where my heart free fell down to my knees, and then I felt the plastic handle through the cloth. I pulled it out and held it up to the light.

"So if I drop this somewhere, I get sucked into a black hole?" I asked.

"That's the general idea, aye."

My eye started twitching again.

"And you're telling me that… that… *this* is my sword?"

Laehn dropped the arrow, just noticing me brandishing my shaving utensil.

"*That* is your sword?" he demanded.

"Welcome to my vacation," Bass muttered.

Laehn sighed and shook his head.

"I knew I shouldn't have turned down that contract up East," he said wistfully.

"I told Mona I wanted to stay in bed," I muttered.

"What was that?" Bass asked.

"Nothing," I muttered. I looked into the fire, crackling and flickering away, the damn thing so annoyingly cheerful, it made me want to throw a bucket of water on it right then, and damn the cold that followed.

Oh, all the irony in that statement.

"How come you know so much about all this, anyway?" I demanded.

"Comes of having a Base Spirit as a friend," Bass replied curtly.

None of us spoke again for a while. I leaned against the tree and traced my finger around the lumps and dents in that wooden bowl. For a long time, the only sound was the crackling of the fire and the occasional toot or two from the mule. The aroma drifted over a couple of times and the fire flared up in response, but other than that, it was quiet.

"What do we do now?" I asked, after what seemed like hours. My voice was sharp after the silence, and even I couldn't help but give a slight jolt. Bass jerked awake and pointed his stick wildly at the shadows.

"We train you," Laehn said, as Bass stood up and started stumbling around, swinging Tom with gusto, "And we make for the Armament. Without it, there is nothing we can do. Unfortunately, Mugatu knows that."

His voice was clear, as if he had been wide awake all along. This guy was starting to give me the creeps, and it didn't help any knowing he didn't like me all that much.

Bass tripped over something in the dark and landed with a strangled curse and a loud thump.

"So we go to this Armament tomorrow?" I asked.

"No," Laehn replied, "We are few and we need help. Tomorrow, we ride to meet the King."

A loud snore cut through the night air. I glanced over at the huddled shape where Bass had fallen on his head, but I was too lazy to get up and go see if he needed help.

"The King?" I repeated, "I thought Mugatu took over?"

"Not yet," Laehn replied grimly, "But he will, soon enough. Eduud was not quick enough to see the threat rising, but nonetheless he brought you along in time. Mugatu had Kernine bring many of the King's men over to his side, but there are still a few more loyal to him, and us. The castle is the last stronghold we have, but it may be over run any day now."

"So we go to the castle?"

"We go to the castle."

We fell silent again. Neither of us made a move to get up and move, and the fire was too mesmerizing, dancing like the traitorous merry fiend it was. Bass snored where he had fallen, and the donkey joined in the rhythm every so often.

And thus the night wore on.

Chapter 5

I woke up with my body all stiff and feeling as brittle as a piece of cardboard forgotten in the freezer overnight. And as if that wasn't enough, my feet and legs had a temperature to match. My arms and back felt like I'd spent the night on top of a bunch of scattered Legos, which wasn't too surprising, given the texture of the tree I'd been leaning against and the pebbles I'd fallen onto sometime during the night.

That pain wasn't why I'd woken up, though; I was awake because Bass had poked me in the shoulder with his stick.

And why had he poked me in the shoulder with the stick?

Because he was Bass.

"Up. Move," he groused, "We have ground to cover."

"I'm awake," I moaned, mustering up the strength to feebly bat away his stick with arms feeling no more useful than branches themselves.

He left me and stumped over to the wagon, which was all loaded and ready. The campsite had been cleared, and I couldn't even tell where we'd had the fire last night.

Something was missing, though. Some*one*.

"Where's Laehn?" I groaned, creaking forward and awkwardly climbing to my feet. The world swayed, and I had to grab onto the tree for a minute before the dizziness passed.

"Out scouting," Bass replied, already in the wagon. Not bothering to spare me a glance, he struck the reins.

"Yah!"

The mule limbering up its hindquarters, set off the customary flatulent emission and began the day's amble. My body was too stiff to bear the jolts and shakes, so, swallowing to keep from giving Bass the satisfaction of hearing me moan, I followed them on foot.

"So when does my towel become my armor?" I called, "I'm hoping it would be much more comfortable than this sack you gave me."

"Your armor is at the castle," Bass replied, his pronunciation mauled by the pipe between his teeth, "We're going there now."

"I thought you said my towel was my armor?"

"Part of it, aye. Your cloak, I'd wager. The rest of it is waiting for you at the Castle."

"My towel as my cloak?!"

"You prefer it as your breastplate? It could be arranged."

"You do realize how weird that's going to look, don't you?" I pointed out, "Medieval armor and a pink towel draped over the back? It's going to look like cheap Halloween costume gone wrong. And I thought I'm supposed to be this beacon of hope for your people?"

"Somehow," Bass muttered. He rummaged around inside the wagon, and I ignored him, fixing my itchy eyes on the pebbles crunching under my heavy boots. I unconsciously raised my hand to scratch at the stubble on my neck. Though I had a razor on my person at all times, I unfortunately lacked the other bare essentials to the art of shaving: a mirror, shaving cream, running water and personal privacy.

I ran the back of my hand over the prickly growth again. To be honest, I'd always wondered what I'd look like with a full beard. Circumstances so far hadn't been too kind to the beard-wielding inclined of the travel agency sort, and Mona wouldn't have tolerated it, no doubt about that. When life handed you lemons, albeit more than a tad rotten…

Out of the corner of my eye, Bass shifted, and his arm moved towards me. Out of reflex, I flinched and ducked out of reach. Experience had taught me that nine times out of ten, such movements were usually accompanied by a brief but intense headache. Right then, I wasn't feeling up for one, so I maintained my half crouch.

"Hurry up and take it," Bass grumbled, "Expecting me to hold onto this all day, are you?"

His wrinkled hand was still stretched out. I threw caution to the winds and braved a look. Rather than the pipe or Tom, his stubby fingers grasped my wooden bowl.

I took it wordlessly, and it was with a measure of disbelief that I beheld a hunk of bread and what looked like soup at the bottom of it, as opposed to the usual indescribable sludge which graced it on all other occasions.

"What happened to…?"

"Laehn had supplies," Bass replied, "And, well. You deserved it. There's some meat in there. Put it to good use."

"I deserved it?" I echoed, grinning despite myself.

"Shut up and eat."

And I did. It was probably because I'd more or less (regretfully) gotten used to how Bass's abhorrent concoctions tasted, but right then ribs and special sauce could not have been better. I licked the bowl clean, surprisingly satisfied.

As was getting to be ritual, Laehn joined us soon after the sun reached sweltering proportions.

"Little to report," he said, his horse falling in step with the mule, "We aren't being followed, and the roads are clear. The enemy has been through here already, though. The towns are empty. Whoever wasn't able to flee to the Castle in time did not make it."

"And what of the Castle?" Bass demanded.

"Untouched, for now," Laehn replied. "It would seem they are waiting for something. Perhaps Kernine is yet to join them."

"Where are they?" I asked, "Are they, you know, still around?"

Laehn looked at me like he'd only just noticed I was walking along next to them.

"We have a clear path to the Castle," he replied, "They have camped on the far side, out of sight. They will not see us approach."

"They should have attacked by now," Bass muttered.

"They will," Laehn agreed. "Before nightfall, most likely."

"Or while we're still inside, if we're really lucky," Bass muttered. He passed a hand over his forehead.

"What of the defenders?"

"They seemed to be arming themselves for the siege," Laehn replied, "I could not get too close. At times like these, one would tend to mistrust mercenaries."

"They won't shoot when I'm there. Probably."

"That's reassuring," I muttered.

We walked in silence, the sun beating down on us as the road leveled out and became harder.

Buildings appeared in the distance, and there was still smoke drifting around as we arrived at the empty shells of what used to be a town. The cobblestoned paths were blackened and stained an ominous shade of brown, and I saw a blackened shape spread eagled on the side of the street.

The wind howled past us, tugging at my cloak and bringing home the stench of smoke and death, and the bile rose.

"Poor souls," Bass muttered.

I swallowed, throat burning, struggling to keep from puking.

"We'd best be out of here as soon as we can," Bass said.

The next fifteen minutes were something out of a horror movie. Houses and stores had been looted and burned, and blackened corpses were strewn about like so many forgotten rag dolls. It didn't take long before I wished we'd gone around rather than through. Arriving too late at the Castle had nothing on having to pass through all the horrors left behind here.

I climbed into the wagon, crouched against the side, bowed my head and screwed my eyes shut. I didn't want to see, but there wasn't anything I could do to block the smells. The nausea rose, and wouldn't stay down.

"See, Alan?" Bass said softly, "Now do you see why we need you?"

The wagon jumped and jolted as we galloped through, but even then it seemed forever before the wind changed and the pungent odor of smoke and decay faded.

The path leading out of the town was still paved, all the way down to the village half an hour away. That, too, hadn't been spared; but this time Bass mercifully led the wagon off the flagstones and into the bumpy long grass.

"Why?" I asked, hollowly, "Why would they do this?"

"Show of strength?" Bass shrugged, "The people might have tried to fight back, the brave fools. Others who had submitted might have survived. Surrendered and then waited for you to free them. It's what they should have done."

We could only go so fast on grass, and as the wagon jumped and jolted around the blackened remains of a farm on the outskirts of the village, we saw it: a tall, shoddily built wooden frame at least ten feet high. It was just two lone poles and a crossbeam connecting them; but dangling off the beam were four rotting bodies, ropes grotesquely pulling back the skin round their peeling necks.

I couldn't hold it in anymore. My stomach heaved, and I threw head over the side of the wagon in time to hurl my breakfast onto the crushed and trampled grass.

Bass wordlessly swung the reins, and the mule picked up speed, coming near to turning the wagon over as it sped out of there. As we thankfully left the monstrosity behind, I kept my eyes fixed at the lump on the horizon.

Laehn alone turned behind to give the village one final glance. His brow furrowed, jaw clenched, and he rode on.

"These people need you, Alan," Bass said, and I heard a very different tone to his voice, one he'd never had before. "You're their hope."

I didn't say anything.

There were two more villages, each one worse than the last, and Bass steered us well away from them. We were a quiet, subdued trio by the time I finally realized the lump which had been sitting on the horizon all the while was, in fact, the castle itself. Hazy and distorted through the heat waves off the baking ground, the only thing I could tell about it was that it was huge.

"It's pretty big, I guess," I said, trying to break the mood. "I mean, I haven't had all that much experience, but..."

"It's meant to be big; it's the King's seat, now isn't it?" Bass pointed out. "That would be the Castle you're looking at. Behind it is the city, where all the survivors are now hiding, and there's a second Keep on the other side."

"There's a city there?" I asked.

"Largest in the Kingdom, as is the Castle itself," Bass replied. "The biggest prize, that is. If Mugatu manages to take it... and it's very likely, from the looks of things... things will become that much harder."

"How could he take it?" I wondered, "It's huge."

"Aye, and here's the problem," Bass growled. "Manpower, boy. Mugatu's been leeching off men for years. It's a five to one on their side, and even so we don't know how many are his behind the walls. There aren't enough men to cover the walls, as impressive as the walls themselves may be. We're expecting a massacre."

I swallowed.

"And we're going there because…?"

"We're going for your armor."

I swallowed again. Awkward silence right then seemed much more appealing than conversations revolving round impending doom.

"Be careful," Bass warned, breaking the silence again with more of that doom, "There'll be traps laid out around here from this point on. Stay in the wagon. The mule knows where not to tread."

"I will follow from behind," Laehn said, pulling away. Bass tugged on the reins and the mule took the lead.

The battlements loomed ahead, and I saw soldiers poke their heads over the top to watch our approach. A couple of them raised crossbows to their shoulders and took aim at us. I still hadn't a clue as to what range those things could shoot, but right then, I was getting to a point where I was really starting to hate crossbows.

After a cautious half hour, we reached the foot of the huge gates without being blown up, maimed, or skewered by half a dozen bolts. Bass leaned back and glared at the top of the wall.

"OY!" he hollered.

The reply was instantaneous, and very, very orthodox.

"Who goes there?!"

"Idiots," Bass muttered, "Like they didn't see us coming from all the way back there."

"The King's Advisor commands you open this gate!" Laehn called up.

"Who now?" I demanded.

"I'm the King's Advisor," Bass replied.

"You're..." I shook my head. "You're...?"

"I have a varied resume. There's a lot you don't know about me, kid," Bass said, smiling, "And a lot you don't really need to. Just remember I pull a lot of weight around, and you might want to reconsider the next time you think about calling me Grandpa."

"Where's your proof?" the soldier yelled back down, interrupting my planned interruption.

"Who else do you think would just waltz up here like this in a time of war?" Bass hollered.

The pause that followed was both spectacularly comical and extremely aggravating.

"Lord Bass?"

Bass sighed and passed a hand over his forehead.

"Are you going to open the damn gate, man, or are we going to have to sit here and wait till Mugatu arrives to knock it down for us?!" he bellowed.

The second pause was distinctly less comical and infinitely more aggravating. The mutters and hushed murmurs floated down like so many flies over a manure field, and over the rest I heard one distinct voice say, "That's probably him, I'd reckon."

The gates finally shuddered and began to open. As the gap between them widened with painstaking sluggishness, I recognized the barrier behind them from a couple of movies I'd rented a while back; a single wall of interlocked wooden beams, with two-foot long spikes at the bottom that revealed themselves as the frame lifted up like a tiger baring its fangs.

I was watching a real life portcullis being raised.

Beyond the wooden killer waffle was a tunnel roughly twenty feet long, with holes spaced evenly along the ceiling all the way to the other side.

"Murder holes," Bass said. He pointed at one of the closest ones, and I looked through it as we passed under. Grim eyes stared back down at us, and I couldn't tell whether or not they were happy to see us. Under each murder hole we passed, I saw more men, most faces hidden behind polished metal helmets. Of the bare headed ones, few faces were not pale and haggard, and some didn't look like they could last a fistfight, let alone a siege.

"What are these holes for?" I wondered out loud.

"What do you think?" Bass muttered, "If the gates were forced open and the portcullis breached, defenders use them to slow the tide down, by pouring boiling oil, shooting crossbows, whatever works. If they're lucky and don't run out of ammunition, they might even be able to block the passage with dead bodies soon enough. Won't last long, but it's something."

My stomach churned. It was easy enough in the semi darkness to see the images in my mind's eye; men shoving forward all around us, packed as tight as crayons in a box, the ones in the front screaming as hell rained down from…

Bile rose in the back of my throat and I barely kept from gagging. Not one of my best daydreams.

"What did you do with that cloth you had around you when you were Summoned?" Bass demanded, oblivious.

"Stuffed it in a sack," I muttered. Relieved at the interruption, I looked back at all the sacks strewn across the back of the wagon.

"… somewhere."

"Find it," he said. "And the razor, too. We're taking them with us."

"Sure," I muttered, "Now you tell me."

I crawled to the wagon's rear and started rummaging around in the semi darkness. Of course Bass had to wait till we'd descended into the depths of semi darkness before asking me to get it.

I pulled it out just as we reached the tunnel's end. Waiting for us stood a portly soldier in red trimmed armor which looked far too tight around… well, around everywhere. Clean shaven, a shame as his quivering jowls could have done the world a favor by never seeing daylight, he wore his salt and pepper hair trimmed short and his helmet under his arm, his chest thrust out the way one only does when they're sucking in their gut as hard as they could.

"Captain Ajold," Bass said curtly.

"Lord Bass," the Captain said, his voice slightly strained to the closely listening ear, "What a relief it is to see you, Sir! We thought you were dead!"

"Well, I'm not," Bass snapped, barely sparing him a glance as the wagon rolling past, "Didn't bother trying to check, did you? I could have been dead, and the Champion with me. You do realize he's the only one who can help us win, don't you?"

"Yes, Lord Bass," Ajold stammered, stumbling after us, "But the manpower… and the siege…"

"No way you could have held out without us, now was there?" Bass snapped, "We were almost caught by Mugatu's soldiers on the way here, if it wasn't for the help from the very same mercenary you said was not fit to set foot in this castle again."

He shot Laehn a look and gulped.

"The preparations," he said, fervently, "And…"

"The past matters not now," Laehn said, ignoring him, "We have come. And we must leave, before the siege begins."

The man paled further.

"Leave? B-b-before it begins?!" his eyes widened, "What do you mean?! We could use all the help we can get, and the Champion…"

"The Champion has a plan, and it doesn't involve being killed here under your command," Bass said. He curtly jumped of the wagon and held out the mule's reins to a soldier who ran up.

The Captain's chins wobbled, and his mouth opened and shut.

Turning away from them, I looked around the courtyard. There was about a thousand feet of open space between the gates and the Castle walls, where we were standing right now. At the top of the short flight of stone steps stood an imposing pair of thick, wooden doors that were now wide open, giving me a glimpse of the wide hallway inside.

"Take us to the King," Laehn said, dismounting at the same time as I climbed off the wagon with the sack in my hands.

Ajold glared at him before and his eyes jumped to me. They flickered toward Bass, and back again at me before his shoulders sagged ever so little and he nodded curtly.

"The King is overseeing fortifications," he said, leading the way up the steps, "Follow me,"

Soldiers bustled past us, arms full of weapons, bundles and barrels. I examined their armor as they passed, but I guess I didn't know enough to tell it apart from what Mugatu's men wore. Thankfully, the cloth and trimmings under their steel metallic bits were red rather than blue.

Color coding. Always helps.

"How are we?" Bass asked, his voice low.

"Food and supplies will last us a few months at full rations," the Captain replied, his voice just as low, "and even if they somehow divert the river, we have enough water to keep for a while. We're terribly undermanned, though, and short on weapons. What townspeople who survived have made it to the city. We're trying to get able bodied men to help on the walls, but we haven't enough weapons or armor for all of them. We set traps all the way from there to here, and scouts spotted the advances…"

Being Champion and all, I probably should have been following the statistics closely as we walked through the Castle, but with all there was to see in there, one didn't need ADHD to find paying attention to mundane chatter a problem. The corridors were enormous, and the rich carpets were thick and luscious underfoot from the inner passages onwards. Every corner had some statue done in metal or stone, and paintings on the walls set in gleaming frames portrayed men and women in all manner of poses Royalty tend to take when being painted.

And the chandeliers; you'd think the era of glass lighting decoration had no business here yet in this time and age, but those blazes of glory hanging up over most of the large halls would slap you in the eyes and tell you to go mind your own business.

My gaze fell on an enormous tapestry on the wall. I'd seen two dozen or more of these on the all over the rest of the Castle, but this one was somehow very different. Weird shapes, colors and words popped out at random, and as I peered closer, the figures melded to form a distinct object: a sword.

Out the corner of my eye, I could see the others drawing ahead. Obviously preferring to not be left behind, I kept moving. Even so, I couldn't draw my gaze away from the tapestry as the colors shifted and the picture changed again. I couldn't make out more than some sort of large rock and dozens of tiny figure on it when it blurred once more.

I reluctantly walked a couple of steps and the scenes morphed yet again: this time a throne, sword and something else, a vague, shapeless object in between them. I continued to walk, even as it transformed faster than I could make sense of what I was seeing. The last thing I recognized was a face… or at least, what might have passed off as an indistinct, almost featureless face. The eyes, though… the eyes were the clearest part of the apparition, and they seemed to follow me, what might have even been curiosity in them as I walked past.

It was the last I saw because it was at that moment when I was rudely interrupted by a wall of metal armor; I'd bumped into Ajold's back. He gave a start and recovered, Laehn rolled his eyes ever so slightly and Bass heaved an audible sigh.

"Sorry, sorry," I muttered.

I turned to look back at the tapestry again, and for some reason I wasn't too surprised to see the visions gone. Once again, it was nothing but a mass of abstract shapes, colors and lines, and even though I willed myself to see the pictures again, nothing happened.

Disappointed, I joined the others. They stood together a little further down the corridor, facing a pair of immense double doors on the wall opposite the tapestry. Each door looked as wide as five Laehns standing abreast, and intricate designs were carved all over them in flowing loops and curls like they'd been painted on with a brush. On any other day I'd have stopped and stared; now, I had something else on my mind.

"Hey, Captain," I said, tapping his shoulder, "What's that?"

He seemed annoyed at the interruption, but followed my thumb back to the tapestry.

"That?" he shrugged, "Don't really know what it's supposed to be. Art, I suppose."

He spun around smartly and clicked his boots together.

"The Throne Room," he announced.

Striding forward, he pushed them open and strode in.

I'm no expert on the subject, but as far as throne rooms go, I'd have to say this one was pretty huge. It was decorated, too, all done over in velvet and gold, with chandeliers dangling off the arched stone ceiling and statues in all the handy little niches in the walls. It didn't take an expert to tell that all this was some pretty expensive stuff.

At the far end sat the two thrones; the silver and scarlet one dominated at the center of the raised platform, three gilded steps above the rest of us unworthy commoners. On its right it sat the slightly smaller emerald green and gold throne, probably where the Queen sat when she graced the Hall with her presence.

I'm not much of an expert on the medieval issues, but I was pretty sure I wasn't a fan of rich, spoiled Kings taking advantage of their people. So, it was with a healthy amount of skepticism that I followed the Captain, Bass and Laehn up the red carpet, through the few people still in there.

As big as it was, the throne room was almost empty; yet I could feel the eyes burning through me as I took that walk, trying to ignore the people who stopped whatever they were doing to blatantly stare. Manners weren't all that big in the Throne Room, after all.

The smaller, green throne was empty, but the red one wasn't, and the man seated there raised his head to look at us as we approached. Tall, broad, and commanding, his white, gold and silver armor gleamed out at me like a reminder of just who I was walking towards.

His brown hair was shoulder length, like most of everyone else's here, and he sported a short but full beard. When our eyes met, I had the feeling, despite myself, that this was the sort of guy you'd want to vote for if he ever ran for President.

Maybe Kings weren't all bad after all.

Right then, though, the King didn't seem all that commanding or confident; just as the doors had opened, he'd been leaning wearily against the side of his throne, an elbow on one armrests and his forehead in his palm, listening as a soldier read out from a list in front of him.

The soldier had stopped reading now, and the King sat up straight as we approached. His gaze flickered on Bass, lingered on Laehn, and then fell on me. His eyes widened.

"My liege," Captain Ajold announced, "Lord Bass has arrived. And with him… the Champion."

The man looked at me, and his beard twitched.

"So. The Champion survived, after all."

"I did, too," Bass grumbled, "What, I don't get a mention?"

"You always survive, my old friend," the King replied, smiling wearily, "It takes more than a stray arrow or a lucky sword to get rid of a thorn as obstinate as you."

"You'd be surprised," Bass muttered.

The King stood and walked down the steps.

"Welcome, Champion," he said, extending a hand, "I am Zaahis, King of the Realm. I thank you for your arrival in our time of need."

I shot a look at Bass, and he nodded. I reached forward and took his hand.

"Alan," I winced as his metal gauntlet crushed my fingers, "Pleasure,"

"We'd have been here sooner if you'd had the decency to send someone over to get us," Bass pointed out.

"We'd received reports of how you and Eduud were ambushed at the Summoning Chamber," Zaahis' brow creased, "They said the two of you were captured, and you'd both been killed on General Kernine's orders. You know I didn't believe them, but still, we had no knowledge of where you could be. Sending search parties out when we were already hard pressed for men… it would have been madness."

"Well, we're here now, and that's what counts, I suppose," Bass muttered, "Where is the Queen?"

"Sent her and the child off with my three finest," he replied, voice strained, "with orders not to let anyone know where they were. Not even me."

"Good," Bass nodded, "Eduud can find her when the time is right."

"And if Eduud would be less than willing, should a Law arise?" Laehn asked.

"I've taken care of it," the King replied, "If… *when*… everything is alright again, I'll send town criers with a special message in their words. They would know to return then."

"Good," Bass said, "Now, about here."

"The siege is about to begin," the King passed a hand over his forehead, "I had myself convinced we wouldn't last through the day."

"Don't get your hopes up too high," Bass muttered, voice just loud enough for us five to hear.

The King's brow furrowed.

"The rebels are camped just outside the Castle and will attack at their leisure," he said, "I've had far too much bad news in the last few days, Bass, I really don't need any more."

"Can't talk here," Bass mumbled, "We need the armor."

The King sighed and closed his eyes. A minute passed before he looked up again and nodded.

"Quickly, then," he said. He snapped his fingers at the guards by the side of the throne.

"I'm going down to the Armor Vault," he said, "I must see to this myself. Let the bugles sound if the enemies are spotted. Do not hesitate to be the first to strike."

He strode down the steps and the golden cloak swished past my nose as he led the way to the door in the wall behind the thrones. As always, Laehn brought up the rear, but Captain Ajold left us, jogging awkwardly out through the front of the room, back to his men.

No one spoke as we strode down the wide corridors. Soldiers passed us back and forth, some acknowledging the King with a quick bow, others too preoccupied to even notice us.

The King stopped by a blank bit of wall and reached up for one of the torch brackets. The ground gave a throaty rumble as he tugged on it, and a space opened in the wall behind us, wide enough for two people to enter abreast.

"Secret passage," I whistled, "Didn't see that coming."

"Some would say that was the point. You're not supposed to," Bass pointed out.

The King took down another torch.

"Shall we?" he asked.

Holding the torch behind him, he led the way into the passage. Bass followed, and I glanced at Laehn. The archer nodded reassuringly.

In movies, you always see the guy holding the torch seem to have no problems seeing in the darkest tunnels when he has the thing aloft. In reality, having that flame waving in front of your face could be the worst thing you could do to yourself in a dark tunnel; the moment you look away from the light you're pretty much blind to anything else. Which is why as King Zaahis led the way into the claustrophobic passage, he held the flickering tor torch up behind him, letting it light up the way ahead.

It blinded the rest of us, obviously, but at least following the bobbing ball of fire up ahead was better than holding the fire yourself and ending up with a bloody nose sooner or later.

The passage was close on twenty feet long, and I was fighting off claustrophobia by the time the walls finally receded. The King held the torch up to a spot on the wall. He tapped the head against a knob, and light flared up and ran round the wall.

It was a small, circular chamber. Halfway up the wall was a small ledge which I supposed was filled with oil or something, because it burned in an unbroken line around the room from one side of the archway we were standing in to the other. Golden light flickered off the stone walls, and off the polished metal directly in front of us.

Assembled on a stand like designer clothes on a mannequin, a suit of armor gleamed. Another smaller ring of fire ran on the ground underneath the stand, throwing up light from below. The whole effect of the light shining off that steel… the one word for it was breathtaking.

"Now isn't that fancy," Bass commented, breaking the spell as usual.

It was silver and green, I saw as I walked up to it. There were green shoulder pads, deep green metal gauntlets, and gold trimmings elsewhere over the silver body. It was beautiful. It was deadly.

It was badass.

"Well, Champion," Zaahis turned, the flickering light giving his pleasant smile a touch of unintentional malevolence, "What do you think?"

"What do you think I think?" I breathed.

He laughed and clapped a hand on my shoulder.

"We'll make short work of this traitor," he said, "And, I forgot to ask. What was it you Chose?"

That was the awkward moment long coming. In my head, I heard the crickets chirp and the penny drop at the same time.

I looked at Bass. Bass looked at Laehn, and Laehn looked at the ceiling and sighed.

"He didn't," Bass said with his usual blunt subtlety.

"I'm sorry, what was that?" Zaahis frowned, "I don't think I heard quite..."

"The Champion did not have time to Choose," Laehn clarified.

The King looked at me, and though it wasn't outright horror on his face, the smile which had been there since we first met slid off like it had been wiped away by a particularly smelly rag.

"Well..." he began, coughed and swallowed, "Well, that changes... everything."

"You don't say," Bass muttered sardonically.

Zaahis thumped a fist into his forehead and began to pace round the small room.

"We can't afford to risk having you here when the fighting begins," he said, "That much is certain. You wouldn't last a minute."

"Thanks for the vote of confidence," I said, not trying to hide the bitterness in my voice, "I'm completely useless, aren't I?"

"At least you're quick at grasping the obvious," Bass offered.

The three of us stood silently as the King paced, the ringing silence punctuated only by the crackling fires running around the room. He sighed and passed a hand over his sweaty forehead.

"Well... now what?" he asked weakly.

"We need the armor, that's what," Bass replied, "And then we need to get to the Armament. It's the only chance we have."

"Does he have a weapon?"

"Aye."

"But the Hill will be guarded. They know you will have to go there sooner or later."

"The best time would be while they're busy with the siege."

"Then you should have come much earlier than this. You have no…"

"We'd have been here much earlier if there had been an escort. And if you'd had done a bit more investing into the Quest budget."

The King sighed and massaged the back of his neck.

"Too late now," he said grimly, "Take the armor and go. We'll try our best to delay them for as…."

He faltered. Seconds later, I heard it too: it was a bugle, the sound muffled as it permeated through the walls. The horn played one long, mournful note before breaking off. A moment or two later, I heard it again.

I swallowed, "Was that what I think it was?"

The King's nostrils flared.

"Time is up," he said, "They're here."

Again we heard the bugle being blown. This time, it was accompanied by the roar of voices, so loud and resonant, it had to have been every man inside the castle yelling at once. My mind whispered how it had sounded like a whole lot of people; barely a second later, it dug up the memory of Bass telling me how they were outnumbered five to one.

My knees started knocking.

"They sound happy," Bass commented.

"They know the Champion has arrived," Laehn said, "They expect him to join with the defense."

"You need to leave," Zaahis said urgently, "Before it's too late."

The bugle blew a third time.

"What about the suit?" I demanded. Something was pounding in my ears, and I couldn't tell if it was my heart or the sound of people stomping past us in the hallway outside.

"Pack it up and take it with us," Bass said.

"No," Laehn countered, "It's already too late. They would know we're here, and so we are not going to be able to leave undetected."

"What do we do, fight them?" Bass demanded.

"Put the armor on. If it is to pass that we fight our way out, at least then you would be protected."

Bass nodded, "Good plan. Get to it."

The King nodded, "Don your armor, Champion. This is the moment."

They looked at me.

"Uh, thanks and all," I hesitated, "I haven't a clue how to start putting this on."

The King sighed, and Bass rolled his eyes.

Laehn thrust the sack into Bass's hands and strode forward. He took a couple of pieces off the stand, weighed them in his hands, examined them in the flickering light, and then turned to look at me.

"Well? Hurry!"

I moved, and then the next ten minutes or so passed agonizingly slowly as I stood there awkwardly, watching him fit one bulky piece over my body at a time. The bugle blew a different note as he was attaching my greaves, the metal thingies that went around my shins.

"They have begun," King Zaahis said, pacing worriedly, the torch still in his hands, "They need me."

"No chance you could hurry it up, is there?" Bass wondered out loud.

The ground shuddered, very likely in response to the muffled explosion a few seconds ago.

"We're going as fast as we can," Laehn said calmly, "Here, strap this round your leg, and we are done."

Though there was heavy duty steel strapped to me from head to toe, I didn't feel any more weighed down than if I'd put on a raincoat. I took an experimental step forward, and surprisingly, it wasn't heavy at all.

"It's light," I said.

"It's meant to be," Bass grunted, taking out the towel and dropping the sack, "It wasn't enchanted for nothing."

"Is that the armor the Champion brought with him?" the King asked eagerly, peering over his shoulder.

"Of sorts," Bass muttered. He shook out the towel, and I watched as the King's smile slid off again. I was starting to feel sorry for the guy.

"That..." he coughed, "Is a very... admirable shade of..."

"It's pink," I said, "Mona picked it out for me. It isn't admirable, it just gets the job done."

"I meant to say... it is a fine garment," he regained his composure, "And if I am not mistaken, it would do nicely as your cloak."

"Looks like that's all it can do," Bass grumbled, "Hurry, clip it on before..."

The bugle sounded again, but this time, it cut off abruptly before it finished.

"That didn't sound too good," I muttered.

"The wall has been breached," the King said grimly, "They are inside."

"We will have to fight," Laehn said, taking the towel off Bass and fastening it to my shoulders, "The castle will be overrun before we can leave."

He handed me my helmet; emerald green lines ran over the sides like a fancy Nike design, and the silver visor gleamed like a pair of 80s sunshades. They watched, almost with bated breath, as I clumsily accepted it and lowered it over my head with such grace as to make an alcoholic after his sixth pint seem graceful.

For a second I paused, hoping an AI would pop up and give me thruster diagnostics; but when it didn't happen, I looked at them through the visor and shrugged.

"It's okay, I guess," I said, my voice hollow.

The spell broken, the King swung his torch around and strode to the opposite wall.

"There's another passage from here which leads out to the streets," he said, "You'll have to hurry."

I spun around and felt the thick towel slap ungraciously against the plates on my back. I'd never worn a cloak with full armor before, and for some reason it didn't feel at all as imposing or formidable as I'd hoped.

King Zaahis prodded at one of the stones, "You'll end up somewhere in the middle of the City. From there, you will have to find your way to one of the gates."

"Wait, hang on," I interrupted as a section of the wall receded, revealing another dark passageway, "You're not coming?"

The King smiled.

"My people need me here," he said.

"You'll die," Bass pointed out, "You won't be of use to anyone that way, now will you?"

"You and I both know one man cannot win this on his own," he replied, "Only the people can do what needs to be done. But to do so, they need to believe one man alone can do what it takes."

He smiled at me.

"They need a hero to believe in. They need hope. And right now, you're more important to them than I am, Champion. You need to be the hero they think they need."

The sounds of metal clashing against metal reached our ears. The fighting had spilled into the castle; the siege was all but over. And it hadn't even been twenty minutes since it had begun.

"But I'm not anyone's hero," I said, trembling even as I tried not to, "I can't fight, or win a battle or command armies or anything. I didn't even…"

"Eduud chose you for a reason," Zaahis said. He smiled, and gripped my shoulder again, "I have faith in you."

Shouts and screams echoed; there was no way they could have been anything but the voices of men slaughtering and of others being slaughtered. They were getting closer, and we had five minutes before they reached us, at best.

"If they see you, we'll lose what chance you have of getting out of alive," Zaahis continued, "And if they have me to deal with, they won't wonder where you are till it's too late."

Bass reached up to put his hand on the King's shoulder.

"You know what to do," he said. It wasn't a question.

"Put up a good fight, and then surrender," the King replied grimly, "Live to strike back another day. I remember. You taught me well, Bass."

"Don't go get yourself killed on me," Bass said.

"You don't have to do this for me," I said, a lump rising in my throat, "You…"

"I do not do this for you," Zaahis said, his voice calm and collected. "I am doing this for my people. As should you."

He smiled. There was no malice in his voice; no regret, no anger, nothing. It would have been better if he had yelled at me, raged at what a failure I was for not Choosing, at how his people were dead and dying thanks to my stupidity.

If only he'd yelled.

"Remember, Champion," he said, "My people are the reason why you're here. Do not let them down."

Bass stumped past, holding high one of the torches he'd pilfered off the wall. Laehn looked at me from inside the tunnel entrance, his impatience obvious.

"Good fortune, Alan," King Zaahis said, still smiling, "With you go the two best people you could hope for. You will succeed."

He prodded at the wall again, and as the door rumbled into place I saw the glint of steel inside the other tunnel. Echoing battle cries burst into a deafening roar as soldiers in blue armor rushed into the into the chamber like a tidal wave, the ones in the lead fanning out and crouching with crossbows aimed.

The last thing I saw as the gap closed for good was the King charging, sword drawn. A brave man; another one who thought I was a failure but still did his best to bring out in me the courage he thought I had.

If only he'd yelled.

Chapter 6

If the first passage was long and uncomfortable, this one made it look like a stroll in the park. Laehn took the lead, sprinting in short bursts and halting long enough for us to catch up to him before dashing off again. Bass was next with the torch held behind him, illuminating the path ahead without the light blinding him the way it did me. He jogged steadily, surprisingly fast enough to leave me gasping for breath after five minutes.

I followed at the back, struggling slightly to keep up, with the hovering flames just ahead blinding me to anything else that might have been in the passage. There I was: in a dark tunnel, running towards the light.

None of us spoke, and I had the feeling none of us wanted to. There wasn't anything to be said, after all.

After eternity and a few more minutes, a loud clunk echoed from far ahead, and a chink of light opened up in the blackness beyond the flames. Laehn had found the other end of the tunnel.

I was the last one to clamber out of the hole, and the first thing I did was to involuntarily fall to my knees and gasp for breath as Bass threw aside the torch.

The transition from the deathly silence to a chaotic roar of voices was disorienting. A pungent smoky aroma lingered in the air, and the skies were choked with the actual stuff. The soundtrack playing was the usual you'd expect from a city being sacked: screams, explosions, shouts, and lots of each.

"Where are we?" I asked.

"The city," Bass replied curtly.

The wall rumbled behind me and slammed shut with a thud of finality. There wasn't any going back, even if we wanted to.

Right then, there in the real world, I wanted to.

The narrow stone paved street was littered in rubbish, and people were running around in panic all around us. Even though I'd just escaped that claustrophobic burrow, the grimy walls on either side seemed to want to suffocate us between them, and a cold hand squeezed at my heart. From where we stood, it looked like we were in a maze of dirty narrow passages, and the end of the street we were on zigzagged into the distance.

Bass reached into the folds of his cloak and pulled out something I'd completely forgotten we had: a long, wooden tube, dangling on the string round his neck.

"Is that the mule whistle?" I demanded. He nodded and raised it to his lips.

I'd been expecting ultrasonic, but the sound that came out of the little pipe could have replaced any single one of the piercing bugles I'd heard till now and no one would have noticed.

"How did that even HAPPEN?" I yelled, jamming my palms over my ears far too late to keep them from ringing like a fire truck.

"It's a mule whistle!" Bass yelled, "You might not have noticed, ours is rather deaf in an ear!"

He screwed his eyes shut and blew again. I yelled as it blared, and Laehn stretched out an arm to steady himself against the wall.

"The mule will come to us if it heard it," he said, voice strained, "And the chance of the soldiers not responding to that, Bass, is very slim at best. Let us not do that again. Please."

Bass nodded, dropped the whistle and stuffed it under the neck of his garment. I made a silent vow to steal it from him the first chance I had and lose it forever.

We stumbled down the street, roads branching out in either direction as we went. Some people pushed past us in a hurry to flee down one of the roads, and I lost sight of them in the curling smoke.

"How are we ever going to get out?" I moaned.

"Follow us," Bass suggested, "Let's go."

Out in the open air, the sounds of war carried far too easily, echoing around the high walls and narrow paths to end up eerily distorted and much more frightening than they would have been. I heard the sounds of falling rubble, voices screaming in pain, the yells of battle frenzied soldiers… it was all too *real*.

This wasn't a movie, where you watch the blood being spilled and hear those screams filtered through your speakers while reclining in your couch with a bowl of popcorn. This was hearing people being killed right in front of you, not too far away.

I was *in* this movie. And these killers were after me, after *my* blood, not the blood of some random character I'd become attached to on a two dimensional flat screen, thanks to good scripting.

And it didn't help how, in my armor, I stuck out like a sore thumb, something which the other two noticed at once.

"Forgot how the damn thing shines," Bass muttered.

"If we could have reached the wagon, we might have used some spare cloaks to disguise him," Laehn said.

"Aye, the mule should have been here by now," Bass said, his forehead creasing, "They've taken over the front, and they're working their way here. Probably blocking its path."

A particularly blood curdling cry echoed over us. Believe you me, you'll never really know what that really means till you hear that brand of scream and feel your blood curdle.

Not a good feeling.

"No doubt now," Bass sighed, "We've lost the wagon."

We pushed and shoved past panicking people, running for the end of the street. The walls expanded into a junction; the streets adjacent to us were twice as wide as the one we were on now, and I could hear the voices down the end of the lane on the left. The path ahead looked the same as the one we were on now, and the smoke obscured the end halfway down.

"We shouldn't stay here," I said, "What do we do?"

"We're going to have to find horses," Bass muttered, "Shame… I'll miss that mule."

He sighed and bowed his head. I shot him a glance, and at the sight of his very real sorrow, I felt a pang and a lump rise in my throat.

"I.… I guess I'll miss him, too," I said, looking at my feet, "That mule was fast."

We stood in silence. It could not possibly become any odder than how that moment was right then: we were literally running for our lives and the enemy almost at our heels, but we still felt the need to bow down in a minute of silence to remember the most disgustingly malodourous mammal to have ever lazily sauntered into our lives.

I remembered the trumpets and many expulsions I had had the unfortunate luck to witness, and just as I recalled one particularly nasty one, I heard a long, familiar toot.

I raised my head.

"Wasn't that…?"

A loud clatter of hooves on stone echoed off the high walls. Round a corner halfway down the street to the left streaked out a white blur, and behind it came the wagon, teetering wildly on two wheels as it barely made it to the street in one piece.

"It made it," I croaked.

The mule bellowed a colossal bray, and its hooves scrabbled wildly in an effort to slow it down as we backed the heck off the road. The wagon fishtailed and swung around before coming to a stop, inches in front of us

I breathed again.

The mule snorted and pawed the ground, and right then, I was happy enough to hug the thing. It gave us a welcoming toot, and I quickly decided that this was maybe not the best time to show such a degree of affection.

The three of us hurried to the wagon, but jumped away in unison when a chubby green face popped over the side, the last one I'd expected to see again.

"Thank goodness," Captain Ajold muttered. He opened his mouth to say more, but then his eyes twitched. He threw his torso over the side and retched.

"What are you doing here?!" Bass demanded as he leaned up again and wiped his mouth with the back of his hand.

"The Gates have fallen and they're on their way," the Captain moaned, "We need to leave before too late."

"What are *you* doing *here*?" Bass repeated, slower and louder on the emphasis.

"Brought you your wagon," the Captain wheezed, "They're coming. Get in already."

"And what about the King?" I demanded, "And your men?!"

"We've lost already," the Captain said, regret etched in his face, "The castle has finally fallen. But you are still our hope. You will need all the help you can get to defeat Mugatu, and I offer myself."

I glanced at Bass.

"One idiot on this trip is too much already!" he snapped, "We don't need…"

"Look, there's nothing more I can do here other than die or be taken prisoner!" the Captain yelled, going from green to red in a heartbeat, "And you need me! They're coming, so let's go!!"

"We can argue the point later," Laehn said, ever the voice of reason, "They come."

He was right. Far down the same lane, I heard the sound of stomping feet before I saw the sun glint off the blue trimmed armor.

Laehn and Bass swung themselves into the wagon, and I took the Captain's hand as he strained to pull me up. Bass fell into the driver's seat and took the reins.

"Yah!"

The mule took off again, passing gas as he bolted, almost like the worlds foulest exhaust pipe.

The men chasing after us on foot flattened themselves against the wall as a trio of horses charged past them. One of the riders had a crossbow raised and was taking aim even as they and we raced along the bumpy, narrow street.

He was on a jolting horse, aiming at a target moving at almost twice his speed, over two hundred feet away and rocking from side to side. No matter how good he was, I told myself, there was no way he would hit any of us.

And just as I had that thought, there was a bolt speeding right at me.

"I hate crossbows!" I yelled.

I spun around, but before I could jump aside, it hit me in the back and sent me sprawling forward. I landed hard, banging my jaw against the inside of the helmet. I laid there for a few moments, contemplating how I was a goner and very aware of the dull throbbing pain in the small of my back and the blood bubbling up just under my tongue.

"What happened?!" I heard Bass yell.

"Crossbow," Laehn answered.

I felt the wagon swerve round a corner.

I wasn't dead yet. I wiggled my fingers and moved my toes, and sat up slowly. The dull ache was gone, and for some reason, I couldn't feel the shaft of wood which should have been nestled between my ribs. Confused, I raised my visor and turned around to see the bolt on the floor, its broken off tip a few inches away.

"You are not even wounded?" Laehn asked. Wide eyed and his jaw hanging, this was the first and probably only time I'd ever see *him* surprised.

Bass looked back at us over his shoulder and chuckled, "Looks like there's some use to your cloak after all, boy."

The Captain's eyes widened, and Laehn was actually smiling. I pulled my towel and took a look at where the arrow had struck the armor. There wasn't even a dent.

Believe it or not, my towel was bulletproof.

The mule took another corner and the wagon rocketed around it, swinging all of us to the side and almost tipping us over completely.

"Hey, watch it!" I yelled.

"Almost there!" Bass called.

And there, at the end of the lane, I could see the outer wall rise up, larger and thicker than any of the buildings around us. As we drew closer to it, stone and brick began to be replaced by wood and tar; homes and buildings were shabbier and poorly constructed piles of firewood.

"Incoming!!" the Captain roared in my ear. It was totally unnecessary; we could all see the huge boulder sailing up over the wall and arcing down towards us.

The mule brayed and put on a burst of speed, and the mass of rock smashed into the ground behind us, turning the street into a fountain of rubble.

"They won!" I yelled, "Why are they still flinging those rocks?"

"It's far too much fun to stop once you start," Bass yelled, "It isn't every day you get to kick back and lay waste to a city, now is it?"

The mule took a quick right turn, leaving my reply hanging in the air behind us, along with the rest of my breath and sanity.

We were moving adjacent to the wall now, and yet we were still over two hundred feet away from it. There was no way we could get any closer; we could see the soldiers pouring into the city but keeping to the wall as the artillery from the outside kept bombarding the city.

"Where do we get out?!" I yelled.

"Another secret passage!" the Captain hollered, "Just down the… INCOMING!"

Time slowed.

The arc of this boulder would have taken it over our heads, and it would have passed by even before we reached it. I watched as it sailed by overhead, as sluggish to my adrenaline pumped mind as me getting out of bed in the morning.

It crashed into the top of a building just ahead, reducing the top half of it to rubble and firewood. The momentum carried it forward and further into the city, but the shattered remains it left behind had nowhere to go but down.

And down would be right on top of us.

The mule was too fast to stop now and, at that point, it was impossible for even another burst of speed to get us past the looming kill zone.

I breathed in.

Time switched to fast forward.

Bass spun and dove at me. His shoulder hit me in the chest and knocked me clean over the end of the wagon. I landed hard on my back on the safe, still ground, Bass on top of me. Laehn was already a few feet behind us, having done the same thing to Ajold.

"NO!" I yelled.

The mule bellowed. Without the weight of four pesky humans, it lowered its head and brought on the burst it needed. Wooden beams and rubble fell down to the street, and both mule and wagon vanished in a cloud of dust.

Seconds later, there was a loud strangled bray, a sickening thud, and a loud, prolonged trumpet of gas.

I sat up again, acutely aware I had done far too many painful sit ups since I'd arrived here. The dust was slowly clearing, even as another rock sailed by overhead, landing somewhere further inside the city.

Bass was already at the pile of rubble, peering through it anxiously.

"Is it okay?!" I coughed.

The mule brayed.

"He's okay," Bass said, his voice as gravelly as always, "Looks like he made it clear of the debris, but the halter pulled him back. He's on top of the pile, and he's fine."

"Can we make it through?" Laehn asked, dusting himself off.

"We've been spotted," the Captain yelped, pointing behind us, "They're coming!"

They were. No horses this time, but the blue soldiers were coming at us in droves, damn crossbows at the ready and spears raised.

"Climb over the top," Bass said, "Come on, move."

"If we can make it through, they will, too," I said, my heart beginning its drum solo in my temples again, "How much farther is it to this passage of yours?"

"Just round the corner," the Captain panted, "but if they see us open it, they will be able to follow, and once we're out, we have no way to outrun them without a wagon."

"Let's worry about that once we're on the other side of this, shall we?" Bass snapped, "Go!"

He clambered on top of the pile, and reached a hand down to pull the Captain up. Laehn was already at the highest point, bow drawn and aimed.

He shot five arrows, seconds apart, and then drew another five. He had a moment's pause, and then fired again.

A crossbow bolt hit a wooden beam by my head and quivered ominously.

"Come on, come on," Bass grumbled, grabbing my arm and hoisting me up effortlessly. The mule was lying on its side on the top of the pile, the halter disappearing under the debris and forcing its head against the side of a wooden beam. It saw us and snorted, like, "About time, already."

The Captain released the halter, and it bounced up again. Hooves scrabbling wildly, it slid down to the other side, a small avalanche of broken wood following in its wake. We clambered down after it, and as I landed hard on my steel clad bottom, I could hear the voices of the men closing in on the other side.

"I have the entrance," the Captain wheezed, on his knees. He grabbed an inconspicuous ring set into one of the flagstone in the corner of the street, and tugged, beads of sweat popping over his chubby face.

"Help me," he grunted.

The soldiers were almost on the other side of the pile of wood. Bass had raised his stick, and Laehn was crouched down, helping the Captain shift aside the heavy stone block. I took out my tiny razor, feeling like a fool.

"We need…" the Captain panted, "more… time…"

"If we could set fire to the wood," Bass said, digging out his matchbox, "That would slow them down long enough."

"With a match?" Laehn demanded, setting down the stone, "By the time it catches fire, they would be over it and after us."

My chest hurt, my legs hurt, the back of my head hurt. I looked from Bass's box of matches, to Laehn's grim eyes, to the mule's long face, to the Captain's sweaty brow…

My eyes shot back to the mule. It stared at me, its expression the mule equivalent of a human raising an eyebrow.

"We have the mule," I said.

"Now is not the time to lose your mind, boy." Bass snapped.

The pile began to creak as men began to climb to the top from the other side. We were running out of time.

"Give me the matchbox!" I yelled.

I don't know what it was that made Bass listen to me for the first time that day. Maybe it was my wild eyes, or the sound of my voice, or maybe he thought how since we were about to die anyway, he might as well let me try out something for once.

He held it out. I turned to the mule, which inexplicably spun around to face its rear to the pile. How it knew my insane idea was anyone's guess; but when it obediently bent its forelegs and waited expectantly, I knew then that this, here, was the elusive now or never moment.

I looked at the Captain, who was as white as a sheet, at Laehn, who took three quick steps backward, and at Bass, on whose face realization was now dawning.

"Are you doing what I think you're doing?!" the Captain demanded.

"Trust him," Bass said savagely, the wild glint in his eye only then prodding me to consider the sanity of this plan.

But by then, it was too late. The soldiers were already on the top of the pile, and I could hear a deep rumbling from within the depths of the mule's stomach.

The Captain whimpered as I struck the match.

"NOW!" Bass bellowed.

I threw it down as the mule let out one of the most ear splitting, nostril burning emissions of its extremely productive career. The match exploded into an inferno, a blaze which washed over wooden debris, bathing the in pile in flames that burned red hot and stank worse than burnt rubber.

The wood caught instantly, an inferno rising straight up in a small explosion. The screaming men who had just reached the top were thrown over the heads of their fellows.

It was a foul, acrid, beautiful equine flamethrower.

The mule gave off a final toot, as if emptying the tank, and sauntered towards the hole in the road, shaking its hindquarters like... well, as they say, like a boss.

The street was on fire between them and us, and the flames jumped to the buildings on either side. At that rate, the entire wooden section of the city would be a furnace within ten minutes, but I was too exhilarated with the fruit of my brilliant idea to care about anything else right then.

Some of the debris shifted within the pile, exposing a hole large enough to look through. The soldiers on the other side saw me and cursed, and yet no man was brave enough to venture any closer.

I took off my helmet and drank in the beauty of it. I let out a victory whoop, which Bass echoed with gusto.

"There are ways around," the Captain called, his voice still trembling. He crouched at the side of the hole in the ground, shaking, "Please, let's go already!"

"He is right," Laehn said, slinging his bow on his back again and slipping the arrows into his quiver, "We must leave while we have the advantage."

He didn't have to say it twice, but as I turned, I noticed movement on the other side of the blaze. I peered out through the hole and saw the soldiers move to either side of the street and stand at attention.

"Alan!" Bass shouted.

"Hold up!" I said, raising a hand, "Something's happening."

Someone was walking towards us, pushing apart the soldiers around like they were nothing. Nine foot tall, built like an ox, wearing a gigantic helm shaped like the head of a bull, the last I had seen of him had just been a silhouette, but I'd have recognized him anywhere.

"It's Kernine!" Laehn called, "We should go, NOW!"

He came, rust colored armor rippling, stained here and there with darker patches of what had to have been blood. A beefy fist wrapped around the haft of a gigantic double bladed battle axe, the blade dripping red and dangling bits of hair and gore off one end.

Physics didn't seem to exist here. That axe shouldn't have been able to have leave the ground.

Through the heat waves radiating off the bonfire, his enormous figure shivered and shook as he walked towards us, like the image of Satan rising from hell.

Even then, in that time of peril, with my knees knocking together, I envied the guy his entrance.

"So," he said, stomping to a halt, a foot closer to the flames than the rest of his men, "You may have not Chosen yet, but yet you do know how to handle yourself. Admirable, I might have to say."

"Keep admiring," I said, barely keeping my teeth from clicking, "You've tried to get to me twice, and yet here I am."

He reached up and took off the red helmet. He was bald; his red face resembled a marble statue which had been carved by an amateur on his first day at pottery class, and been dropped quite a few times since then. Scars ran up and down his cheeks, and his small, beady black eyes were trained on me.

He smiled; with the combination of his missing teeth and the color of the ones remaining, he really shouldn't have done that.

I decided I liked him better with the helmet on.

"Commendable though you may be, I give you this warning," he snarled, his cold, eyes burning in hate, "Other Champions have failed before you. Tyrants have ruled for years after the Champions Summoned to fight them were killed. You will fare no better."

My pre-prepared retort died on my tongue. What he said did not make sense.

He saw the look on my face, and his scowl turned into a mocking smile.

"Oh, I forgot. You wouldn't know that, now would you?" he said.

"I wouldn't know what?!" I demanded.

"Boy, come on!" Bass yelled, but I could hear the note of desperation in his voice, "He's trying to stall you till his men come through from the other side!"

Kernine laughed out loud.

"Go, by all means," he roared, "Listen to Bass. Of course, he wouldn't want you to know, now would he?"

"Alan, come on," Bass said, and this time, he was definitely pleading.

Of course, I stayed.

"He wouldn't want me to know what?!" I demanded.

The pile of wood shifted, sending gouts of flame leaping up.

"What did they tell you?" Kernine asked, his voice loud and mocking, "That you were special? How you were the first and only?"

I turned to Bass, crouching by the hole with his face as pale as I had ever seen.

"You aren't the first Champion," Kernine said, "And you probably won't be the last."

I looked back at him, confused and afraid, "What are you…?"

"You don't have to believe me," he said, pointed through the hole, "Ask them."

"Bass?" I asked softly.

He looked away from me.

Kernine laughed again, his voice echoing off the walls and streets.

"Go," he said, gesturing, "You have won yourselves another day. And you will have much to discuss, I'm sure. Go."

He turned and stomped away. The soldiers around him exchanged confused glances, but when he raised his fist, they turned as one and scurried after him.

"Bass…" I said, my voice shaking, "What did he say?"

The pile of wood shifted again, and this time collapsed inwards on itself on one side. The hole was gone; but what I had heard kept echoing.

"Alan," Laehn said, "Come."

I glared at him, but he was right. As the fire leaped to the other buildings all along the road, I jammed my helmet over my head and ran towards them. I dropped through the hole, landing in another claustrophobic stone burrow, and Bass followed.

Laehn closed the stone on top of us, and I was blind.

Chapter 2

Once again, I sat at a campfire with only the crackling flames and occasional odorous toot to break the quiet. The long grass was knee high on either side of the road, but we'd cleared a camping site and stomped flat a small circle in which we sat.

Night had fallen by the time we'd finally climbed out of the passage and into a countryside dark for miles around. It hadn't been easy to start a fire, but thanks to foresight, Laehn and Ajold had managed to salvage some of the wood from the wreckage which hadn't been burned, and Bass had somehow managed to save two sacks out of the load in the wagon; one with the pot and the wooden bowls, and another one with the ingredients to his brew.

As Bass struck the match, I wondered for the first time where the matchbox had come from, and what it was doing in a time where matches had no place being.

The conversation leading to someone explaining what exactly Kernine had been talking about took its time coming; the others avoided my gaze and only spoke when they had to, their words clipped.

I didn't want to ask them if what I'd heard was true; given their reactions, there wasn't a doubt. I didn't want to hear their explanations, in any case. Mona was on my mind; she was always on my mind.

Right then, though, as I looked at the wizened old man on the other side of the fire, the question in my mind was why I hadn't knocked Bass unconscious when his guard was down, tied him up and threatened to starve him or something him till he sent me home.

If they'd being lying to me all this time, I reasoned, then they'd been lying to me about not being able to send me back, too. They needed me for some reason to finish off this Mugatu whom I still hadn't even met; and so they obviously wouldn't want me to go till I finished the job.

Maybe the whole thing about Eduud and his portals was a sham, something to keep me satisfied till they got me to do what they wanted.

Bass hadn't wanted me to listen to Kernine, which was darn well apparent; they didn't want me to know what I knew now. I wasn't the only Champion; there had been Champions before me. And they had died.

So I wasn't some Chosen one after all, unlike what every single person had led me to believe all along. I could die anytime, anywhere. I might have almost been close to dying already.

I lost track of how long we sat there. I hadn't bothered taking my armor off; there was something prodding me in the shoulder, but I didn't bother shifting to budge it. With my not-too-pleasant thoughts keeping me company, it could have been anything from fifteen minutes to an hour that I'd been sitting there.

As the flames threw flickering shadows on their faces, again I asked myself the other question which kept returning for encores: should I fight them and make a break for it?

I eyed them, one by one.

Bass, busy filling his pipe, done with stirring the pot which now hung over the fire. Many times had I seen him move faster than any old man had any business to, and I doubted my chances with him even if there had been a way to separate him from his stick; I'd never seen the two apart.

I shifted my gaze to Captain Ajold, looking as worried as always, legs crossed and jowly face fixed on the fire. He may have been rotund and had the courage of a mouse, but he had his sword and some reasonable amount of experience if not skill with it, if his rank had anything to go by.

And then there was Laehn, sitting there in silence, polishing his bow with a cloth. He was Laehn. Enough said.

Bass stuck his pipe in his mouth and began to ladle out the brew. He handed me a bowl, and I shook my head.

"Eat," he said, "And then we'll talk."

I took it. He passed bowls to the others, and then sat with his own.

"Look, kid," he said, finally, "It would never have had anything to do with…"

"I still had a right to know, didn't I?" I snapped.

Bass's brow furrowed.

"Everything I have said and done," he replied slowly, "I have said and done with good reason."

"Even when that meant LYING to me?!"

The tentative grip I'd been having so long on the tidal wave of emotion was lost. The dam broke, and the anger and hate all poured out, mixing and churning in my head.

"You LIED to me!" I bellowed, "Lead me on, fooled me into thinking I was important, tore me away from Mona, leaving her all alone there… all so I could be your damned SCAPEGOAT!"

I hurled the bowl and its contents into the fire, which flared up and sparked. Ajold jumped back in shock, and Bass closed his eyes and sighed.

"It was wrong of me…" he began, but I wasn't done yet.

I couldn't sit still. I jumped to my feet and balled my hands into fists.

"WRONG of you?!" I yelled, "WRONG?! You never cared about me, about her! You only cared about your damned Quest and your damn people who had NOTHING whatsoever to do with me! I could die right now, and you'll only go get some other witless oaf to do be your little puppet!"

"You could die right now, and then most of us will die with you," Bass snapped. He wasn't lying; there was something in his voice that rang true. Still, I wasn't about to sit down just yet. I started to pace, wanting so badly to punch something, and yet afraid of what they'd do to me if I dared.

"You're our only hope, boy," Bass said, his voice still sharp as a knife, "You're the only one who can defeat Mugatu. I had no control over your being here, no more than you do. But now you're a…"

"Why should I believe you?!" I demanded, "How can I, when all you've been feeding me for so long was a goddamn LIE?!"

"We did not lie to you, Alan."

Laehn narrowed his eyes at me.

"We did not lie," he repeated, satisfied he had my attention, "We only did not tell you all of the truth."

"WHY?"

"For your own good." he paused. "And for ours."

My chest was heaving. I turned back to Bass, who was looking up at me with what might have been sadness in his eyes. I wasn't about it buy it just yet, though.

"Now that it has come to this," Bass sighed, "it would be foolish to go forward without you knowing the rest."

"And how will I know you're not making this up?" I demanded.

"Listen," Laehn said, "and judge for yourself."

So many questions leaped up, demanded to be asked, but I only managed to wrap my head around one and force it into words.

"What did he mean when he said there were Champions before me?" I demanded.

"Sit down," Bass offered, "And try not to start shouting again. Kernine's men are still looking for us out here."

Captain Ajold looked right at me for the first time since we'd left the city. The look in his eyes... he was pleading.

I glared at Bass, and then at Laehn, who had gone back to cleaning his bow. The fire crackled, and over somewhere in the darkness, the mule gave another toot.

I clenched my fists and sat down again.

"Good," Bass said. He took another deep puff, and blew the smoke upwards.

"Aye, Kernine did not lie," he said, rummaging in the sack and bringing out another bowl. "There were Champions before you. And Tyrants, too, like Mugatu. There always has been a Tyrant who rose up, and there always will be Tyrants to rise up. And for each one, there will be a Champion. And that person will be from your world."

"Why our world?" I demanded, "Why couldn't someone from here do it? Like Laehn, like you...?"

"I don't know," Bass shrugged, ladling stew into the fresh bowl, "Our worlds have always been linked. Time and time again, when a new villain tried to conquer a realm, or raise armies from the families of the poor to make war on peaceful neighbors, or charged enough taxes to buy himself a gold plated warship, which, of course, sank majestically the first time it set sail… come to think of it, that one drowned on the ship before we ever got around to Summoning a Champion for him, if I recall correctly."

He drifted off, looking nostalgically into the distance.

"Can we focus, please?" Ajold interrupted.

"Sorry," Bass cleared his throat, shuffled forward and offered the bowl to me. I looked at it skeptically, and my stomach growled, despite myself. Swallowing my pride, I took it from him, avoiding his eyes.

"Whenever someone new rose up to try and take over," Bass continued, sitting back down with his pipe, "Eduud would always be the one to decide whether or not to bring in a new Champion from… from your world. When the Champion came, he or she would Choose one of the three powers, and then would make war upon the Tyrant he or she was brought to defeat."

I watched a lone spark jump off the fire and float around before vanishing into nothing.

"And not all of them survived to defeat the Tyrant, did they?"

"No," Bass admitted, "Not always. Sometimes they died, sometimes… well, sometimes pretty badly."

"Even the ones who had made the Choice?" I asked.

The three of them looked at me.

"What?" I demanded.

Ajold and Laehn turned to Bass.

"You're the first Champion in a long, long time," Bass said slowly, picking his words with care, "who didn't make the Choice immediately after arriving."

"What do you mean, the first?"

"Exactly what it sounds like," Bass replied, "Every Champion for as long as anyone can remember has Chosen minutes after being brought here. Most did not really understand what each Choice represented; some were lucky in picking the one which suited them most, and some weren't. But they… *all…* chose."

"And they died?"

"Even ones who made the Choice suited to them died at the hands of a Tyrant smart enough to defeat them," Laehn said, "And some who made what everyone thought was the wrong Choice succeeded, with help and luck."

"What happened when a Champion died?"

"The Champion Summoned would be the one person who would ever have a chance to defeat the oppressor," Bass said, "If he failed, then there would be no one else who could. And so the Tyrant would win, and rule."

"Didn't anyone else try?" I swallowed.

"Oh, they did," Bass replied with a mirthless laugh, "They never would win. The oppressor would live out his days in glory, doing as he pleased unopposed, until he died. Then, the cycle would begin anew, and another Champion could be Summoned for his successor."

"Why only one Champion?" I demanded, "If the first one died, why not bring another to deal…"

"Only one Champion could be Summoned to do battle with each oppressor," Bass interrupted, "and no more. There were Laws written at the start of it all, and that was the way this one was written; and Eduud has overseen the Laws since the dawn of time, as it were. It's how it has always been done, and if anything, Eduud is a stickler for the rules. You've seen him in action, you should know."

A distant chorus of 'WILT THOU, CHAMPION…" echoed in mind.

"Don't remind me," I muttered, "So after all this, you're saying I could die?"

The question hung in the air like a limp rag dangling inches in front of everyone's faces.

"Yes," Bass said, his classic acidity shining through once more.

"No," Ajold said, at the exact same instant, "Of course not."

I looked at Laehn, the voice of reason.

"From the time you arrived, the outcome of your survival has been slim," he said, "That you have survived thus far… it cannot be more than a mixture of sheer luck and carelessness on the part of the enemy. You may have something in you that will take you to the end."

He paused and shrugged. "Or not."

"That's reassuring," I muttered.

"All odds have been against you from the beginning, boy," Bass said, "Mugatu knew well how the system worked; he's been planning this for years. He knew the steps to take to prevent a Champion from rising, and he followed them to the letter. Had all gone well for him, you'd have never had made it this far. But here you are. All this has to count for something."

"But how?" I demanded, "How could someone plan all that out, to the dot?"

"Because," Laehn said. "He was once a Champion himself."

If he had reached out and clubbed me across the face, I doubt I'd have been half as shocked I was right then.

"Years ago," Bass said, giving me time to recover. "Centuries, actually. We had one of the worst Tyrants to ever rise up. No one knew from where he came, and no one knew where his armies would strike. He conquered the realm with an iron fist like no Tyrant had before or has since."

"Eduud Summoned a Champion, the only person who could have defeated him," Laehn said, "He Summoned Mugatu."

"Or Frank," Bass interjected, "As he was known back then."

"Frank," I repeated. "Seriously. The all-powerful Mugatu was once called Frank?"

Bass shrugged.

"He called himself a hero when he first came. Goodness knows, we needed a hero then. We all believed him; Eduud would never have Summoned wrong. He defeated his Tyrant, and the descendant of the old Kings was found. The Royal Line was reinstated and Frank... Mugatu... stayed on, an idol, loved and hailed by all. He grew rich, powerful, and had friends in the right places; no one saw what he was building up to."

"Not even you?" I asked. This story wasn't what I had expected to hear, but it didn't mean I had to believe a word of it.

Bass sighed. "No, not even me. Why would I? He saved my life once, and risked his own to save the life of the man who would become the King, the same man who was Zaahis' great grandfather. Was it all a ruse to get him into where he could strike? Who would have guessed?"

"What's all this to the two of you?" I demanded, "Where do you come in? If the odds are so bad I'm liable to drop dead anytime within the week, why hang around with me when there'd be crosshairs on your backs, too? Why not run and save yourselves while you can? And don't tell me you're here because of a conscience; you might think me a fool, but I'm not that naïve."

Bass smiled.

"I have a large personal stake in the whole affair," he said. "Believe it or not; I was once where you are now. I know better than anyone else how hard it can be for a Champion on his Quest."

"Sure you do," I scoffed.

"You'd be surprised," he said, "But then again, I was a Champion, too."

As you'd expect, this second bomb had as much effect on me as the first, but this time I recovered faster.

"YOU?!" I demanded.

He smiled, "Aye. This would probably explain to you my rank and why I'm so close to the King."

"You're... you're from home, then?" I stammered, "From... Earth?"

Bass chuckled.

"Aye," he said, "Back there, I was called George. George Bass, surgeon, and an explorer, back when there was still so much to explore."

"Where were you from?" I demanded.

"A little island called Britain," he grinned.

"Your accent is anything but British," I pointed out.

"I've been here for a few dozen centuries, son," Bass puffed out a smoke ring, "The accent faded a long time ago."

I'd taken my first mouthful of brew, just in time to send it out in a fine spray all over the fire.

"How *old* are you?" I choked.

Bass puffed on his pipe.

"Not a clue, kid," he said, "And at this point, I don't think it really matters."

"But… how is it even possible?" I licked my dry lips, "You… you should be…"

"Dead, I know," he agreed, "I don't feel older than sixty. I don't know why, but I age slower, much slower than I should. We all do; us Champions who survive and stay behind, I mean."

"Survive and stay behind?"

"Not all of them die," he shrugged, "And not all of them want to go back home after they're done. The ones who stay back and do not die in battle or in any accidents… they keep living. And so will you, if you decide to stay."

"Out of the question," I snapped, my temper returning to push my amazement out of the room. The tension returned for a while, and no one spoke. Curiosity got the better of me, though, as it always does, and I eventually looked up at them.

"How did *you* get here?"

Bass jerked awake and shook his head.

"Oh, me?" he coughed. "Don't think I'll forget that in a hurry. It happened when I was halfway to

Tahiti on the *Venus*, back when the year was 1803. Took my boat out one evening for a spot of quiet fishing, and the next thing I knew, I was being sucked into a whirlpool. Woke up half drowned in the Summoning Chamber, with my boat in splinters and this..." he raised Tom, "being the biggest piece there was."

"That was your weapon," I said, "The blade from the forges of your land."

"Aye," he ran a hand fondly over the rough surface, "That quote doesn't have to be literal, as it happens. It came with me from my land, so it was what I would use to bond with the Armament. When I did, Tom turned into a staff, one like you'd never hope to see, Alan. I'd Chosen Skill, and it's what's kept me going all these centuries. You've seen I can still hold my own in any fight."

"And why do you call it 'Tom'?"

Bass chuckled.

"The first boat I had, somewhere around 1790 or thereabouts, was tiny," he said, "so I called it the *Tom Thumb*, sort of an I joke with my first mate. Had another boat roughly the same size, not too long after, and called that the *Tom Thumb* as well. Granted, the *Venus* was the one I took when Eduud Summoned me; but I'd been on the lifeboat when he did, and it just so happened I named the lifeboat *Tom*. Call it sentiment. This piece of timber is all what's left of the third Tom."

Hunger gnawed at my insides. I picked up the bowl again and took a huge gulp. There are times when you're hungry enough so even the vilest concoction tastes good; this, though, wasn't one of those times.

"How come it's a stick again?" I asked, drawing the back of my hand over my mouth.

"The Armament bonds with the Weapon for as long as the Champion is in need. When my time was done, it remained with me for a few years," he shrugged, "When the next Tyrant tried to rise, I wasn't the one to defeat him, as you'd understand."

"Only one Champion per Tyrant," I said, "Yeah. So Eduud Summoned another one?"

"Aye," Bass nodded, "And the moment he did, the Armament left Tom and returned to where Champions claim it from. The new Champion was the one to defeat the new Tyrant, not me; didn't mean I couldn't help, though."

I licked my dry lips with a drier tongue, and turned to Laehn, who was polishing his bow again.

"Are you a Champion, too?"

He smiled one of his rare smiles, Bass chuckled and Ajold laughed in the background.

"No," he said, "I am from here. What skills I have are what I learned in my travels and my training."

"You wanted to know why his face changed," Bass said, and Ajold stiffened. Laehn gave Bass a hard look, and the old man shrugged.

"Well, he knows now, and it would help him understand."

Laehn's green eyes narrowed.

"Laehn has been training for combat all his life," Bass said, "And for most of his life he has been protecting and aiding the King and his men. The last Champion, a few decades ago… his Tyrant was a mage, and a powerful one. Laehn joined us in that campaign."

I glanced at Laehn out of the corner of my eye; there was look of murder on his face as he carefully swiped down the bow. A part of me wanted to tell Bass to stop, that I didn't really want to know. The rest of me, of course, was too curious for its own good.

"The final battle dawned," Bass continued, "And the Champion became too eager. He made a mistake, and the mage attacked. Laehn used a shield to deflect the spell, and saved the Champion's life. It rebounded, though, and took him in the face.

"What did it do to you?" I whispered.

"Not this," Bass said, waving a hand at the archer's long, straight blonde hair and the still-so-prominent ears, "This is what Eduud was forced to do to save him. If he hadn't, Laehn would have died, and painfully, at that. Eduud almost never does anything other than Summoning Champions… and sending them home. It's part of the Law how he not interfere."

"Magic?" I asked, "That's a thing here, then? And not just for Eduud and his portals?"

"Aye," Bass nodded, "And now you know why Laehn wanted nothing more to do with Champions and their Tyrants anymore."

"But you're still here, now," I pointed out.

"Don't push it," Bass warned.

"Now we have concluded that tale," Laehn stiffly interjected, "May we move on?"

Bass cleared his throat, and I coughed. The fire crackled, and the mule sounded off.

"So you're like, what, a thousand years old?" I asked.

"Give or take a couple hundred," Bass chuckled, "You'll age slow too, kid. If you decide to stay."

"I thought I made it clear," I said, anger returning, "The only reason I'm doing this is so I can go back home. I'm not staying back here, Bass, and you're not going to make me."

A flutter in my chest, suspiciously resembling a sob, forced me to break off in mid rant.

The three of them looked away from me again, and the silence resumed.

I shook my head.

"None of this makes any sense," I muttered.

"Oh, don't you start again," Bass griped, "So far, has anything you have seen or done made sense? You set fire to a pile of wood using a mule's natural gas and a box of matches, for crying out loud! And that's an indestructible towel you have draped over your shoulders there."

He did make a fair point.

"About the matchbox," I said, finally seeing light shed on the sore point pricking at the back of my mind.

He nodded, "Aye, not the sort of thing you'd expect to see around here, eh? When some people cross over, they bring new things with them. A box of matches was one of them. Technology here is slow, but they're quick to copy anything and spread it around if it's good enough."

"I assume that's how you knew what my razor was," I accused.

"Aye," he said, smiling.

"So, let me see if I have this right," I said, "You hang around till a Tyrant pops up, and Eduud Summons a Champion. Then you train that poor victim and send him off to kill or be killed."

"Pretty much," Bass agreed.

"What do you do in the meantime?"

He shrugged.

"After I killed General T'Channs, the Tyrant I was summoned to kill, I've helped with other Champions on their Quests," he said, "And I had mentors, sort of like you have me, only not as good."

"Modest, aren't you."

"I became the King's Advisor when my elders died, left or decided to leave the wars behind," he continued, "Over the centuries, I've seen Kings come and go, Tyrants rise and fall; and I've seen Champions fail and the realm plunge into darkness for decades or more. All that, and here I am. Anyone with sense fears me; as they well should."

He inhaled and blew out another cloud of smoke.

"Oh, and yes," he added, as an afterthought, "I keep bees."

"Bees?" I echoed.

"Bees," he clarified. "Always wanted to try keeping them when I was… home. I never could find a chance till I arrived here."

"Sure it was," I muttered. I raised a hand to my forehead and rubbed hard at the dull ache just above my eyes.

"Why didn't you tell me this at the start?" I demanded.

"None of the Champions I mentored ever learned the whole story till after they had defeated their enemy," he said, "You had enough happening to distract you with whomever you had to defeat. Confidence in invincibility, even if it didn't exist, sometimes gave one the push they needed to succeed where they wouldn't otherwise."

"And overconfidence in powers they didn't have could kill them just as quickly." I pointed out.

"Knowing all this, and how you could die, how others before you had died; tell me, Alan. Do you really feel better now? Are you any more confident about winning?"

He gave me a cold, hard look. I stared back into his eyes, and then lowered my head. He was right. It didn't. I'd probably have been better off not knowing I wasn't invincible.

"You're the first one to both *not* Choose *and* find out about the legacy before you faced your Tyrant," Bass said, "This one's new for us all, kid."

No one spoke for a while. A cold wind picked up, and I instinctively wrapped my towel/cloak closer around me.

"Did they ever get to know?" I asked, "Other Champions?"

"Aye," Bass nodded, "If they survived, it was Eduud's role to tell them all. And then, he gave them their second Choice; to return, like some did, or stay here, like myself and the rest."

"Why would anyone want to stay?" I demanded, "When we have lives over there?"

"Everyone has their reasons, boy," Bass said, "Some found their new lives here better than what they'd had before. Others were ready for a new beginning, and being a hailed hero for the rest of your days… that's always nice."

"What was your excuse for staying, then?" I asked, "Surgeon and adventurer like yourself?"

Bass smiled at me, and this was one of his sadder ones.

"I'm an explorer," he said simply, "And this was a whole new world for me to explore."

Something did not feel quite right, the way he said it. Not that I had become psychic or anything, but

I could tell he wasn't telling the truth; or at least, not all of it.

"No, that can't be it," I said.

Bass's eyes hardened, and he looked away from me and into the fire.

"I had my reasons, boy," he said, his voice harsh, "And they're nobody's business but mine."

Captain Ajold shifted uncomfortably, and Laehn sat a bit straighter. The lull and calm which had started to settle was gone again; tension had built up between the four of us again.

I cast around for a change of subject. I knew I had promised myself I wouldn't believe a word of whatever excuse they were about to make; but you had to admit, this story had to be believable, even a little bit.

"The armor I'm wearing," I said, "Is it the same one you…?"

"No," Bass said, sounding relieved at the change of subject; the electricity seeped away, "No, this armor was created especially for you. It was part of the enchantment Eduud cast when you were Summoned. You're the only one it would ever fit."

"And what happened to yours?"

"Gone," Bass replied, wistfully, "Centuries ago. I wore it to every battle and war I had the misfortune to fight in, and it saw plenty of wear and tear after a couple dozen decades. These things don't come with spare parts, and there's a pity. Look after yours well, boy. The only one you'll ever get, and you'll never wear a finer."

I nodded.

"So what's this Armament you keep talking about, anyway?"

"It's where we have to go next," Laehn said.

"There's no way to explain it," Bass said, "You have to see it for yourself. It will bond with the blade you brought from home; it will turn that useless razor into the weapon you will use to kill Mugatu."

I swallowed.

"Do I have to kill him?" I asked.

Bass sighed.

"Believe you me, boy," he said, "That's the very same thing I asked Eduud when he brought me here. I'd never killed a man before, either. But I had to. He forced me into it, and it happened."

I took a deep shuddering breath, and let it go.

"Do it for Mona's sake," Bass said, his voice ironically kind.

"She wouldn't want me to kill a man for her," I snapped.

"It's the only way you'll ever see her again," Laehn said, his tone cold.

I glared at him.

"I never asked for this, and you all know it," I snapped. "And none of you deserve to talk about her. So don't."

"We never asked for you, and you know it," Bass replied curtly. "You're all we've got to work with, and we're all you have to keep you alive. These people need you; for what it's worth, you're their hope Alan. So pull yourself together and be a man. The sooner you end this, the sooner you can get going."

I don't know why I turned to Captain then, but when I did, I saw him gaze into the fire, his face troubled. It was understandable for him to be worried, given the odds which all of a sudden seemed much, much greater than when we had first set out from that safe house, miles away. But the look on his face; it bothered me in a way I couldn't put a finger on.

"We had enough for one day," Bass said, "And we've a ride ahead of us. Get some rest, kid. We'll talk more tomorrow."

And that was it for the night.

Chapter 8

I didn't need Bass to wake me the next morning; thanks to good old force of habit, my eyes popped open just as the sky began to lighten. The others had already woken; the campsite was clean, down to where the fire had been the night before. Laehn was missing, as usual; but this time there were two new horses tied to the tree, snorting and turning up their noses at the mule, who'd decided for some reason that the grass just around there was what it needed for breakfast.

The mule was a plain old bully.

The horses weren't bare; they had all kinds of fastenings and bags hanging off straps attached to their saddles. And these were no ordinary plow horses; these were of the huge, ride-into-battle variety.

I looked over to where Ajold stood, reaching under his belly to adjust the belts on his breastplate, apparently just finishing with donning his armor.

"Where did those come from?" I asked.

"The horses?" he replied, straightening his tunic, "Laehn went out and found them for us. He took the third out scouting."

"'Found' them?"

"It's Laehn," he shrugged, "I've learned not to ask."

"There are two of them," I pointed out, "And three of us."

"We don't need another horse, we have a mule," Bass called. He walked up behind me, leaning on Tom and trailing smoke off his pipe.

"And you're the one going to ride it, I suppose?" I queried.

"I am," he replied.

I raised an eyebrow.

"I thought it didn't take riders."

"It does when it trusts you," Bass replied, smugly.

"Of course it does," I muttered. I groaned, stretched, and climbed slowly to my feet. My eyes fell on where I'd piled my armor the night before, and yesterday's events came back in a rush, bringing with them soreness in every part of my body.

"I'm going to need help putting this on again," I groaned.

"Learn to do it yourself," Bass said, sitting against the tree, "You'll have to, eventually."

I looked over helplessly at Ajold, who shrugged and walked over.

"Watch while I do this," he said.

It took considerably longer than the first time, but it was finally done. With just the pot and the bowls to carry on, we left the camp and headed East.

"Where to now?" I called over to Bass, a fat man on a fat mule, a sight as comical as it gets, "Where's this Armament?"

"We're heading there," Bass replied, "And why do you bother asking when you know you wouldn't know where it was even if I showed you the map?"

"Making conversation," I said sourly, "So what's next? Find the mystic Oracle and get its blessing? Slay some beast and steal its powers? What quest will I have to complete after this one?"

"Bond the Armament with your Weapon, and then you face Mugatu," Bass replied, "We're just about done."

I swallowed, "Okay then."

Bass chuckled, "Alright, Alan. Now you know what you know. Any other questions you might want to ask?"

"You're getting all chatty for some reason," I pointed out.

Bass shrugged, "It's a long ride. Like you said, I'm making conversation."

I inhaled.

"Okay, then. How many other Champions are out there right now?"

Bass's smile faded.

"Three."

"Just three?"

"You, me, and Mugatu," he said sourly, "Aye, there were more. Many more. He had them systematically wiped out as he rose to power. Some we thought were accidents; the rest he had executed the moment he showed his hand."

"You...?"

"I was lucky," Bass snapped, "Or else I'd be dead, too. As of right now, I'm the oldest living Champion here in this realm. Probably the oldest person around, too."

"He wants to be the only Champion left, then."

Bass shrugged, "Aye, you could say that."

I nodded, and spared a glance at Ajold, who was watching us and listening in silence.

"So how many were there? You said you mentored a few."

"Champions?" Bass asked, "Aye, I mentored a lot. Can't remember how many there had been before me, and I sure can't remember how many came after."

"Any names?"

"Well, there was that Lewis Clark fellow; Agatha Christie, she was one of those who went back home; Glen Hyde; Amelia Earheart..."

"Come again," I interrupted, "Amelia Earheart? Like the pilot?"

Bass turned, "You knew her?"

"History books," I said, "She was famous. Went missing in her plane..."

"Aye, the contraption she was in when Eduud Summoned her," Bass said, "We didn't have the fuel she needed to make it fly, though. She was a feisty one."

"What happened to her?"

"She died," Bass said, and a look of pain passed over his aged face, "Killed helping another Champion fight his Tyrant."

"They keep coming then," I said, "These Tyrants. Even after Mugatu… there'll be another, won't there?"

"Aye," Bass sighed, "But he won't be your problem, kid. Your time is now."

"But he'll still be yours," I pointed out, "And your time was long past."

"It's a dirty job," Bass replied. He gave me a slow, sad smile., "But someone has to do it."

"But why-?" I began.

"What else would you like to know?" he interrupted. I looked at him, and he looked at the horizon, steadily ignoring me.

I let it go, and another question I'd been wondering about came to mind.

"If Eduud knew the armor was at the castle, why didn't he send us there instead of the safe house?"

"We didn't know if it had been overrun or not," Bass replied.

"I thought Eduud could do that kind of stuff," I protested. "Know where people are, for instance."

"At certain times and for certain reasons," he said. "But one Law or another interfered at that point, so he sent us to where we would be safest. And it happened to be my house."

I couldn't think of anything else to ask, and Bass seemed to have grown tired of indulging me. Out of boredom, I started patting around the bags that were attached to the horse I was riding. In one, I found a packet of hard biscuits, and in another a small, hardy knife.

"Where did he get this horse?" I wondered.

"Off a wandering guard patrol, probably," Bass replied.

Ajold drew a sword out of a sheath attached to the horse.

"Aye, this is from the Castle armory," he said, "These were probably Mugatu's men."

He slipped it into the sheath, and undid the straps.

"Here," he said, tossing it to me, "Until you get your Weapon."

"Careful you don't cut yourself," Bass said. He chuckled.

I awkwardly leaned forward to attach it to my saddle. When I looked up, I noticed a speck growing larger on the meadows ahead.

"Is that Laehn?"

"Aye," Bass replied.

We watched and kept riding as the speck grew larger. The archer came into view, riding a horse similar to mine, minus the baggage. He slowed to a stop as we approached, and then turned to join us at our trot.

"Nothing to report," he said, "I trust you find the mounts to your liking, Champion?"

"Yeah, thanks," I said.

"Any idea on what happened at the Castle?" Ajold asked.

"None," Laehn replied, "I saw no one. The City is fallen, Captain, of that much we can be certain."

"What do you think happened to the King?" I asked, my throat dry.

"He'd know not to be a fool enough to get himself killed," Bass replied, "And since Mugatu knows I'm still with you, he'd want to use Zaahis as leverage. We'd best hope he doesn't decide to kill the King just yet."

"How much farther to the Armament?" I asked.

"Three day's ride," Laehn replied.

"Why is everything so far away?" I grumbled. A fly buzzed past my face and began to start dive bombing me again.

"It's how things are here, kid," Bass said, "Get used to it."

"So what is it?" I asked, waving my hand irritably, "Some kind of Castle?"

"Aye, you could say that," Bass replied, "But it's more like a mountain, or a rock, if you would."

"It is a place of many names," Laehn added, "It has been known as The Hill of Reclamation, The Mound of Recovery, the Heap of Retrieval, the Mass of…"

"You get the point," Bass cut in. "It's usually deserted, but don't expect that when we get there though; Mugatu would have his people all over it, waiting for you."

"And we're still going there?"

"Aye," Bass's brow furrowed in thought.

"What is it?" I demanded.

"There's no knowing what your Weapon's going to be till you touch it to the Armament," he said, "But right now, you couldn't fight to save yourself with a common sword, I'd wager. You need training."

"As you've been saying since we first met," I snarled, ducking as the fly zoomed past again, a small, demented buzzing missile, "but you never did anything about it, did you?"

"Laehn can start you up today, and every day for as long as you're here," he said. "That sword Ajold gave you should serve."

"Lovely," I said.

And they were true to their word. When the afternoon sun grew too hot to handle, Bass and the Captain lounged in the shade, watching while Laehn taught me to spar. 'Taught' was too strong a word to use, though; what happened was he swung his sword, I missed with mine, and it ended up with me aching all over.

That night, Laehn commandeered a wagon from a village on the way, along with some food, clothing and small tools, including a shovel, though goodness knew what we were going to need it for. We trained at midday, and again at night, and when bedtime finally came, I collapsed onto the grass on my face, glad the day was over.

Hindsight proved me too hasty with that sentiment; the next few days were even more grueling. Laehn didn't ease off; no matter how many times I messed up in my form or my pose, he'd correct me, two dozen times in a row on the same move if he had to. He never lost patience with me; but I lost mine with just about everything else plenty of times to make up for it.

At the rate I was going, it looked useless to keep trying; I was useless. But we still went on, thrice a day for a few hours at a time, even when I begged to stop. In a word, training sucked.

Two days passed, and it was on the afternoon of the third when Bass announced that we'd reached the Armament. We didn't train that day; the last thing I needed was to go into a very real fight with aching bruises all over. And, though no one said it, we all knew it didn't seem like there had been any improvement at all.

I rode and rested all day; when evening fell, Bass told me to get some sleep before we woke up for the assault.

You think it's tough to fall asleep the night of the one big exam, the important interview, or that life or death board meeting? Fine, I wouldn't really know last one, but let's just leave it for the sake of argument.

Think about the last time you tossed and turned on a night when you really, *really* needed to get as much rest as you possibly could.

And that was just for some interview or meeting. This was actual life or death I was supposed to be resting for. How easy do you think it is to fall asleep under conditions like that?

I'll tell you: it's damn near impossible.

I'd have asked Bass to knock me unconscious, (he'd have only been too obliged), but the only thing stopping me was the thought of the headache which would last for a day or two afterwards. Assuming I lived through the night.

Of course, I eventually did fall asleep; and of course, it was about five minutes before Bass shook me awake, a couple of hours past midnight.

"It's time," he said.

The fire was out, and I could see the eerie silhouettes of the others moving, silently clearing away the site; Laehn's tall and thin, and Ajold's shorter and more rotund.

The wind blew cold on my skin, raising goosebumps and making me shiver involuntarily.

Laehn helped me into my armor, and I lowered the helmet over my head. Bass gave me my old robe, complete with the hood. I pulled it on over my armor and let the cowl fall over my helmet, my heart doing a drum solo in my ribcage.

"Keep that closed, and don't let the metal shine, or they'll see us coming from a league away," he warned.

I nodded. He peered into my eyes through my visor and smiled.

"Aye, we're going into battle," he said softly, "And you'll be a fool to not be afraid, lad. Stay behind us and listen to what we say. We will be in and out before they know it."

I nodded again.

The cleanup was done, and we mounted our horses. Bass hitched the mule to the new wagon, climbed aboard and lead the way. No one spoke; I doubt I'd have been able to reply. My tongue was a stick of sandpaper in my dry mouth, and my throat felt like it had sealed itself closed.

The wagon slowed to a creaky stop.

"This is as far as we can take the horses," Bass said, "We're going in on foot. If we need them in a hurry, we have the whistle."

"If we blow that again, we'll wake the countryside," I pointed out.

"By the time we'd need blow that again, we'd have already woken the countryside," Bass said, cheerfully.

I dismounted and fell knee deep into the high grass. I crouched, tugged the hood lower over my face and breathed. Calm, I told myself, keep calm.

My heart and lungs chose to mutiny.

Rolling mists swept over the ground. I could see hazy lights in the distance, but beyond that I could make out nothing else. I tied the cloth over the lower half of my face and turned to the others, half hidden shadows vapor as they lashed the horses to a tree.

The mule we left free, still hitched to the wagon. Bass patted its neck, and it gave him a soft toot in reply, and then sat down as if to wait for us.

Laehn was already on all fours, a dark, silent spider-like shadow through the grass towards the faint lights. The said grass was soaked in dew, cold and wet on my hands as I followed him. The condensation soaked into the cloth of my cowl, causing it to cling to my helmet like wet tissue

We advanced on all fours, kneeing pebbles and making wars on colonies of ants. None of the others said a word; we were like a ninja stealth team, and I couldn't help but feel a thrill run through me for a few minutes as the thought crossed my mind.

Laehn's shadow stopped moving; his body stretched out and flattened against the ground. I swallowed, looked at my itchy fingers, then apprehensively drew up to him and did the same.

The mists chose to part with uncanny timing, and I looked up into the hideous monstrosity of a structure roughly the size of my ratty apartment building and just about as attractive. It squatted a little over a few hundred feet away, the ground in front of us sloping slightly to its base.

It was hard to make it out clearly in the cloudy moonlight, but from what I could tell, it was a big, rocky lump that jutted out of the ground and rose straight up, rather like an upright rectangular Lego. A Lego dropped by one enormous kid, just waiting to be trampled by an equally enormous foot.

Holes dotted the structure, sprinkled sporadically across the face of the rock like those on Swiss cheese, only smaller. Lights flickered through some of them, mostly the ones near the bottom. Most of the ones higher up were dark.

At the very top, there was what looked like four torches, burning bright at the corners of the roof. I squinted at them and counted the moving shadows of what could have been three of four people moving around up there. Archers. Obviously.

At the base was a large opening, flanked by a double row of torches and two guards, both in blue, both clad in full armor with weapons at the ready… and both asleep at their posts. Lights at the window-like holes flickered every so often as shadows cut across them; there were more men inside. Of course there were.

Shrouded in the haze and with the eerie lights all around it, it loomed over us, foreboding and unfriendly. I'd expected this mission to be dangerous; what I hadn't been counting on was the Hill itself being one terrifying structure all on its own.

"Hill of Reclamation," Laehn breathed, totally unnecessarily.

"I can see that," I hissed.

He chose to ignore me, his eyes still trained on the hideous structure.

"The torches on the top," he told me, "They guard the Armament. That is where you must take your Weapon."

Of course it was the top; the hardest place to get to, after all. I eyed the guards by the entrance, slumped against either wall.

"How many do you suppose are in there?"

"More than seven and twenty," he replied.

"How do you know for sure?"

"That's how many arrows I have,"

Ask a silly question; get a silly answer, my mind piped. I whacked it down with a cudgel.

There was a slight rustling in the bushes behind us, and Bass joined us on my left. A loud thump, a curse and heavy breathing preceded Captain Ajold as he painfully crawled up on Laehn's right.

"Shall we?" he puffed.

"About time someone asked," Bass grumbled. He leaned up on one elbow and screwed a knuckle into his eye.

"They're going to know we're here before too long," he said, "But every second they don't is one person less standing between him and the target."

He didn't need to specify the 'him' or the 'target'; they knew. And as I sat there, my metal clad knees slipping on the drenched cloth beneath them, despite the fear and the cold sweat on my brow, a thrill of excitement sent needles up and down my spine.

This was a huddle. The game plan. Where the plan was made, moments before we swooped into beautiful execution.

The moment, that feeling, did not escape me.

What did escape me, though, was the plan.

"…and we get out." Bass finished, "Alright, get ready…"

"Sorry, could we go over that again?" I whispered.

Bass closed his eyes and shook his head.

"Short version. Crawl there, wait till Laehn kills the guards," he sighed. "Get inside, make it to the top. Prevent bugles from being blown. If they raise the cry, keep going. Just don't die. We'll handle the rest."

He looked at me, eyes grimmer than I'd ever seen them.

"And follow me," he said, "Whatever happens, follow me."

Not for the first time, my hand drifted down to the cold sword hilt on my belt.

I nodded.

"And… go."

Laehn pushed up from the ground and leaned on one knee. Slowly, deliberately, he drew his bow, and took out two arrows; one he fitted to the bow, and the other he held in his right hand as he used it to draw the string.

The others were already moving down the slope at a low run. I ducked my head and did the same. Halfway down, I heard the soft whine of two arrows passing by overhead; the guards at the door buckled and fell, moments apart from each other.

The other two reached the door and crouched on either side. I panted and wheezed my way up to Bass, and knelt down behind him.

We sat till Laehn approached, bow at the ready. He ducked into the doorway alone, and I heard his string thrum thrice. There was a long pause, and then a soft whistle.

Ajold and Bass ducked in, and I followed.

It was a wide room with a low ceiling, very likely not man made and definitely spooky. Torches mounted at random points along the uneven walls threw shadows everywhere, and I imagined a soldier inside every nook, waiting to pounce at us.

Two were dead; one on the floor just a few paces away, and another a little farther away, against the wall next to a dark hole that had to be a doorway.

Laehn jogged towards the far end of the hall, and there, in the shadows at the base of a roughly hewn staircase, was the third. The guy would have been invisible from the doorway; it could have been a lucky guess or Laehn probably had superhuman eyesight. Either way, I was glad he was on our side.

We filed into a narrow corridor, and Bass took the lead. He ducked around the corner, and there was an indignant "Hey!" followed closely by a dull, wooden thud. Ajold and I joined him as he carefully lowered the limp body to the ground and dropped it without as much as a clink of armor.

We climbed higher, into the next floor. Just a few paces away from where the staircase ended sat a table, glasses, a large bottle, and three bawdy guards. Three quick arrows were all it took.

I followed them as they jogged past the corpses, struggling to keep the bile threatening to rise from reaching its goal. Laehn moved with the bow in his left hand and five arrows in his right. As he drew and fired, I watched him, more to ignore the men being killed at arms-length away from me than out of interest in technique.

I lost count of how many soldiers we put down, and how many staircases we climbed; the latter being somewhere around seven or nine. It was one narrow, unnerving passage after another, and the climb never seemed to end.

The air inside was pressing down on me; I felt waves of nausea rise, maybe from the claustrophobia, but much more likely from all the spilled blood. When Laehn finally paused at the base of the last flight of crude, uneven stone steps, it was with no little relief that I recognized inky blackness and felt cool night air filter through my helmet's visor to caress my sweaty face.

"I counted five guards when we were outside," Bass muttered, "Could be more or less. Take them out as we go up. Ajold, keep the rear. The two of you come up when we give you the signal."

I tightened the grip on my sword, clean and fresh as when I'd first drawn it. I hadn't spilled a drop of blood, for which I was grateful; even Ajold had downed a couple who had sprung up on us from behind. The night had been far worse than I'd been preparing myself for, that was for certain; and it was hardly done yet.

Was I a coward for not wanting to take a life? Did I even care if I was?

Bass nodded, and Laehn sprang out. Bass followed him a heartbeat later. I heard a bowstring hum twice and a dull wooden thud.

Again, the long, strained pause. My pulse echoed in my ears, like a drum, beating, drowning out…

"Clear," Bass rasped.

Ajold nodded at me.

"Go," he said.

This was it. I swallowed, inhaled, and then I climbed.

Chapter 9

The air filtering through my visor was so crisp and cold, it stung my eyes.

The moon was still hidden behind thick clouds, but the huge torches I'd seen from below threw enough light and more to brighten up the place like a shopping mall. A shopping mall at a time somewhere close to midnight on Halloween, if one were to phrase that more accurately. The mist crept in, too, winding its way around everything, making the rooftop look like the setting for a spooky story with the walls just ahead drifting in and out of view.

Just perfect.

I moved away from the stairs. I was in a corner of the roof, and one of those immense torches towered up over me; twice as tall as I was and about as thick around as my waist, it looked like it had impossibly been wedged into rocky wall. Given the magical circumstances of where we were, however, maybe it might have not have been as impossible as all that.

At this height, a numbing wind cut through my cloak and the chinks of my armor, but the flame didn't waver or even flicker. Sweat dripped down in the midst of my itchy beard, but as hot as it was, I dared not take of my helmet just yet.

Roughly fifteen feet away, the rooftop faded into the haze. Even so, three balls of dull light hovered unnervingly in the near distance; the flames of the other three torches permeating through the vapor.

Waist high walls ran around the edges, with sections broken off at random points giving it the look of uneven battlements. The mists made it look like a body of water floated just beyond those gaps; my feverish mind suggested I stroll over and take a look over the edge.

I backed away from the edge and turned around. I felt more than saw the ground slope gently from under my feet towards the middle of the rooftop; or maybe it was a trick of the light and the moisture in the air.

Bass stood a few feet away, wraith-like in the gloom, Tom held aloft, gaze wary.

"What's wrong?" I whispered.

"Hold," he replied. "They could be hiding anywhere."

With a rustle and a slight jangle of metal, Ajold climbed up behind me, brandishing his sword. I looked for Laehn and spotted him on the third pass, standing at the very edge of where the stone began to vanish, the vapor wrapped like a blanked around his waist. He glared intently into the haze, bow in left hand and the glint of metal in his right.

"Go," Bass said.

Laehn nodded. In two steps he was gone, and Bass, Ajold and I were alone. If two steps were all that were needed to make him completely vanish, then there could have been eyes all around us and we wouldn't know.

This had been a bad dream from the start. Now, it was closing in nightmare status.

Bass strode after Laehn, and I hurried behind him, trying not to fall on my shaking legs. The only good thing I had going was how Ajold behind me, and he seemed just about as jumpy as I was, if not more.

Misery loves company.

Walls emerged; roughly seven feet tall and standing randomly in front of us, and not one of them running any longer than five or six feet. It was as if they'd been dropped there all over the place and left standing, dominos being set without a pattern.

They could have possibly formed some sort of meaningful design together if you looked straight down on them from above, but how exactly you'd have been able to get high enough to see them in this age and place was anyone's guess.

As you'd guess, I wasn't paying as much attention as I should have been to what was happening right then, with my mind wandering the way it was.

"Get over here," Bass hissed.

He and Ajold were already at the closest wall that faced us, their backs to it and weapons at the ready. I jogged over, holding my sword out clumsily.

"Now what?" I whispered.

"Wait," he breathed hoarsely, "Stay out of sight. There might be more of them."

I rested against the wall, the metal on my back sliding on the layer of cloak between it and the stone. Closing my eyes, I let my head fall back till my helmet touched the wall. I breathed.

Ajold tapped my arm, and I opened my eyes as Laehn walked out through the mists. His bow was still in his hand, and his dagger dripped blood.

"Only two," he said.

Bass frowned.

"There should have been more," he said, "Mugatu knows we'll have to try for the Weapon sooner or later."

"It's a trap," I said, my heart sinking, "They're trying to lure us in."

"It's always been a trap," Bass said, running a hand up Tom's length, "They know that we know that they know. But do we know that they know that we know that they do?"

I looked at Ajold, who shook his head.

"It is going to happen, one way or another," Laehn said. "We need the Armament."

"We can't just walk in, can we?" I said.

"We could use you as bait," Bass mused, "But then they'd have seen there were four of us who came in. Trying to trap them won't work."

"You're particularly ingenious tonight, aren't you?" I said.

My voice ended in a very unintentional squeak, and I faked an unconvincing cough, which probably sounded phonier than a cat being nice without an ulterior motive. Something prodded at me to speak again, an unshakable need to convince them that I wasn't as afraid as I looked.

"We're here now," I said, the fool that I was, "So we might as well get it over with."

Laehn nodded.

"Follow me."

He led the way along the wall and turned the corner. I let the others pass, and just before I followed, I gave my head a good bang against the stone, one it thoroughly deserved. I'd have kicked myself, too, but worse than having to follow them into the mists unknown would be to find myself alone in those mists unknown, and I hurried after them.

It took me a minute to realize it wasn't just a random pattern of short walls here; this was a maze. And with the vapor distorting the light and twisting the shadows, the only thing that would have made it worse would have been random holes in the ground.

There weren't holes. Dear God, I hoped not.

Laehn moved through the sinister shadows with feline grace, his half formed silhouette my only guide through the mass of cold wisps. I lost count of how many near heart attacks hit me every time I lost sight of the others when a corner or found myself at a junction. After forever and five minutes later, I walked through a wall of gray and bumped into Ajold again.

The air was clearer here, and I saw that we stood at the edge of what had to be the center of the maze; a large, square chamber, with one yawning doorway on each side. It the center of the room was a waist high pedestal, and when my eyes fell on what floated a couple of feet above it, all the worry, fear and adrenaline that had been taking residence in my mind for the last week packed up and left.

"Is that...?" I breathed.

"The Armament, aye," Bass turned to me and smiled.

We four stood in silence, awed by sight of the glowing plinth, bathed in the faint light of the four torches and the moon that now decided to take a peek.

Clearly hovering well above the surface of the pedestal was... something. It looked like a ball of light, only it wasn't a ball, or anything else definable. Its shape continually shifting, its color kept morphing into hues I'd never seen. Its light blazing and dulling with no decipherable pattern, the thing was one kaleidoscope of never ending beauty.

And this is coming from someone who knows next to nothing about art.

The size of a bowling ball, it just hung in midair, as if suspended by an invisible string. Loops of colored light trailed out of it, drifting like long hair underwater for a few seconds before dissolving into vapor, only to be replaced by more.

If the whole portal deal hadn't been enough to convince me how magic was real, this cinched it; it beckoned to me, calling out. It was benevolent, it knew I needed it and it wanted to help. Don't ask me how I knew that… all I did know was as I stumbled to it, everything what had happened till now seemed worth the trouble; all the deaths, the pain, the fear; all we'd lost and taken seemed fair.

It was a price I would have paid over and over again, just to keep looking into that magnificence.

"Touch your razor to it," Bass said.

His voice sounded like a long distance call with a lousy connection. It was annoying, unnecessary, and hardly relevant, but I reached my hand under my armor and into my pocket anyway. My eyes never leaving the Orb, I pulled out the razor and held it up.

"Welcome," a voice rasped, "Took you long enough to get here."

If there was one thing which could have broken the spell, it was that voice, and the thing it belonged to.

Behind me, Bass swore, Laehn cursed, and I spun around.

They had all followed me from the wall in a drunken trance right up the Armament; and behind them, just in front of the doorway we'd used, he stood there in his bull shaped helmet and all his rust red hulking mass.

Kernine.

"Better late than never, Champion," he said, his voice muffled by that hideous helm. The Armament's light gleamed off his armor, and off the steel of the men forming ranks behind him.

The stamping of feet echoed out from behind the narrow walls, and the ground shuddered underfoot. I turned around as the blue soldiers marched into the chamber and filed into formation, blocking the three other exits.

"Come now, old man, you'll give yourself a heart attack," Kernine drawled. "You of all people knew this was a trap."

Bass's scowl dragged his busy eyebrows even lower.

"Your mistake, Dog," he spat. "You won't leave here alive."

"As much as we would all like to stand and chat," Kernine replied, "I'm not really in the mood. Get them."

Kernine's minions yelled, lowered their spears and charged.

Ever seen those sort of movies where there's always a tense standoff, and then everything explodes into insane violence? It's easy for guys watching with their popcorn to understand what's going on there; the camera is considerate enough of your viewing pleasure to focus on one choreographed fight at a time.

In contrast, someone in a real life brawl would be lucky if he could make sense of where his own fists were, let alone who the owner was of the brass knuckle decked one currently on a crash course with his nose.

And mind you, these were *swords*.

Bass roared and charged at them, Tom whistling as it spun in a blur. Laehn was Laehn; he loosed arrows and slashed his dagger in turns, never in one place for more than a moment.

Rotund as he was, Ajold tried valiantly to leap to my side, but was waylaid by three soldiers that dove at him and knocked him to the ground.

And even in that frenzy, my mind couldn't resist wondering how long they had been itching to do what they were doing now. After all, they'd ditched their spears and were punching every inch of him with their bare fists with quite a bit of enthusiasm..

It takes a special kind of pent up torment to want to do that to your former boss with your bare hands, especially when you have plenty of spears handy.

The battle raged, and I just stood there, razor in one hand and sword in the other, acutely aware of just how much I would have appreciated a considerate camera. Soldiers ran past me and were thrown the way they came almost instantaneously; Laehn sprinted past me, more of them hot on his heels; and for some odd reason, no one was paying me any attention at all.

You have to admit, that was rude.

"ALAN!" Bass bellowed, his voice booming over the cacophony of battle, "Bond your WEAPON!"

I felt like he'd rapped me on the head with his pipe again.

My mind snapped to focus, and with it came the adrenaline and the fear. I spun around, and Armament gleamed at me, beckoning. The razor was there in my left hand; all I had to do was to reach out and touch it.

I leaped.

"NO!"

Kernine's voice snarled in my ear; I felt hot breath through the holes in my helmet, and pain as something hit me with the force of a van doing sixty.

I skidded across the stone floor and smashed into a wall. Pain kept me conscious; I opened my eyes and saw him standing, a demon between me and the Armament, its light turning him into the silhouette that had been all I'd seen of him the first time we had met.

We had come a full circle. Funny how it happens, isn't it.

My mind skipped to reality, and I realized my hand was empty. The sword was gone; I'd dropped it in the fall. All I had against his bulk was the razor.

"Come, Champion," Kernine snarled, "Come, bond with the Armament."

I gasped as I stood , the pain agonizingly sharp and brutal. Nothing was broken, as far as I could tell; inside my armor, I was just bruised.

The battle still raged around us, but right then, it was just him and me.

He stood there, watching me as I lurched forward. I took one step and the world cartwheeled, forcing me down on one knee.

Kernine threw back his head and guffawed.

"Nice armor," he said, "It is such a pity that even inside it, you amount to less than *half* the man my weakest soldier is."

His raised an immense arm and curled his sausage fingers over the handle jutting over his shoulder. He drew the gigantic axe off his shoulder and swung it lazily, showing off the sound it made slicing through the air.

"Come," he said, "Try and bond the Armament. Finish this quickly for us and for yourself."

My brain kicked itself into overdrive. The ultimate adrenaline rush, a gibberish of extremely distracting voices in my head, the last thing I wanted right then.

I need a weapon. Need to reach Armament.

Need to pass him to get there.

There's no way to pass him.

Where others go?

Where grammar go?

I was arguing with myself in my mind, and not too surprisingly, I was losing that, too.

I swallowed. The others were lost in the fighting, and if they'd seen me, they'd have been here by now. I didn't dare break eye contact with the conceited barbarian to try and see where they were.

Need pass him.

Pass him if he no there.

Duh. How I make him no be there?

Get him to be somewhere else.

A stroke of genius in the words of a lunatic.

Kernine slammed the axe's haft against the ground, the stone splintering beneath the impact.

"Come on, you coward!" he roared.

He thinks you're a coward.

Use that.

How?

Do what cowards do.

I was open to any other ideas, but I was out of time, and Kernine made my decision for me; he lowered his head and charged.

I deafened myself inside my armor with a shrill scream and rolled out of the way. He bellowed as he swung his axe, missing my head by inches and driving a hole in the wall.

He swung again, and I dodged; the blade hit the ground, and the shock ran up the handle. Stunned, he took a step back and shook his head; that was all I needed.

"No!" he roared.

I scooted in between his legs, I pushed myself back up and then I ran. I ran like I'd never run before, streaking across the room in what I hoped looked like an epic, shining silver and green blur. Kernine's footsteps pounded behind me; I stuck out my right hand, razor squeezed tight in my fist.

The Armament erupted in intense, blinding color; Kernine snarled, and I screwed my eyes shut and kept running. My hand plunged into warmth; the heat intensified and ran up my arm like a horde of ants.

I didn't know what I'd really expected when I touched the razor to the colorful floating orb; whatever it was, though, I'm pretty sure it didn't involve my feet leaving the ground.

I yelped, opened my eyes, and there I was, hovering two feet off the stone floor. The explosion of light caught everyone's attention, and they all turned to me as my legs lifted up and floated out behind me, higher than my head, the cloak flapping in a wind that had picked up round the orb.

And speaking of the orb; I was tethered to it, my wrist was sunk deep inside the depths of dazzling light. The loopy tendrils floating around drifted towards my arm, wrapping lethargically around it, and the warmth rose with each one added to the tangle.

"NO!" Kernine howled.

"YES!" Bass roared.

"YEEEEEEEEEEEOW!" I hollered.

The fighting had stopped. All eyes were on me, suspended like a puppet in an embarrassing retro superman pose, complete with cape. Laehn paused and looked around, a wriggling soldier in a headlock under his arm. He looked up at me, shrugged, slid his dagger over the exposed throat and then turned to watch without interruption.

The orb flashed, blinding bursts of colored light that forced everyone to turn away. The light didn't affect me, but the razor in my already scorching grasp started to heat up rapidly. I was holding fire in the shape of a plastic handle; fire that was searing the flesh off my palm.

I screamed.

I couldn't let go, I couldn't move, and it still burned, the loops of light wrapped around my arm pulsing in time to my screams.

Bass's voice. Somewhere in the deathly quiet audience, I could hear him mutter.

"... forgot to tell him about the pain, didn't I..."

I screamed again, and the supernova in my palm started to thicken, to grow. It expanded, opening my fingers as it did; now the size of a comb, now a remote control, now a baseball bat, the edges jutting out of the orb on either side in blinding lump of light.

And all the while it still burned, and I screamed.

And then it was over.

Whatever force it was what held me up gave way, unceremoniously dropping me out of the air to land in a stupendous belly flop. The ringing clang my armor made jerked me out of my stupor; the pain was gone, and my hand looked as unharmed as it had been when I'd last seen it. I painfully sat on my knees and looked at the flat metal club I was holding, roughly five inches wide and only about three feet long.

And that was all it had become. There wasn't anything else to it; I was holding a plain, steel colored metal club.

I searched for Bass, and found him in the middle of the crowd, looking down at me along with everyone else.

"This is it?" I demanded.

The orb's light was gone; it sat there on the pedestal, no longer hovering, an ordinary black bowling ball innocently pretending it hadn't cost the lives of all those soldiers that night for nothing.

I slowly rose to my feet and looked at Kernine, standing within charging distance, torso heaving like he was either having a seizure or blowing a particularly resistive invisible balloon.

I swallowed, and looked again at the club in my hand.

"DIE!" he bellowed, and his roar broke the spell. The fighting began anew, and chaos closed my friends away from me again.

He reached up to yank his helmet off. The small beady eyes glowered, and the yellow teeth bared in a snarl that made him so much more frightening than he already was, which is saying a lot.

He let the helmet drop, lowered his head and ran at me. I stumbled backwards and my heel hit something jutting out of the stone.

I lost my balance, and I fell.

The bottom of the club struck the ground the same time my elbow did; the shock prompted me to let go of it just in time to save my fingers from being sheared off by the blade that swung up and out, Swiss-army knife style.

Kernine's eyes widened, and he tried to slow down; a bow twanged, and a frenzied heartbeat later there was an arrow in his knee.

He howled; his momentum still carried him forward, and all I could do was brace my Weapon against the ground, hold the blade up and throw my arm over my eyes as his immense bulk toppled onto me.

The sound I heard as he impaled himself on my blade, a foot in front of my face; I'll never forget that, nor how he screamed in my ear, spraying me with spit and blood.

He rolled over, his momentum yanking the thing out of my grasp, and landed with a heavy crunch of crushed metal; he bellowed, the agony in his voice painful to witness.

The soldiers lost heart; they ran, fleeing into the shadows, abandoning their commander to his fate. I sat up as they went, but I wasn't too interested in them. My eyes were on Kernine as he rocked on his back, slamming his giant fists on the ground in torment.

He screamed a curse into the night and grabbed the handle, and roared again as he tugged. Fascinated, I watched as three feet of bloodstained metal emerged;

he threw it aside and rolled around to stumble to his feet.

Blood gushed out through the hole in his armor; he staggered and pressed a fist against the jagged tear. It didn't cover the wound, and the blood oozed freely.

His unfocused eyes cleared and fixed on me. I read the menace in them; he was going to kill me slowly, even if it was the last thing he ever did.

I was still on the ground when he took his first step towards me. My legs weren't working; I couldn't stand. My heart jackhammering, I scooted backwards in panic as he advanced. Blood gushing down his armor with every step, he limped to me.

The arrow had broken off halfway down the shaft when he'd rolled, but the head was still deep in his flesh. His leg buckled, and before he could regain his balance, it gave way. With a bloody oath of pure rage and murder, he fell. I watched as he reached out desperately, but the only thing he was close to was the Armament.

Kernine landed on the pedestal and his weight and momentum shattered its base like a sledgehammer; it shifted and fell aside, leaving him to land hard on his back at where it had stood.

The orb had rested on the surface of the pillar since the moment it had done its job; now, with the pillar gone, it hovered in place directly over Kernine's torso. He looked up at it, and I followed his gaze.

For a moment, it looked like nothing had changed. Then it shifted, trembled, and began to vibrate.

It didn't take a genius to figure out that whatever coming next wasn't going to be nice.

"Get out of the way!" I yelled.

There was nothing for me to hide behind and no time to run to the exit. All I could do was turn around and cower under my towel.

The explosion seconds later was soundless, but the floor resonated from the blast, and I heard stone crumble as a ripple of air rushed past me. Dozens of tiny bits of debris peppering my towel like tiny bullets, and I felt the impacts from inside my armor. More ricocheted off the walls all around me, like tiny machine guns going off everywhere.

The wind died, my towel went silent, and it was over. I swallowed and turned.

There was no black bowling ball, no collapsed pillar, and no humongous fallen lap dog. Under the light of the four torches, all that remained in the center of the room was a smooth crater, the first perfect scoop in a freshly opened tub of ice cream.

I slowly rose to my feet and looked up at the sky. The clouds had wandered off, and the mists had faded. The moon shone over the rooftop, an omen of peace.

I took off my helmet and, at long last, felt the wind on my sweaty brow.

The soldiers had all gone; and the others, my friends, my team, had probably chased after them. There was silence; the dust was settling, the battle was over, and somehow, we'd won.

"We did it," I whispered.

I heard a boot scuff gravel behind me.

I turned, and there stood Bass, leaning on Tom, the same way I'd seen him when we'd first met, so, so very long ago. He smiled.

"We did it!" I exclaimed.

Bass's smile quivered, and, his whole body trembling, he slowly lowered his head to look down at his chest.

I was imagining it; no, I wasn't. There was something dark staining his robes. Many, many small splotches on the fabric, stains that were growing larger, joining into one big patch of...

"No," I said.

He looked up and into my eyes, still smiling.

I barely registered letting go of the helmet; it bounced on the stone, the sound echoing as I ran to him. Bass' arm jerked, and his fingers let go of Tom; his knees buckled, and he fell.

The stick clattered against the stones, the sound of the wood mingling with that of the clang of my helmet. They rang together in my ears, echoing, repeating, mocking as I dropped on my knees by his side.

He was trembling. I touched his robe, and my hand met warm, sticky blood. Nausea and terror mingled in me, my mind wanting to float away, escape from this hallucination.

His eyes closed, Bass heaved in a labored breath.

"Bass," I said, "Bass. Bass!"

He looked up at me, his smile now a contorted scowl of pain.

"Yeah, yeah, I hear you," he muttered thickly, "I'm not dead yet."

His chest spasmed, and he wheezed in, a painful gasp of breath.

"LAEHN!" I screamed, "AJOLD!"

"Not so loud," Bass snapped, but his voice was fading, "You're giving me a headache."

"We… we need to…" I was hyperventilating.

We'd won. We'd done what we came for. This was not happening, it *couldn't* happen…

My head spun. He was bleeding to death, slipping away in front of me, and there was nothing I could do, nothing I could think of, except watch him die.

"Someone!" I yelled.

Bass reached up, but his hand fell short. He tried again and this time I took it, but when I tried to put it on my shoulder like he'd been aiming for, he held onto it, squeezing as tightly as he could.

"This is not fair," I stammered, "We won. You can't… you're not supposed to…"

"Listen… to me…" he choked, "You… idiot."

I closed my mouth and nodded. I realized I couldn't see him anymore; my eyes had blurred. I blinked, and my vision cleared as the tears rolled down my cheeks.

"This… always going… to happen," he wheezed, "I knew… I'd never… make it…"

"Then why did you come?" I demanded, "Why didn't you stay where you were?"

"You…" he rasped, "Needed… me."

His hand was shaking, shaking violently. He was going, fading, his life draining out with the blood pooling around him, soaking into the cloth at my knees.

"You're… their *hope*,"

His voice was weakening, and his fingers were losing their grip.

"I was… hard on you," he whispered, "I… shouldn't…"

I choked on the lump in my throat.

"You did what you had to," I whispered.

His jowl quivered; there was fear was in his eyes as his shaking hand closed on mine with renewed strength.

"Choose…" he wheezed.

He coughed, an agonized, heart wrenching sound, and drew in one last, shuddering breath,

And he was gone.

The moonlight ridiculed me now; the wind was icy cold.

The night was so, so very still; I knelt by Bass's body with my head lowered and I cried.

I lost track of how long I was there; it could have been hours. Laehn eventually arrived; I didn't know when he had turned up, only that he was kneeling beside us, hood lowered and head bowed in respect. Ajold was there, too; he was on his knees behind me, but it was all I remembered. I didn't bother turning around to look.

I'd seen death before; I'd had deaths in the family; I'd even stood sad and solemn at my father's funeral, just a few years ago.

This was Bass. I hardly even knew the guy, and now he was gone. And it felt so, so much more intense.

"Come," Laehn said quietly, "We must leave."

He put his hand on Bass's neck. His fingers found the string and he pulled on it gently till the whistle emerged, dangling on its end. Respectfully, he removed it and left us.

I heard him blow it from out by the torches. The sound thundered over the empty countryside, a low, mournful note; a note of death, despair and sorrow it was to me, long after it was gone.

Chapter 10

A blur.

That's all it was. A haze of motion and color and darkness.

I was lost, even as my arms moved and my legs walked. I might have helped them carry Bass down through the Hill, or I might just have been standing there, watching as they did it.

I couldn't remember; but when my mind finally snapped to reality again, I was in the back of the wagon, fighting down intense nausea, the blood all over my robes, dry and congealed on my hands.

Bass's blood.

His body was on the floor next to me, wrapped in spare cloaks. I tried to not pay any attention to it rolling obscenely from side to side as the wagon jumped and jolted, the two horses galloping in time with the mule. Laehn lead the way, and Ajold covered our rear as we ran away, away from the Hill, away from the death and destruction we'd caused, the lives we'd taken and the bodies we had left behind.

And we ran some more.

Day was breaking when the mule began to slow. We climbed a low hill, and as Laehn and Ajold dismounted, I awkwardly climbed over the edge of the wagon and dropped down on shaking knees.

I walked away from them and sat cross legged on the grass. The sky grew brighter as they lowered Bass's body to the ground; a new day, a new age. Laehn found the shovel among the tools in the wagon while I removed my armor, and I took it from him.

The sun rose as I dug, perspiration freely running over my arms and down my back. My sweat mingling with the dried blood on my palms, making it run fresh, dripping into the soil as I worked. Laehn stood and watched in silence, neither complimenting nor criticizing my efforts. Eventually, he took the shovel from me when I paused to wipe the perspiration slicking my forehead and wordlessly continued.

I sat down and watched as the hole grew deeper. Ajold went next, puffing and panting freely, and then it was me again. We took turns as the air grew warmer and the world grew lighter. I let my mind wander again as we worked. I went back home, to Mona, to her arms and the smell of her hair. I heard her laugh at my stupid jokes, I saw the color of her eyes as I stared into them…

I lost track of time. I worked, I sweated, I sat, and then I worked again. The pain in my arms, the ache in my back; I welcomed it. Far, far worse was the other pain, the one that was more than physical: the pain in my chest.

By the time we had dug a decent sized grave, it had been morning for a few hours. We hadn't time or the material for a coffin, and we couldn't carry him around till we did. I climbed down into the hole, and using our cloaks as a sling, we lowered him into it.

Ajold handed Tom down to me, and I curled his stiffening fingers around it and crossed his arms over his chest.

"Thank you," I whispered.

I was never one for too much sentiment. We didn't bother with a sermon or anything fancy. The moment Ajold had pulled me out of there, Laehn had started to throw the dirt in, and we helped.

We broke a plank off the wagon for his tombstone, and it was a simple enough epitaph we etched into it; "Here lies George Bass: Hero, Friend, and Champion to the end."

Our labors done, we stepped back and looked down on it in silence.

"He didn't deserve this," I muttered.

"We shall return when this is done," Laehn said, "We will build a tomb here as befits his deeds and who he was."

"When this is done," I echoed, my voice hollow, "If we survive past it."

"What now?" Ajold asked. "What was the plan once you bonded with the Armament?"

I looked down at the flat club hanging off my belt. Ajold had retrieved it somehow before we'd left. What had been a simple disposable razor was now a bizarre gigantic version of the old cutthroat my grandfather's barber used to prefer.

As bad as I was with the sword, a simple enough tool in its own right, I hadn't the faintest clue how in the world I was meant to hold the thing it had become, let alone use it to fight. If ever there had been a tool far too unwieldy to ever exist, this would be it.

"Alan?" Ajold coaxed, lassoing my wandering mind and pulling it back to the harsh, grey reality.

"I… I don't know," I confessed.

"What do you mean you don't know?"

"He never elaborated," I said, turning away from the grave. "If he had a plan, he didn't tell me. All he said was that after bonding my Weapon with the Armament, I'd face Mugatu."

"Does it mean you're ready now?" Ajold insisted, "Will you do battle with him? But… but how? And when?"

"If I knew, I'd be telling you right now, wouldn't I?!" I snapped. "That's what I've been saying! I don't know!"

I looked away and my gaze fell on Laehn, standing just a few feet apart from us and yet worlds away, eyes fixed on the grave. I hadn't heard him speak since we'd been on the roof of the Hill, where he'd blown the mule whistle. Now he stood there looking like he was fighting a silent war in the battlefield of his thoughts.

"Laehn," I said quietly.

He looked up at me, green eyes dull.

"If he had a plan," Laehn replied, his voice heavy, "Bass kept it to himself,"

"Assuming he even had one," I said, kicking at a clump of grass. "He might have been counting on making it up as we went along."

"That sounds like him," Ajold sighed.

"So what DO we do?" I demanded, "We can't stay here. Where do we go?"

Laehn shook his head.

"Bass gave the orders," he said, "I followed them, and gave him my counsel when he asked. What he planned for now… I don't know."

"So what, we attack the Castle?" I asked, skeptically, "Please tell me we have other options?"

"To go there now would be suicide," Ajold said. "Doesn't matter if you're ready or not, there are too many guards there. You'll never get in."

"We must hide," Laehn said, "Stay out of sight of his men."

"For how long?" I demanded.

"Till you are trained, and till we can raise an army of the people," Ajold replied, grimly, "I agree."

"That would take months!" I cried, "Years!"

"Well, what did you expect?" Ajold demanded, exasperated.

"I left my wife behind without so much as a goodbye," I snarled, "And all the while I've been here, the only reason I've been helping was because it's the only way to free Eduud so he could send me home. Bass said…"

"Bass is dead," Laehn interrupted, his voice harsh, "And he said you would return home as soon as you have defeated Mugatu. If you see a way to do it, one which we do not know of, please tell us. We await Mugatu's downfall as eagerly as do you."

His fists were clenched, but his eyes weren't on me. He glared at a patch of grass by the side of the grave, and something about the way he stood told me that he was avoiding my gaze. I glared at him, trying to find the words to yell in his face, but as angry as I was, I couldn't argue his logic. What he said made sense. As much as it drove a red hot knife through my heart, it made sense.

"Whatever we decide to do, we can't stay here, can we?" Ajold gestured at the mound of dirt.

Laehn ran his eyes over the crude wooden marker again. His brow furrowed in thought, and then he sighed and shook his head.

"Eventually, we will have to find a place to call home," he said slowly, "But for now, we must hide till we can find such a place."

"So where do we go?" I demanded, though not as calmly as I'd have wanted to.

"There's a place nearby," he replied, "I have friends there, and they will shelter us for the time being. I am loath to bring the danger to them, but we have no choice."

"We're on the run here, and Mugatu's people are everywhere," I said, cautiously. "Can we trust these friends of yours?"

He finally found reason to glare to my face.

"I trust them with my life," he said. His voice was even, but his eyes spoke otherwise; the glint warned me that the last thing I wanted to do right then was provoke him.

"We are out of options. It will only be for a few days, until we are ready to move on again."

"We can decide what to do next from there," Ajold pointed out, oblivious to the sparks which were just beginning to die.

Laehn eyes softened, and his expression changed. It was when Ajold gave me a similar look that I realized they were waiting for my call.

They were both soldiers in their own right; they followed orders, not gave them. Somehow, it left me with having to be the one making decisions. It left me in charge.

No, I didn't like it.

"Let's go," I said, "And let's make it fast."

I didn't bother putting my armor on. Instead, I wrapped it up in yet another spare cloak and stored it in the back of the wagon. The clothes Bass had first given me on my first day here had burned with the first wagon; but Laehn had made sure to swipe some clothes when he had stolen supplies, so I had something to change into.

I drew the quintessential hood over my head and followed on horseback as Ajold drove the wagon and Laehn took the lead on the other horse. The third horse trailed after us, its reins tied to Laehn's saddle. We were probably going to sell it at the next town. I didn't know, and I wasn't really bothered to find out.

It was a mixture of reasons I gave myself as to why we brought the mule along; it was fast, it was smart, and it was a walking flamethrower. After everything we had gone through together, it didn't seem right to leave it all on its own to roam around in the middle of nowhere.

And then there was the final reason that kept returning to peck at me; at the very beginning, before we'd even left his safe house, Bass had introduced the mule to me as my 'steed'. Somehow, someday, he'd expected me to ride it into battle. Even if the mule ever agreed to let me climb on its back, I still wasn't half sure whether or not I wanted to.

The notion of 'nearby' to Laehn wasn't the same as the one I'd had; to him, it meant a hard ride of over a day and a half away, with few breaks, if any, in between. Evening was about to fall on the second day of Bass's funeral when we rode into a small, quiet village. As was habit now, I drew the hood lower over my face as we rode in.

Eyes turned to us, wary and suspicious. Some ignored us after a first look, and others kept glaring, but when Laehn raised his head ever so slightly and threw a faint nod at a group of men lounging on a fence, the tension seemed to ebb.

He hadn't been kidding about having friends, that much I saw. Most of the people kept away from us, but one man walked past him almost by accident, and their hands met for the briefest second before he walked away and vanished back into the crowd.

Ajold and I were ignored, which suited me fine. A child came running up and tugged on my cloak as we slowed to turn a corner, and his mother gave me a shy smile before pulling him away.

I spurred my horse into a trot and drew up to Ajold, driving the wagon at walking pace behind Laehn, who lead the way with his head bowed.

"Who are these people?" I asked softly.

"I've only been here a couple of times with the men," Ajold shrugged. "They never gave the King any trouble, but then, not many of the villages did, either. Other than that, I don't know much about them."

"They're friends," Laehn said, hardly raising his head. "Know that. It shall serve."

We walked deeper into the village, down narrow winding roads and past small, neat wooden homes. Laehn finally reined in at an old but wide and sturdy wooden gate, set in a simple, waist high picket fence. He dismounted and nodded at the house.

"This is it," he said, "Leave the wagon there, Captain. The mule knows its way to the stable."

"How does…?" I asked, but he'd already pushed open the gate and led the horse inside. Ajold shrugged, so I slid off the saddle and pulled my horse through the gate after him.

The well-kept garden was small, though just large enough to have two full sized horses stand inside without smothering the humans in between them. The path was just the gap between the grass on either side of the yard, and it ran straight from the gate to the small wooden house like it meant business.

Laehn looped his reins over one of the rough spokes on the fence and gestured for me to do the same. As the mule said goodbye with its usual flatulence and began to drag the wagon away, we followed Laehn up the path and to the small door.

He paused when he reached it, and glanced at us. For some reason, it looked to me like he was bracing himself to do something extremely unpleasant.

"Well?" I asked.

He ignored me, turned around and knocked three times.

And we waited. It was a while before we heard sounds from behind the door, and when we did, it sounded like someone skipping playfully over wooden floor.

"Who is it?" a female voice demanded, shrill and singsong like.

Laehn closed his eyes and took a deep breath.

"Arhaza, it's me," he said.

The door creaked as it opened inwards a crack, but slammed shut almost immediately. Laehn turned his face away from us, but not before I saw the scowl.

"Who are you?!" the voice demanded.

"Arhaza, open the door. We don't have time for this."

"I don't believe you!" the girl called, "No beggars allowed!"

Laehn slammed his palm against the door. It shuddered violently, and the girl's laughter escalated.

"If you don't open this door before I count to three, I will open it for you and string you up by your ankles." Laehn snapped, "AGAIN. And this time, I'll leave you there all night."

"No one's home!" the girl piped gleefully.

Laehn slammed his palm against the door again, and the girl laughed harder.

"The heck…?" I muttered, "Who IS that?"

The peals of hilarity diminished abruptly, and I heard another voice from inside; this one a woman's, and fortunately, not as amused.

The door creaked open again, and I saw a pair of eyes gleam from within the relative darkness inside.

"Yes?" she asked.

"Mother, it's me," Laehn said, "And… friends."

The door swung open, and I had my first glimpse of Laehn's mother seconds before she threw her bony arms around him in a passionate hug; like him, she was tall and thin, but her skin was dark, unlike him, and her hair, though black, was graying.

Laehn returned the hug, and if I didn't know better I'd have sworn I saw tears glint near his eyes when she finally let go of him.

As she faced us, I saw a thin, faded scar under the edge of her left eye, running across her cheekbone and into the hairline at her ear. Her eyes, unlike her sons, were brown; and they were narrow and suspicious as she scrutinized us, barely looking over Ajold but staring long and hard at me. Just when I thought she was about to yell at us to get off her property, she gave us a tight smile and pushed open the door.

"Come," she said, "hurry."

Beyond the door was a refreshingly cool, cozy living room. There was an empty fireplace on the side, wooden stools, a stout table on the other end and two doors leading further in. Counting this one, I'd only been in two houses since I'd arrived, the first being the tiny room Bass called a safe house.

Taverns, bars and Zaahis' castle didn't count for this observation, and that there was probably the first time all three places would have been used in the same sentence.

All in all, it was a fairly large house, I suppose, by medieval standards.

Laehn sat down on one of the stools, and gestured for us to follow suit. His mother vanished into the house. The moment she was gone, I reached out and grabbed Laehn's arm.

"Why didn't you tell us it was your Mother's home you were bringing us to?" I demanded.

"It's my home," he replied simply, "And we had nowhere else to go."

"I thought assassins didn't have homes?" I hissed.

Laehn's nostrils flared.

"We don't," he replied stiffly, "But before I learned my craft, I lived here."

I closed my eyes and shook my head.

"I'm sorry," I said. "That was out of line. I shouldn't have said what I did."

He looked at me coolly. For a second, I thought I'd done it; I'd finally pushed him over the edge. Then he nodded.

I leaned forward again.

"This is wrong," I insisted, "We should never have come here. Your family doesn't need the danger we're bringing with us."

Laehn smiled.

"You know what I do for a living," he said, "My father did the same. Our family was born and bred in danger, Alan. The villagers are our allies; they are *your* allies. And I need not remind you of how sore a need you have of those now."

"Allies fine, but this your *family*."

"No man or woman here would betray us," he smiled reassuringly. "You have my word."

"I'm not talking about being betrayed," I said, "I'm talking about them getting hur…"

I broke off and pulled away as his mother returned, a pitcher in one hand and three mugs in the other. It was plain water she poured into them, but I'd never been as happy as I was then to feel it slide and soak down my desiccated throat.

"Thank you," I said, holding it out for a refill.

A thin, freckled girl bounced into the room as I gulped it down. She could hardly have been over twelve. Between the cheeky grin she flashed me and the twinkle in her brilliant blue eyes, I'd have kept a firm grip on my wallet if I'd had one.

"Who are they?" she demanded, glaring at me.

"Now, Arhaza," her mother admonished, "You mustn't speak to the Champion that way."

I coughed, embarrassed.

"No, it's… it's okay," I said. A few moments passed before I'd registered what she called me. "You know who I am?" I asked, surprised.

Her expression hardened and her eyes grew cold.

"I may not fully approve of my son's choice of life and what he does with his skills," she said stiffly, "But I am aware of how important his service is to the King and who he keeps company with. He is his father's son; he will do what he must."

I swallowed uncomfortably.

"Even so," she said, bowing her head slightly, "It is an honor to have you in our home, noble Champion."

"The… uh, the pleasure is mine," I said.

No one said anything, and my ears began to burn. Toying with the mug in my hands, I racked my brains for something to say.

"I, um, I wish this had been at a better time, and under, uh, better circumstances."

No one replied, and Laehn's mother turned around and busied herself with the fire. Maybe I should have just stopped there and kept my mouth shut, but I'm not a fan of awkward silences. One was brewing right then, and neither Ajold nor the girl seemed about to spark conversation.

I had to say something.

"I kind of get the feeling," I said, twisting the mug some more, "That, well, you don't like Champions all that much, do you?"

Her back stiffened.

"You know of the Champions before you?" she demanded, glaring at Laehn.

"Kernine,"he replied, "Mugatu's hand. He told Alan plenty to make him doubt. He had to learn of the truth, so we told him."

She looked at me, and I shrank into my seat, mentally kicking myself.

"My husband lost his life defending a Champion," she said, "and my son almost died with him. He may be alive, but he is not without his scars."

I nodded, a lump rising in my throat. I felt like an idiot, and rightly so. Of course I wasn't welcome here. Bass had told me Laehn had wanted nothing more to do with Champions before I'd turned up. No matter how nice they were, they hated me.

She must have sensed my thoughts right then. Her face cleared and she smiled, a real, genuine smile for a change.

"No, Champion," she said, reassuringly, "As much as the Laws, the Tyrants and their Champions have taken from me, I bear neither anger nor ill towards you. We all do what we must, and it was by no means your fault or your choice to be here now. You are in need of help, and you are welcome."

Relief flooded through me; after the last few days of sorry and fear, relief was new. It felt wonderful. I smiled and nodded.

"Thank you," I whispered.

"Lord Bass was the only other Champion to visit our home," she continued. "No other one ever came here, or knew of Laehn and his father's home. It was kept a well-guarded secret, and we have Lord Bass to thank for that."

She paused, brow furrowed.

"Why is Lord Bass not with you?" she asked, "Where is he?"

Laehn's face darkened. He looked away from her.

"Bass is dead," he said flatly, "Two nights ago. The Hill of Reclamation, after we'd fought off Mugatu's men and the Champion bonded with the Armament."

His mother gasped and put a hand on her heart. The girl, deep in the midst of covertly reaching into Ajold's pocket, stumbled and fell over, tearing Ajold's pocket as she did. On her knees, she looked up at Laehn, her eyes wide as tears began to gather, lip trembling.

Laehn closed his eyes and nodded.

She heaved in a sob, picked herself up and ran out of the room with her hands over her face.

"He was like a father to her," Laehn explained, his voice strained as stifled sobs permeated through the walls, "Our father passed soon after she was born. She hardly knew him. Bass was what a father would have been to her."

No one said anything else as Ajold clumsily reached down and scooped up the debris that had fallen out of his pocket. I'd tried, but the awkward silence prevailed nonetheless.

Fortunately, this time we were saved by the door.

"The damned mule is in the stables again," a voice complained from the outside, "but couldn't he have the *decency* to put those horses…"

The door slammed open and the speaker was already halfway through his next complaint when he paused halfway through the door as his eyes fell on us.

"Oh," he said. "Hello."

"This is Elrik," Laehn said, "My brother."

The introduction wasn't necessary; the resemblance the boy had to his mother and sister was uncanny. His hair was as dark as theirs, his skin the same as his mothers, and like them, his eyes were bright blue. His face, though, was long and pointed, and his hairline started low, just like Laehn's.

It hit me with a jolt. What was standing in front of me was Laehn himself; Laehn as he would have looked like before the accident that forced Eduud to change his appearance.

"You have a brother?" Ajold demanded, "I didn't…"

"Well, can't blame you. No one knew," Elrik sighed, "Because no one needed to know."

"How old are you, boy?" Ajold demanded.

"Ten and nine this winter," Elrik replied, slamming the door shut behind him, "And who would you be?"

"Captain of the King's Men," Ajold puffed out his chest.

Elrik stuck out his lower lip in mocking respect and nodded.

"And Laehn's here, big surprise. That should make *you*," he turned to me, "… the Champion."

Elrik looked me up and down, and he didn't seem particularly impressed by what he saw. By now, though, I was getting used to it.

He turned to his brother and shrugged.

"What, you started bringing work home, now?" he asked.

"Watch your tongue, brother," Laehn snapped, "We are in no mood for your..."

"Where's Bass?" Elrik interrupted, looking around.

Laehn clenched his jaw.

"Well?" Elrik demanded, "Please don't tell me he sent you and didn't come this time."

"Elrik," his mother said softly, "Lord Bass is dead."

Elrik paused, and the color drained off his face.

"Oh," he said, "I... I was at the town... but no one... no one said..."

"No one knows," Laehn said, "Not even Mugatu."

Elrik stood in the doorway, unsure of whether to come in or go back out. He made his decision; slamming the door, he dropped the sack he had slung over his back and joined us on another one of the stools.

"For what reason are you here?" his mother asked, looking at me. It wasn't a demand, or a challenge. She simply wanted to know.

"We don't have a plan," I replied, "And we're out of options. We needed a place to stay and to think our next move. Laehn brought us here."

Laehn's mother closed her eyes, sighed and nodded.

"He was right to do so. You are welcome here, Champion. This village will keep you safe."

"Thank you," I said, "I mean it. But for how long? How long will it be before Mugatu sends his men door to door?"

"You will stay for as long as you need," she said.

"That's nice, and everything," Elrik interrupted, "But you're not planning to sit and hide for the next century or two, are you?"

He looked around at us.

"Bass may have had a plan," Ajold said, "But he neglected to mention it to us before… before it happened. Now, we're trying to pick up the pieces."

"Kernine is dead," Laehn said, "The Champion took care of him. This may put their troops in disarray until Mugatu chooses a new one."

"It's not a lot, but it's something," Elrik said, "As long as you can act soon enough to make use of it, that is."

"Look," I said, standing up. "It's dangerous wherever we are. And I don't want to cause your family any more harm than you've had already, Mrs…. Mrs…"

Mrs. Laehn was all what popped into my head, but I had a feeling calling her that would have felt more than slightly awkward.

Fortunately, she saved me.

"Call me Ennah," she said, "And no. We have been living in danger, ever since Mugatu showed us all the snake he truly was. Danger is no stranger here, Champion. Not for a long time. But having you here, alive and well... it's the hope we needed to continue. You are welcome to stay here for as long as you need to, and whatever it is you decide to do, the men shall give you their aid. This is their Realm as much as it is your Quest. You are not alone."

I looked around at them, hope daring to flutter in me.

I was among friends.

Chapter 11

Days passed; weeks, I suppose. When we'd first come there, I'd never wanted to stay more than a few nights, or at least till we found somewhere else to go. Somehow, it was taken for granted we weren't leaving. For as long as we had to, Laehn's home was where we would hide.

Waking up in a bed after months of using rocks as pillows; sitting with Ajold, Laehn and Ennah and listening as they devised strategies and cast them away again; watching Elrik and Arhaza argue day in and day out; no matter how entertaining, thought provoking or distracting they were, none of it took away the hollow in me.

Bass was still gone, and try as I might, I couldn't get over it. Maybe a part of me didn't want to get over it. It wanted to keep in the hurt and the sting, fuse the ache with the pain that stabbed whenever I thought of Mona.

Nothing was going to bring him back. His raspy voice, his crude remarks and the godawful brew; I guess it's true you don't realize what you have till you've lost it.

He was gone, but Mona wasn't. Somewhere, somehow, at the end of this madness, I clung to the hope that I'd see her again. Excuses ran through my mind; what I could possibly tell her to explain all the time I'd been away. The truth… she'd never believe the truth.

And then I'd try to forget it all, and focus on what was important, how I was going to go home, somehow. It was probably the only thing that kept me going.

As the days added up behind me, I didn't stay cooped up inside the house; Laehn, Ajold and even Elrik took turns training me inside the large stable behind their home. I tried a couple of times with the hideously cumbersome thing my razor had turned into, but I gave it up for lost. With the blade retracted, it was nothing more than a short club; but when I tapped the bottom and the blade swung out, I didn't have a clue on how I was supposed to hold it, let alone swing it around and hurt someone other than myself.

With the sword, though… I couldn't say I was a star pupil, but I definitely was improving. Somewhat. And it had to count for something.

The villagers more or less knew who I was, and we took the fact for granted, even though they never spoke to me or made eye contact when I was out. It was obvious they had to have guessed it. After all, I was with Laehn, and they all knew what he did for a living. They never saw me train, though; Laehn and Ajold made sure of that. The last thing any of us needed was for them to see just how much of a clumsy oaf I was. Morale always was a tricky thing.

Every few days, Laehn and I would ride to the neighboring town, where we'd mingle with the people and listen to the news. There rarely was any we found useful; only how the few men still openly loyal to the King were scattered, and Mugatu's forces were almost, if not totally, in control.

The biggest blow came when we caught wind of a few holdouts and towns garrisoning themselves against him and openly declaring war. We didn't waste time. Provisions were packed, the horses were brought out, and we prepared to ride out and join them. Just as we were leaving, though, word arrived that Mugatu had attacked.

They hadn't lasted a day.

I felt like a homeless junkie, with no future and my life dead in the water. What separated me from the junkie, though, was the guy had that next fix to look forward to, the fleeting sensation of bliss, no matter how brief it was.

All I had to look forward to were the sword bruises I had coming.

After a while, I found myself spending more time with Elrik than I did with his brother. He was a whole different person, and at times, I even wondered if they were even related. As arrogant, cocky and self-assured as he was, truth be told, I liked the kid. He was as good as Laehn was with a blade, and despite myself, I started to enjoy training with him. And yes, this was in spite of constantly having to swallow my pride and get my rear handed to me by someone six years younger than I was.

Like now.

"You okay?"

"No," I groaned, "I think you broke my hip. Again."

I closed my eyes and let my head fall to the floor. Elrik rolled his eyes and grabbed my arm.

"Wait!" I cried, but he pulled me to my feet and, in the same move and with no warning at all, he hurled me against the wall.

Did I say I liked him? I hated his guts right then.

I slammed into it shoulder first and scrabbled at the wood to keep from collapsing again. My knees wobbled.

"Stay up!" he said, and lunged.

My hand moved out of muscle memory, and I parried his blow with a sharp crack of wood.

"Nice," he said.

"Hang on," I gasped, "Need… to breathe."

He shrugged and let up, allowing me time to push away from the wall and wipe my hair off my forehead. Uncut since I'd arrived, it had grown long enough to wear in a ponytail now, which I did. That, along with the rich beard I know itched at all night, made me look like a scrawny hippie in the land of no color. Of all the things that had happened to me, going Bohemian wasn't one I'd expected.

I wondered what Mona would have thought of the look. After all, she'd only she'd ever seen it cropped short. As she traipsed through my thoughts again, I immediately cast for a subject, any subject, to take my mind away.

"So," I said, "You have any other siblings we might run into?"

I guess I'd been hoping the question would have thrown him off, and I swung before I'd finished speaking, to try and catch him off guard. He sidestepped and I blew past, looking like an idiot again.

"You've already met all the surviving ones," he said.

It took a few moments for that to sink in.

"I... I'm sorry," I said.

"Don't be," he waved a hand, "It wasn't your fault. I had two more brothers; the oldest was with Da and Laehn when they confronted the mage. You know. The last Tyrant."

"Bass told me the story," I said, "Something about how Laehn used a shield to deflect some spell? And Eduud had to... well..."

"Had to make him look like some freak to save him?" Elrik finished, "I'm frankly surprised he told you. My brother isn't particularly fond of the story... and I guess you can't blame him. I suppose he wasn't there when Bass was telling it to you."

"Actually, no, he was."

Elrik raised an eyebrow.

"Bass always did as he pleased, didn't he?" he said, and sighed, "Yes, that's what happened to Laehn, and why he looks like... like how he does now. But what he probably didn't tell you was it was Da who was meant to be protecting the Champion; Laehn and Aeoril were there to help."

"What happened to them?"

Elrik turned away.

"Same spell hit them, too," he said, "And... it wasn't very pretty. They had been hurt too badly to save. Laehn still blames himself for it."

I swallowed the painful lump that was determinedly rising.

"I'm... I'm sorry," I said, thickly.

"My other brother," he continued, "He was younger than Laehn, but still old enough to page at the Castle. He died when the mage started his attack."

He looked at me, and then swung. I was too distracted to dodge or parry; the wooden training sword slammed into my forehead and I saw stars.

"Don't let your surroundings draw your attention," I heard him say, his voice echoing weirdly, "I thought we told you that a long time ago?"

I peeled my eyes open and watched the roof swim around in circles. Elrik's face popped into my line of sight, grinning but slightly worried.

"Sorry," he said, "I might have been a bit too enthusiastic with that one."

"It's one way of putting it," I groaned. I sat up and looked at him.

"Your family has a lot to do with the Champions, the Kings and Tyrants, don't they?"

He reached down and I grabbed his hand.

"Aye, we do," he said, helping me up, "It's a complicated history. Da's father, and his father before… sometimes I feel like our generations were born to serve the Kings. Damn fools can't look after their own damn selves."

"That's a bit harsh, don't you think?" I asked.

"You think I'm wrong to be harsh?" he demanded.

I nodded, "I guess you're right."

Elrik took a step back and started to twirl the sword in his fingers.

"Tell me about your wife," he prompted, "You've mentioned her once or twice in passing, mostly in complaints. What's she like?"

I didn't comment on the change of subject, given the topic, but I didn't like where he was trying to take the conversation to, either.

"I don't really like to talk about it," I muttered.

Elrik shrugged.

"I told you about my two dead brothers and my father," he pointed out, "That's not something you talk about lightly."

I looked at him, standing there. He was nineteen; not more than a kid, and yet the way he spoke and the things he said… they made him seem so much older. Tragedy and loss made men of children, I suppose.

I wiped my sweaty hair off my face again and leaned against a wooden pillar to catch my breath.

"What do you want to know?"

He shrugged.

"Well, the beginning is always a good place to start. How did you meet?"

"In college," I replied. The memories returned, unbidden, and despite myself, I realized I was grinning, "Oh, she hated me then."

"College?"

"Um…" I cast my eyes around the stable. How do you try explaining the concept of college to a kid from the medieval age?

"It was a place… where we studied," I said, lamely.

"Studied what?"

"Well… stuff. Mostly useless, though."

Elrik stepped forward and swung again.

"You say you met her there?" he said, "Do you mean to say that women… they studied as well?"

"Yeah," I grunted, "they did,"

"What did they do?" he asked, curious.

"Well, the same as us guys, mostly."

Elrik turned a quizzical face to me.

"Your world is strange," he observed.

I laughed, "Oh, you have no idea, kid. Believe it or not, women do a lot more back home than you'd ever imagine."

"That would explain your… skills," Elrik chuckled, "You most certainly did not learn how to fight."

He swung, I parried, and then we were at it again. Five minutes later, we broke off.

"Yeah," I agreed, panting and nursing a bruise on my rib, "We could have used some sword wielding one-oh-one over there."

"How did she become your betrothed?" he asked.

"Way to dive back into the subject," I said, the throb on my chest making me wince, "But it's a heck of a story. Yeah, there was the hanging out, the flirting, the playing hard to get, and the jealousy dating. Everything you'd expect."

Elrik shook his head, his eyes uncomprehending.

I laughed, "Well, you wanted to know. Sue me if you don't get the colloquial."

"I still don't understand," he replied.

"We dated… um, I courted her, I guess you'd put it… for three years," I said, "My buddies weren't ready to bite the bullet just yet. Can't say I blame them. But I knew she was the one. The feelings were real, kid. You only get that once in your life, and when you do, you don't let it go. So three years ago, I asked her to marry me. And she said yes."

"What's a bullet?"

I looked away, sighed and shook my head.

"Never mind."

"Did your parents' consent?" he pressed.

"Yeah, well, my mother wasn't too thrilled, but the old man was stoked. We married the year before he passed. I'm glad he got to see it," I smiled, "Her folks… not so much. I wasn't what you'd call the ideal son."

"You're doing it again, Alan."

"Pick up a dictionary, kid."

Elrik sighed, giving it up for lost. He struck a pose, forcing me to jump to the defensive before he attacked again.

"Have you any heirs?" he asked in between blows.

I laughed hollowly.

"Heirs to what, my cubicle and the office chair with the broken wheel?" I shook my head, "No, not yet. She said we weren't ready, and she was right."

Elrik nodded, and then lunged. I was getting tired, and I was missing with my swings about as much as I kept missing his sword when I tried to block him.

We broke off again, and he let my catch my breath.

"She was the real deal, Mona," I said, "She was patient; so patient. Three years of trouble, and she never complained, not once."

Elrik's brow furrowed.

"Trouble?" he echoed, "What kind of trouble?"

"Finally," I said, with a hollow laugh, "A word you understood."

"That's one every man understands," Elrik said, shrugging, "What was the kind plaguing you?"

"What else?" I stabbed moodily at a bale of hay, "Money. We started out so hopeful… and then I ended up with a damn desk job. She was going for a degree, and she helped out as an assistant at a vet clinic down the street. She didn't make much, but together we managed to scrape through every month. We had each other, and that was enough for her."

I sighed.

"I'm probably fired, too."

"Okay, this time you had to have been making that one up," Elrik said, "You *what* now?"

"I lost my job," I said, "They'd have thrown my papers in the bin weeks ago."

"The desk job?"

"You're catching on," I grinned, and then sighed. "Mona wouldn't mind," I said, "She always was telling me to get a move on from there, anyway. She stuck with me, no matter what. And then I left without even saying goodbye," I paused, "It was our anniversary. We had a dinner planned."

Elrik scuffed at a pebble.

"I'm sorry, Alan,"

I swallowed.

"Sure, we had a tough life," I said, my voice breaking, "And maybe it wasn't how I'd have planned it to go. We hit speedbumps. But she was there. She was always there. And now, it's been…I've lost track of how long it's been since I got here."

Elrik didn't move.

"And the last she saw of me," I whispered, "To her, it would have looked like I left in the morning and never returned. Like I ran away. She'd never believe it… but after all this time…"

I choked. My throat clenched painfully, and I couldn't go on.

"I think we've sparred enough for now," Elrik said quietly.

I nodded gratefully and handed him the sword. I turned away, my eyes stinging, but not before he saw the tears.

*   *   *

I needed something to distract me, so the moment Laehn suggested we pop into the town for a spell, I was ready.

It was late afternoon when we rode in, hoods lowered. The streets were nearly crowded, which was odd, especially at this time of day. There was a feeling of unease in the air, palpable enough for even me to notice. Laehn's brow was furrowed when I looked at him.

"What's wrong?" I asked.

He shook his head and shrugged.

We dismounted and joined the people walking about. I tried to listen to the hushed whispers, but I couldn't catch more than a handful of words. 'Messenger,' was one, and 'Champion' was another.

The whispers and voices cut abruptly, and I could hear the sounds of hooves galloping, somewhere nearby.

"Way! Make WAY!" a voice hollered, and like a curtain, the crowd of people parted, clearing the street for half a dozen horses to gallop in, a gold plated, two horse carriage in their midst. The crowd surged into the street, closing the gap as they stormed into the town square and circled, clearing space.

I searched for Laehn and found him, shoved by the crowd on the opposite side of the street. His eyes narrowed, and I followed his gaze to the double door of the carriage, where some of the blue soldiers had dismounted and were moving into formation.

They stamped their feet in unison, and the door began to open.

I braced myself to run. This had to be Mugatu's new lieutenant, and the moment I was recognized, they would be after me. My heart began to race, and I tried to move away. The crowd jostled me, holding me in place, and, my legs trembling, I turned to watch as a guard stepped out first and glared at the crowd pressed packed tight around the square.

A thin, reedy man stepped out next, and behind him, another guard.

I heaved a sigh of relief. It was just a lousy town crier.

The man swallowed as he looked around the crowd, timidly hugged a jeweled box to his chest. The soldier behind him prodded him with his crossbow, and the man started walking. The guards escorted him to the square and up the steps, eyes sweeping over the crowd, probably for any sign of troublemakers.

On the wooden platform serving as an improvised stage, the man handed the box to one of the soldiers, opened it, and took out a scroll.

My eyes flickered to Laehn. He was watching me, and the moment our eyes met, he nodded.

On the platform, the man held out the scroll and drew it open. Holding it high, he looked over the crowd and licked his lips nervously.

The soldier nudged him again, and he cleared his throat.

"HEAR ye, HEAR ye," he hollered, "By DECREE of our most illustrious Lord, KING Mugatu, First of his Name, Cleaver of Pathways, Conqueror of Kings, MAN of the People, let it be known that the Usurper, former King Zaahis, First of *his* name, (with good reason), is hereby found GUILTY of incompetence and unKingly conduct, and as such, has been SENTENCED to be HUNG from a ROPE till DEAD."

My intake of breath merged with the collective gasp of the assemblage.

"What of his trial?" an old man hollered, "On what grounds is he to be…?"

"SILENCE!" a soldier roared.

"Down with Mugatu!" a woman screamed.

Her mistake. A crossbow snapped, and the crowd parted around her as she fell, the voices dying to a murmur. I swallowed and inconspicuously lowered my hood further, trying not to look like the most wanted man in the Realm.

The announcer attempted a nervous laugh, pulled out a handkerchief and wiped his forehead.

"Ahem, yes. His CHARGES are as follows," he continued, voice much higher pitched than when he started out, "ONE; USURPING the throne WITHOUT public voting OR consideration for others so inclined to do so. TWO; Spending TOO much on the poor…"

His words blended in with each other, their absurd meaning lost to me.

This was it then. It was all over.

As the man kept reading out the ludicrous charges, and Zaahis' voice played in my mind, over and over again. He'd asked me to look after his people for him. I had failed, and now he was going to die. Like Bass, he was going to die.

"Twenty nine: INCOMPETENCE regarding to the CARE of HORSES within the royal stables AND their handling."

The dull murmur from the crowd was picking up again and the soldiers on the makeshift stage visibly loaded and raised their crossbows, glaring at the loudest voices.

The man dabbed at his forehead again.

"For these charges and more, FORMER King Zaahis has been found GUILTY, and is to be EXECUTED at NOON, a week from now."

I'd heard enough. I turned and pushed through the crowd, away from the square. Others were leaving as well; the crowd was thinning out. Out of the corner of my eye, I could see Laehn doing the same, heading towards me.

"Unless," the man cried, "the one who calls himself the Champion were to rightfully SURRENDER and PRESENT HIMSELF before to his Majesty King Mugatu."

I paused.

Don't turn around, my mind screamed, *They'll know it's you!!!*

I didn't turn, but I couldn't force my legs to walk away, either.

"Should this Champion present himself before the King's Men or the King himself," the crier hollered, "former King Zaahis WILL be released without harm. He and his family will be exiled, and their lives spared. One week has the Champion been given to make his decision. Hear ye, hear ye, tis the Champion's choice."

The last thing I wanted to hear.

The crier, apparently done, hurried off the stage with palpable relief, the guards forming a shield around him as they escorted him to the carriage. The people muttered and shook fists, but no one said a word till the carriage had started moving and the horses were galloping out of there.

The crowd of people parted, clearing way for them to pass again, and the press of bodies caught and held me long enough for Laehn to squeeze his way to my side.

"Alan, wait," he said.

The people were yelling now; women were crying, and the men were shaking their fists at the soldier's backs. I ignored Laehn, and pushed past more people, struggling to get back to where we'd left the horses. I felt a hand on my shoulders, and fingers pinched hard enough to make me wince.

"We need to think through this," he said.

"I've thought it through," I snarled, trying to pull free, "I'm turning myself in."

He squeezed harder, and my arm started to go numb.

"Have you gone mad?" he hissed.

I kept walking, and he followed, hand still pinched on my arm.

"Alan, stop," he ordered, "Don't be a fool."

"Alright, let go before you take my arm off," I yelped.

He loosened his grip, but kept his hold on my arm as he dragged me away from the crowds.

"Turning yourself in will undermine everything we have fought for, everything we've accomplished," his eyes flashed, "All the lives lost... and Bass... it would all be for nothing. Would you want that?"

I glared at him.

"Ever heard of sunk cost?"

I used his confusion to pull away from him and try and lose myself in the crowd. For what it was worth, I might as well have had tried disarming him and using his bow to shoot down a crow.

I felt his steel grip on my shoulder again, and I tried to pull away again. This time, he didn't let go, but steered me out through the streets to where we had tied the horses.

"We've been doing nothing for too long, now," I said once we were out of earshot, "I'm not going to sit around and grow old and die here. My wife needs me."

"These people need you," Laehn said.

"If I turn myself into Mugatu," I said, "I can ask him to send me home. Both our problems would be solved."

"You would abandon these people to their fate?" Laehn demanded, enraged.

"I never asked to come here!" I snapped.

Laehn let go of me in disgust.

"Go, if you want," he said, "You know your hope is a lie. Mugatu will kill you, Alan. As long as you still live, you are a threat. It would not matter whether you were in this world or your own."

My breath caught in my throat.

"So I die, then," I said, softly, "If there's no going back for me. At least this way, Zaahis will see his family again, even in exile…"

"You are the Champion," Laehn insisted, "And if you die, the hopes of all men, women and children die with you."

"It's happened," I said, "Champions have died before."

"But not to a Tyrant who was once a Champion himself," Laehn said, agitated. "You know he will not age for centuries. He may never die, and he may rule the Realm for time immemorial. Are you willing to…?"

"I'm not willing to anything," I snapped, "I never wanted any of this, remember? You brought me here, and now Bass is dead and the Realm is lost and I'm never getting home! That is ALL I ever wanted, Laehn, to go home. You never once stopped to think how I felt, did you? Did any of you?"

His nostrils flared.

"You say you do this to save King Zaahis," he said, his voice quiet. "You are naïve to believe Mugatu would let the King leave. Zaahis is bait, nothing more. Mugatu is trying to draw you to him. And once you're there, he will kill you both and be done with it."

"Then what do you suggest we do, huh, Laehn?" I yelled, "What's YOUR idea?! Let Zaahis die and keep hiding out here?"

Laehn's jaw clenched.

"No," he said, "We attack."

Chapter 12

"We WHAT?"

Horrified was not a good look on Ajold. Jaw dangling, eyes wide, he looked from Laehn to me and back again.

"The other alternatives are I surrender," I said, "Or we let Zaahis die. Laehn abhors the first one, and I can't say I'm too happy with the second."

"You'd be mad," Elrik agree, "But to be fair, you'd be mad to do any of the three."

"You cannot expect Mugatu to keep his word," Ennah said, "He is a traitor, a coward who will do whatever it takes to keep his power. You and the King are too dangerous to keep alive."

Ajold ran a hand through his thinning hair. He'd lost weight over the weeks, and a lot of it. Either the food didn't agree with him, or the tension didn't. And after weeks of Bass's gruel, Ennah's cooking was heaven.

"We're talking about storming the Castle," he said, "*My* Castle. With all the men Mugatu has in there… there is no way we'd survive. Laehn, we'll never make it inside."

"We never said anything about storming," Laehn said, "We will sneak in undetected."

"Oh," Ajold threw up his hands, "That makes so much sense. What are you, suicidal?"

"Wait, what?" I demanded.

Laehn fixed his gaze on me.

"This will end with you facing Mugatu in single combat," Ennah said, "As it always does."

As far as I could remember, this was something that had conveniently been left out of conversation.

"Come again?"

"You're going to have to defeat Mugatu on your own," Laehn's brow furrowed, "It will be your blade which kills him, or none at all. I thought Bass told you this?"

I was having trouble breathing. The walls of the living room closed in on me, smothering, suffocating. I had to get out.

I stumbled to the door and threw it open.

"Where are you going?" Ajold asked.

I took a couple of steps away from the door, and I couldn't hold it in any longer. Bending over just in time, I hurled a good portion of Ennah's excellent breakfast back into the light of day.

Arhaza wandered through the gate just as I shakily leaned against the wall and screwed up her nose at me.

"You're going to have to clean that up," she said accusingly.

"Trust me," I muttered, "It's the least of my worries."

The door creaked behind me, and Elrik walked up.

"Better?" he asked

I snorted.

"Take your time…" he began, but I pushed past him and stumbled back into the house. My legs trembled all the way back to my stool.

"Alan, you will face him," Laehn said as I fell onto it, "This will happen."

"Okay, look," I said, "You've all been trying to train me. You've seen me fight. You know how bad I am at it. What makes you think I can do this?"

"You're the only one who can," Ajold pointed out.

"You keep saying that, but it doesn't mean it's true."

"You have survived the odds this far," Laehn said.

"Sheer luck. You were there."

"You killed Kernine," Elrik said.

"No, no wait," I raised a hand, "That was Laehn. He…"

"It was your Weapon what pierced him," Ajold said, "We all saw it."

"It was the Armament that killed him!" I exclaimed, "Him, AND Bass! If you're going to say I killed Kernine, you're going to have to say I killed Bass, too, because that's how they BOTH died!"

I'd made my point, apparently. They looked away and I simmered on my seat.

"It will come down to you or him," Ennah said quietly, "And it does not matter if you are ready or not. You *will* be the one to kill him."

"And if not," Laehn said, "No one else can. If you fail, we are all done."

I passed a hand over my face.

"You're asking me to die."

"You were prepared to on the way here," Laehn pointed out.

I glared at him, and he shrugged.

"Supposing I agree with this," I snapped, "How do you plan on sneaking into it undetected, anyway?"

"The passage we used to escape the Castle the first time," he replied.

For a moment, just a moment, I felt a slight thrill. Then it was gone, and I was sane again.

"They'd have seen us use it," I said, "And either blocked it up or laid guards around it."

"They wouldn't have seen us use it," Ajold said, rubbing his chin thoughtfully, "The fire was too large to look through."

"How many others know about it?" Elrik asked, "Would Mugatu…?"

"No one knows," Ajold said confidently, "It was just Bass, Zaahis and myself who knew about it. And the only reason I do is because Bass himself showed it to me when I became the Captain."

"Even so, there'll still be guards at the other end," I pointed out, "Patrols and such. Not to mention the fact that this passage opens halfway down the city; we need to get into the Castle, and there are way more guards there."

I breathed in a shaky breath.

"And we all seem to be ignoring the fact," I continued, my voice trembling, "that I'll have to face Mugatu… *on my own!*"

"Who said you would be on your own?" Laehn asked.

"What, you coming with me?" I demanded.

He smiled.

"I have been with you since the start of your Quest," he said, "I will admit I did not think I would be here this long. But I have, and so I shall promise you this, Alan; you will have me with you at its end."

My mind flashed to that moment in the tavern, the first time Laehn had promised to help me. So much had changed then, and we had come so far.

"Thank you," I said, and this time I felt the shivers running down my spine.

I looked up at the others.

"You'll need a diversion," Elrik mused, "Draw their attention away from the city."

"An attack on the front Gates," Ajold said, "At sundown. The Gate faces Southwest, and the sun would be in their eyes. And if they're busy looking over the Gate, they will most certainly have their backs to you."

"Whoa, hold on, there," I interrupted, "Attack the Gate? With what army?"

"Yours," Ennah said, raising an eyebrow, "Of course,"

I cleared my throat and shook my head.

"Come again?" I said, "You're saying I have an army now?"

"The village," Laehn said, "The towns. You're the Champion. They will answer your call."

I blinked.

"And…. for some reason, you didn't think about mentioning this before?"

"We did," Elrik said, rolling his eyes. "You weren't listening."

I ran my fingers through my hair, and then did it again.

"That's suicide," I said. "No matter how many of them come. And even if we get in… there's no guarantee I will win. You can't expect me have them risk their lives for…"

"You keep asking us to think from your point of view, Alan," Laehn said, his voice cold, "But have you ever once tried to look at it through the eyes of any man or woman here? This is their life, all they know. If you ask them to risk it for the sake of their children, the sake of their homes… they will fight. They deserve to fight. Give that to them."

"If they want to fight and die so badly, why don't they do it already?" I demanded.

"Because they're afraid. They need hope. They're waiting to be lead, a figure to rally around," Laehn jabbed a finger into my chest. "They're waiting for *you*. The Champion. *You're* the one Eduud Summoned. We will fight, we will die. But *you* should be the one leading them."

"That's just it! Why me?" I yelled, "WHY. ME?"

"You've heard the answer to that before, many times," Ajold said, calmly. He gripped my shoulder and squeezed. "But only because it is true. Only you can defeat Mugatu. Eduud would not have Summoned you if he didn't think you had it in you."

"You, because you are their hope, Alan," Ennah said. I looked at her, and I saw Bass behind those words, the ones he'd said to me so very long ago.

I glowered, and then shook my head.

"Alright, fine," I snapped. "Might as well die in a blaze of glory rather than as a hunted fugitive."

"Why die at all?" Elrik grinned.

"If we're going to do this, we're going to have to recruit people," I said, ignoring him. "Assuming we do send out this call they're waiting for. What's to stop the word from spreading to the Castle? The last I remembered, we supposed to be in hiding."

"I think it's better if they do find out we're coming," Ajold said. "And if we could encourage the rumors, exaggerate them… we could make them focus wholly on the wall. Draw their attention away from the passage."

"More men at the wall makes it more dangerous to the ones attacking," I pointed out.

"Sacrifices are made in war," Ajold said with a shrug, "We're not meant to succeed. You are."

"Doesn't mean you have to die for nothing," I pointed out.

"It won't be for nothing," Ajold replied. "And we won't die. At least… not all of us."

He shrugged, "I think I can handle commanding an army. They made me Captain for a reason."

"You don't seem to get it, do you?!" I demanded angrily. "Even if we do get inside, past the guards and everything… what if I *don't* beat Mugatu? What if I die? And all… all this," I waved my arm around, "All this will be for nothing."

"We know, Alan," Elrik said.

"We're only going to get one shot at this," I yelled. "If we fail, there's NO coming back!"

"We *know*," Laehn repeated, slowly.

I slammed my fist against the wall. It accomplished nothing but send pain across my knuckles, but it didn't lessen my determination any.

"If we fail, we're going to doom the village and anyone else foolish enough to join us to whatever fate Mugatu deems fit as punishment," I said. "Are you willing to risk that on them? I'm not, Laehn."

"But we are," said, Ennah spoke finally, her eyes cold. "Mugatu will not age, and he will not die unless by another's hand. YOUR hand."

I closed my mouth. With Laehn's mother, I'd learned to let her say her piece before interrupting.

"This is a chance you will never get again," she said. "Now, he is distracted by the very trap he is baiting you with. Use that to your advantage. Play him. Go, but on your terms. You can do this."

"We may fail," I said, "We may…"

"I do not want my sons and daughter to grow up in a world where that man is ruler," she snapped. "And their children, and their children's children… my legacy will live under his rule. I will not allow it. Nor will anyone else."

Her eyes flashed.

"And don't you DARE say again you will fail," she warned.

"Now is the time, the only ever time to strike," Laehn spoke. "Only now will they expect you to make a foolish mistake, and only now can you turn it back on them, trick *them* into making the mistake."

I hung my head.

"You'll never break through the Gates," I said. "Not even if you had a hundred men,"

"We don't need to break through them," Ajold said. "We'll just keep them busy long enough for you to slip in. When you're through, we'll fall back."

"There's another thing," I said, as a thought hit me. "If I'm not going to be at the Gate with you, Mugatu will find out, and he *will* smell a trap."

"Oh, but you will be there," Ajold grinned, "The people need you to lead them, after all."

I scratched my head.

"Um… I thought the plan was for me to sneak in from…"

"Yes," Ajold's smile widened. "And so you will. But the people need you to lead them, and so you shall."

"I thought you said *you* would lead the army," Laehn frowned.

"Exactly!" Ajold crossed his arms and leaned back triumphantly in his stool.

"He'll dress up as you," Elrik said, slapping his hand on his thigh. "And fool everybody. It's brilliant! I didn't think of that."

"Are you crazy?!" I demanded. "This whole thing as madness from the start, but this… this…?"

"It can be done," Ennah interrupted.

"We are of the same height, after all," Ajold pointed out. "And I have… well, let's just say I'm… maybe not as heavy as I used to be."

I looked at his sagging jowls and the folds of skin on his neck.

"There's one way of putting it."

"All you need to do is keep your face covered," Elrik said, excited.

"And the armor?" I demanded. You couldn't blame me for being skeptical. There was no way that this was going to work out.

"Nothing some color and light rework on his armor can't fix," Elrik replied, "It's easy."

"I have a bad feeling about this," I muttered. "It doesn't seem right. What if they see through the ruse? Even if they do get fooled, there's still so much more that can go wrong."

"Not if they think this is some foolish, last ditch do-or-die effort," Elrik said. His grin slid off his face. "Which, now I think about it, is exactly what this whole discussion is."

The five of us exchanged glances. Ajold shrugged and Laehn sighed.

"You will need help to keep up the deception," Elrik continued. "I'll fight with you, Captain."

"Absolutely not!" Laehn snapped.

"What do you mean, 'keep it up?'" I asked, at the exact same time.

"You will not involve yourself in this," Laehn said. "You are a boy. War is no place for you."

"I'm a man and you know it," Elrik said coolly. "I will do as I will. Others risk their lives for this. So shall I."

"That is not your decision to make," Laehn stood. "You have your mother and sister to keep look after, to keep safe."

"You decide to fight if you want to?" Elrik asked, "You were younger than me when you started training, and I am just as good as you are, if not bett-"

"Elrik will fight," Ennah said quietly. She closed her eyes.

"Mother?" Laehn demanded, aghast.

"I will not deny him the right to choose what he will," she said. "And should the Champion fail us, it is better if we do not survive than we should endure the Tyrant's wrath."

Elrik nodded, "Thank you, Mother."

Laehn scowled, but didn't say anything.

"Now that we're done," I broke in, "What did you mean when you said 'keep up the deception? From whom? The enemy?"

They exchanged looks.

"Tell me you're not going to lie to the men fighting with you," I said, aghast.

"The only way they will make it look convincing is if they think they fight behind you, and not anyone else," Ajold said. "And… well, it's the only way they'll fight at all."

"War must be won by any means," Ennah said, crossing her arms. "And if it is by deceit we win, deceit it shall be."

"It's what Bass would have done," Laehn said harshly. "And you know that."

He'd played the Bass card; there was nothing more to be said.

I closed my eyes and hung my head. The buzzing in my ears intensified, and my head was beginning to ache.

I raised my head to see them all looking at me.

Again, it was my call, and what happened next… whatever happened, it was entirely on me.

This Champion job really, really sucked.

"Let's do this," I whispered.

It was like the entire village had been waiting for me to do something, and the moment Laehn and Elrik began to spread the word, it felt like the very air was surging up in rebellion.

Messengers rode off to the closest villages and towns, the word of war riding with them. From there, Laehn told me more would set out, calling men to us.

And they came.

In tens and twenties, in groups and alone, men and even women poured into the village, bringing with them food, weapons, horses, and more wagons. These were country folk, and I had no trouble believing that most... if not all... had never used a weapon against another in their lives. And yet, here they were, ready for war. They were answering the call.

My call.

We'd only a week before Zaahis would be executed, if what that town crier had said was true; and from what I was told, it was a four day's easy ride from the village to the Castle. With an army, small as it was, and most of it on foot, it would take a couple of days longer.

We'd still get there in time, we theorized, but we'd only have the time for one shot, one assault on the walls to throw all we had at them. If that messed up, there would be no second chance.

I could hear their voices from outside, floating in through the open window my room. I listened as I moved, fitting on my armor one piece at a time. I hadn't touched it since we'd come here, and I'd only worn it twice since then.

This was the first time I'd ever fitted it on all by myself. And it wasn't at all as easy as Laehn or Ajold had made it look.

The march to the Castle would begin in the morning, Ajold had said. Now, this was for show, to let them see who called them. They needed to see their Champion, who they were following.

I attached the towel/cloak, and picked up my helmet. I looked down at it, at the sleek green lines and the silver visor. I ran a finger over the scrapes and scratches etched into the metal, the ones I'd put there in the battle on the Hill.

Movement in the corner made me look up to see Arhaza leaning against the door and beaming at me.

"Ma said they're waiting," she said.

"I'm coming," I replied.

She kept staring at me, eyes wide and worshipful.

"What is it?" I asked.

"You don't look so sad anymore," she said.

I chuckled.

"Yeah, this armor is something to look at, isn't it?"

She shook her head.

"Not the armor, silly," she said, "I meant your face. Your eyes."

"What do you mean, my face?" I demanded, reasonably mystified.

She stuck her tongue at me, turned around in a whisk of hair and ran away. I shrugged and looked down at my reflection on the back of the helmet.

The mule was waiting for me in the garden, saddle and trappings set. The others stood around, solemnly watching as I stomped out of the door and into the waning sun.

The mule raised its head, mouthful of grass, and greeted me with its usual flatulent familiarity.

"Why the mule?" I asked.

"That mule is your steed," Laehn replied.

"I have to ride it?" I asked, "I thought the point was to make a good impression on them?"

"It's the way it is," Ennah said.

I looked at it and swallowed.

"I've never ridden it before," I said. "Bass... Bass said it needs to trust you before..."

"Just get on," Elrik said, rolling his eyes. "We'll find out if it trusts you any moment now."

It didn't move as I reached out and grabbed the reins. Hesitatingly, I raised one foot and paused. When nothing happened, I threw caution into the winds and hoisted myself up and into the saddle.

It was with a collective intake of breath that we waited and watched to see its reaction.

It chewed, and it tooted. It swished its tail, but stood there.

I guess it was official. The mule trusted me.

I rode into the front of the village, and from my vantage point, I watched as the sea of faces turned to look at me. There were dozens of them, at least five hundred there, and from far away, out beyond the furthermost buildings, I could see more coming.

Laehn and Ajold walked on either side of me as the mule worked its way through the throng. They saw me; some eyes were hard and angry, others were wide and frightened. Their gazes bored through my helmet, metaphorically drilling holes in my literal armor. I didn't know what they were expecting, and even though I wracked my brains, I couldn't even remember a line from any of those rousing orations I'd seen in movies.

"What do I do?" I whispered.

"Something," Ajold hissed.

"Keep your visor lowered," Laehn advised. "Let the ones who haven't seen your face think of you as more than a man."

More deception.

I swallowed, and then punched my mailed fist into the air.

One of the men cheered, and it was the spark that set off the rest. A deafening roar rose, and men bellowed and yelled. Then there were words; they were chanting.

"DOWN with the Tyrant! DOWN with Mugatu!"

"RISE for the CHAMPION! FIGHT for the KING!"

The words echoed, thundering into the air. You couldn't listen and not be affected; no one could. They were there for me. They were my people.

"TOMORROW!" I bellowed. My visor was down, and my voice echoed around in my helmet, deafening me. I didn't think anyone had heard me, but the voices quieted, starting at the people in front of me, the silence working its way to the outer edges.

I cleared my throat and tried again.

"TOMORROW!" I yelled, "WE MARCH!"

"AYE!" they bellowed.

"WE MARCH FOR THE KING!" I screamed.

They roared their approval. Caught in the moment, I drew my sword and held it high to a chorus of bellows.

Something tugged at my leg, and I looked down, distracted.

"That's enough, Alan," Laehn said, just loud enough for me to hear over the voices, "Go back to the house. We will follow."

I nodded, and pumped my fist again, to renewed roars.

They were chanting as I cantered away. I caught the words, and I felt that tingle rise, even as the lump of fear pressed hard on my chest.

"CHAM-pion!" the voices boomed, "CHAM-pion! CHAM-pion!"

Night fell, but I couldn't sleep. After hours of tossing, I yielded and sat up in bed.

The outside air beckoned, and I answered.

The wind was cold on my skin as I pushed open the front door, and it was pretty darn refreshing on my hot skin. My hair fell uncomfortably over my shoulders, and I considered cutting it before the battle as I stepped onto the soil.

In all the time I'd spent there, this was the first I'd left the house after everyone had gone to bed. The garden, the dirt road and the world beyond the gate… it all seemed so different at night, lit up by the milky moonlight.

I walked to the middle of the garden, feeling the little pebbles and wet blades of grass between my toes. For no reason, I crossed my legs and sat in the grass.

"How did it come to this, anyway?" I muttered.

I looked around at the silvery world. So peaceful now; another deception in a land full of empty promises and certain death. And to death it was I would lead these people to tomorrow; of that, at least, we all were sure.

I chuckled. I'd kept thinking to myself how change was coming to me… and boy, had it. A far cry this was from the ratty apartment with the leaky plumbing and faulty wiring; and it couldn't get any more different from the small, predicable wood and plaster cubicles in the small, predictable office.

I breathed, and a plume of vapor billowed upwards, vanishing into the night.

A notion to visit the mule popped into my head, and I considered it for a few minutes.

"Oh, to hell with it," I muttered.

I hoisted myself up, dusted the wet grass off my rear and set off around the side of the house. I saw the stable, and I saw the door ajar, and light flickering from inside.

I didn't know if whether or not Ennah kept a torch burning there through the night; the light didn't seem large enough to scare me into thinking that the stable was on fire, but I was still cautious as I jogged over to the door.

I peered around it, and to my relief, it was just a torch in a pail. A tall, thin shadow against the wall caught my eye. I looked around and saw someone there, facing away from me.

"Laehn?"

He turned, his hands protectively held up against his chest.

"I didn't expect you to be awake," he commented.

"Couldn't sleep," I said, pushing the door open. I walking in and nodded at his hands, "What you got there?"

He held them out; cupped in his fingers was a pigeon.

"Don't tell me," I said, "Sending a message?"

"Replying to one," he said, walking past me to the door.

"Who from?"

Outside, he ran his hand softly over its feathers before giving it a gentle toss. It flapped wildly and took flight, rising rapidly and then merging with the darkness.

"Allies," he said as I joined him, "If we are lucky."

"From where?" I asked, "And how many?"

"Old friends of Bass," he said, eyes on the dark sky where it had gone, "They had… a falling out. A long time ago."

"Will they help us?"

Laehn sighed, "I do not know. We can hope."

We didn't say anything for a long time. He finally sighed and turned to leave.

"Laehn," I said, and then paused.

He turned.

"Yes, Alan?"

I swallowed.

"Will I win?"

He looked at me. The wind whispered, cold on my bare back.

"We shall see," he said, "Let us hope."

Chapter 13

With all the enthusiasm they'd shown at my less than inspired speech, I have to admit I'd been expecting my people to be awake and ready to leave at the crack of dawn, waving flags and singing songs of war.

But people, wherever you go, will be people.

By the time Laehn and I had taken our place at the front, gotten the force in order and, in my case, done more air punches and yelled random inspiring words like "victory!" and "death!", it had to have been somewhere around 10 in the morning.

And even then, it was a slow start. I rode the mule, my armor gleaming in the sunlight, my head slowly cooking inside the helmet as I pretended to lead the way. Laehn kept pace, towering over me on his horse, busy with actually doing all the leading.

Behind us, the people fanned out, tramping behind us on foot in absolutely no order whatsoever. This wasn't an army; this was a mob. My mind reflected unbidden to all I knew about mobs and their effectiveness, and the only images that came up were of them always being dangerous when crowding inside some enclosed area and only being effective when they outnumbered the enemy.

The one we had was going to be outside the walls, and they were nothing more than cannon fodder in their makeshift armor and modified farming tools. And I wasn't going to even consider the other point.

"We're leading them to their death," I muttered.

"We have had this discussion," Laehn replied, "And we have settled it."

My fist clenched, but I didn't say anything more.

"It looks like we gained a couple of dozen more overnight," Ajold said. "And more are on their way."

He walked on my other side, clothed in plain brown, his cloak flapping in the breeze. His armor was still with Elrik, not yet ready for display.

"How will they know where to catch up with us?" I asked.

"Specified waypoints and villages on the way," he replied, "They'll rendezvous with us as we go along."

"We'll never make it in time," I said. "We're barely walking here."

I turned around to look at the six hundred or so people ambling along, laughing and talking among themselves. This wasn't even a mob; it was a family picnic. And literally everyone was invited.

"We will reach the Castle," Laehn promised, "And in time to save the King."

All I could do was believe the guy.

He was right, though. We picked up speed as the day wore on, and if Ajold's estimates were right, four more days would be all it took to reach there.

We stopped at midday, and then pushed on till nightfall. The days blended into each other; sleep, eat, march, and repeat. The men didn't complain till the third day, and yet we pressed on. We passed villages, but we didn't have to go close. The people there and the ones from elsewhere who'd joined them were waiting for us on the path, yelling and waving their weapons as they caught sight of us. At each village we passed, the elder bowed to me and pledged his allegiance, and his people, to my cause.

With every man who joined us, my feeling of guilt deepened; Ajold, on the other hand, couldn't keep his joy down.

Dawn rose on the sixth day after the town crier had kicked us into action. By the time the sun had reached its peak, I noticed a lump standing out on the horizon.

I shaded my eyes with my hand, but I couldn't make it out in the haze.

"Is that?" I croaked, throat as parched as the dust we were kicking up.

"It is," Laehn replied.

"About time," I wheezed.

"Aye," Ajold agreed, a six foot mound of sand and dust walking alongside us. "I say we get closer and then make camp. We need to time the attack so we can bash them just as the sun sets. We're going to have to circle around the left if we want to reach the front Gate."

"They're tired," Elrik said. "They're going to need rest before the attack."

"We haven't time," I rasped sourly, "And this is the last sunset we get."

I turned in my saddle and looked over my army, straggling after us in disorderly droves for as far as the eye could see. The ones who noticed me turn gave out a ragged cheer, waving their weapons and punching the air. I pumped my fist again to encourage them, feeling sick in my stomach as their cheering redoubled.

"Quick march to where we camp, then," Laehn said, sharply. "They've seen how close we are. Use it to push them."

"Lead the charge," Ajold said to me.

My visor was down, but I'll bet they knew I was scowling even if they couldn't see it. I drew my sword again, and the mule reared up on its hind legs.

I gave them the wordless battle cry, swung my sword, waited for their answering roars, and then I fell forward as the mule took off at half the speed it usually went at. Like sheep being led to slaughter, they followed, screaming and yelling, following nothing but blind hope.

The wind made my cloak flutter, stinging my eyes as it filtered through the slits in my visor.

How dare you call yourself a Hero? You're leading them to their graves, my mind whispered, *How does this make you any better than Mugatu?*

It doesn't, I replied, gritting my teeth.

*   *   *

The tent was cramped and stifling, and I'd have given anything to have done this out in the open air. But here, so close to the Castle, we didn't want to give the men too good a look of me and my real armor before Ajold rode out to take my place.

"This is it then," I said, clenching my fist.

Elrik, Laehn and Ajold were with me in the tent; Ennah had stayed back at the village with Arhaza and most of the other women. She'd wanted to come, but as intimidating as she was to argue against, Laehn had won that dispute.

"Preparations are complete," Elrik said. "We're as ready as we'll ever be."

"Ajold's armor?" I asked.

"There's no way to tell it isn't yours from a distance," he replied. "The coloring isn't an exact match, but it should pass. The pieces, though, and the shapes of the individual parts… it's a good thing most folk here aren't all that familiar with armor to tell the difference."

"And the soldiers on the wall would have probably never seen it properly," Ajold added.

I focused on my breathing. Inhale; one, one thousand, two, one thousand, exhale.

"The battering ram is almost ready," Ajold continued. "We'll be ready to move out as soon as it's finished."

If they were going to storm the wall with an angry mob of villagers, the least they could do was to make it believable. Littering the meadows surrounding the Castle were chinks of timber and half cut logs of felled trees, the remains of what Mugatu's army had used to construct their siege weapons when the Castle had been attacked the first time around.

Under Ajold's direction, the villagers had gathered what they could from the moment we'd stopped moving. For the last two and a half hours since we'd camped, they had tirelessly worked on building a sizable battering ram on wheels, Ajold looking on and giving the orders. Makeshift as it was, even I had to admit it looked fairly impressive. The last I'd seen it was just before I'd ducked into the tent some ten or fifteen minutes ago, and from what I could tell, it was just about ready.

Whether or not it would work was something else entirely.

"What of the men who will be joining you?" Ajold asked.

"I handpicked them myself," Laehn replied, "They were not happy to hear the truth. But they knew it had to be done."

I rubbed my forehead, "I've been thinking. Why don't we send everyone in through the passage? Attack from the inside?"

"It was the first thought that occurred to me," Laehn replied, "Along with the first reason as to why it would not succeed."

"Which is?"

"You'll never get into the Castle," Ajold replied. "The moment they knew you were inside the walls they'd barricade the Castle from within. They'd trap your people in the City, divide them, and then cut them down one by one."

He sighed, "That's what I'd have done if it were me in charge."

"This plan will work," Laehn said, standing up and walking. "Trust in it. We have come this far."

I watched him reach the end of the cramped tent, turn around and pace to the other side, head bowed, hands behind his back. It was a few moments for my distracted mind to wrap around the fact that Laehn was pacing; Laehn, always so calm and collected, always the cool head.

I'd never seen him pace before. And with a shock sending tremors through me, I realized Laehn was just as nervous as the rest of us. Probably even more so.

Watching him reach the other end of the tent and spin around, I realized I couldn't take it anymore. The waiting was getting to me, to all of us. I had to act, to do something before my mind exploded.

"Is it time yet?" I demanded.

Elrik rose, walked past us and pulled open the flap of the tent.

"Aye," he said quietly, eyeing the horizon, "It is time."

Ajold and I stood up together, and as I drew the robe and hood over my armor, he let his fall to reveal his almost-matching armor. Standing together, it was pretty easy to tell the difference; the green lines and trimmings on the silver metal weren't in the exact same spots, and even the shade of green Elrik had used on Ajold's armor was different from the one on mine.

But to someone who'd not seen too much of my own suit to know how to tell the difference… the two would probably seem identical, especially from a certain distance. For the first time since we'd come up with this flimsy plan, I actually felt a twinge that this might work.

Ajold put his helmet on and walked over to me. We stared at each other as he stuck out his hand. I swallowed and tentatively reached out and took it.

"Thank you," I said.

"Thank *you*," he replied. "Good fortune to your blade, Champion," he eyed my belt and grinned, "Whichever one that might be."

An air of finality took hold then. I'd been putting off the thought, but now it couldn't be held off any longer. This might very well be the last time I ever saw Ajold or Elrik again. I gripped his hand harder.

"And you," I whispered, "In the field."

His eyes crinkled in a grin.

"To victory and to death," he said. "Tonight, we take one and them the other."

He let go of my hand and turned to Laehn. They gripped each other's shoulders and nodded wordlessly. Ajold shut his visor with a clang and strode out of the tent. I heard his voice as he yelled, and the voices of the men who replied.

Elrik grinned as he came up to me.

"You look like you're dead already," he teased, "Lighten up."

I grabbed his hand.

"Good luck, out there," I said.

He laughed.

"Look after yourself, Champion," he replied. "Don't let my brother infect you. You should know better than that."

Laehn walked over and glared down at him. Just as I thought he was going to punch his lights out, for old times' sake and all that, he stunned the both of us by reaching out and hugging him.

"Watch your back, little brother," Laehn said, letting him go and squeezing his shoulders. "Take yourself home to Mother. Protect our sister."

"Do it yourself," Elrik stuck his tongue at him. He turned to me and nodded.

"With luck," he said, "Tonight you'll go home, too."

He strode through the flaps after Ajold, and they were gone.

The silence inside the stifling tent was so loud, my eardrums were splitting. Ignoring me, Laehn picked up and examined his bow, twisting it around to let the light play over it. Satisfied, he slung it over his shoulder and picked up the two quivers, tying them both on either side of his belt. Next, he sheathed his dagger, and then drew the cloak around his shoulders.

Finally, he looked up and caught my eye.

"What?"

I blinked.

"Nothing."

He nodded and pulled the cowl over his hair, throwing his face into shadow once again.

"We have given them enough time," he observed. "Let's go."

The wind was cool on my cheek, and from the look of the sky I could tell there was about an hour and a half left till sunset. It hit me then, just how much I had changed in the few months, how much I had learned and seen.

Tonight, I might be going home. Finally, I was going back to Mona. I didn't want to dwell on it, but my mind started to annoyingly wander back to when

I'd meet her, putting words to my mouth that seemed just right, how I'd explain everything to her.

I didn't want to think about that. And yet, I did.

The first time Bass, Laehn and I had come to the Castle, back when we had our own wagon, when I still didn't know how messed up everything was going to get, we had approached it from the opposite side. Then, the path we had taken was paved with stone slabs running all the way to the gates.

On this side of the countryside, the path was still paved with stone. But unlike there, the grass everywhere else was all knee high and incredibly itchy. Lucky for us, the men had thrown up their crude tents all around the camp, and they had trampled the grass flat all around within our little area.

Beyond, though, like an unofficial perimeter, the grass still rose up thick and strong, defying us to desecrate their itchiness. Of course, it was exactly where Laehn was headed, flitting from tent to tent, out of sight of the army as they assembled with their backs to us a few hundred yards away. Ajold bellowed commands, resplendent in his counterfeit armor, overseeing as they fell into as spectacular a disarray as none but an untrained mob can achieve.

Apparently giving up order as a lost cause, I heard his tone change, and as bellows and roars of what seemed to be approval followed, I guessed he had launched into a speech. I could hardly make out what he was saying over the murmuring crowd, the intermittent cheers and the hollowness of his closed helmet, and I paused by the edge of the tent.

"Alan!" Laehn hissed.

"Hang on a minute," I called, "I want to see this."

Ajold pointed at the people, slammed a fist against his chest, and then pointed at the Castle. The men roared as he awkwardly pumped his fist in a hideous rallying gesture.

"That's just terrible," I said, aghast, "Why couldn't he have just punched the air like I did?"

"He did it exactly the way you do."

I avoided looking back at Laehn. "Oh."

Ajold drew his sword and waved it wildly to a chorus of cheers. He walked away, disappearing behind the crowd, and then the army began to move. Far up ahead, I saw him on top of the white donkey, sword raised high as he led the way to the castle.

"Will the color hold?" I wondered, "After all the trouble the donkey gave us... it really didn't like being whitewashed, did it?"

"It will hold," Laehn replied, as calm as ever, "It shall not rain tonight."

We waited there, crouching against the side of a tent as the men slowly followed Ajold out the camp and up the road. Roughly seven hundred men and women had joined us; and here I was, hiding, watching as they marched to their deaths.

"This is wrong, Laehn," I moaned. "They're going out there to die because of me."

"We are not having this conversation again, Alan," Laehn snapped. "It's happening now. Get moving."

He grabbed my shoulder and dragged me away from the camp. We plunged into the grass, and I waded after him. Not too far away, six horses milled about together, and an albino mule kept them company, much to their discomfort.

As Bass once said: it was an acquired taste, after all.

Unexpectedly, I fell out and into a hidden clearing, where five men sat in the midst of the grass they had flattened beneath their bulk. They gave me silent looks, and I was taken aback by the hostility in their eyes. Laehn crouched on one knee in their midst, looking over the top of the grass at the army.

Clearly, he'd picked the biggest and the meanest in the village to break in with us; burly and ox sized, they flaunted two sharpened woodcutters' axes, a staff, and a pair of mismatched swords.

"Hail, Champion," the staff wielder spoke.

I looked back at them and ground my teeth.

"You know how this is going to happen, don't you?" I demanded.

Three of them scowled.

"This wasn't my idea," I said. "If it was up to me, none of those men would be out there…"

"But they are," Laehn interrupted coldly, "So I suggest we stop talking about it every few minutes, and make sure what they are doing for us isn't wasted."

The men muttered. They weren't happy, which wasn't so bad since neither was I.

"What now?" one demanded.

"The army is leaving," Laehn replied. "We should stay in the grass, off the path. When we find the passage, we'll have to hurry."

"We have to get into the Castle before they get to the Gate," I added, and he nodded.

They followed wordlessly as Laehn mounted his horse and I pulled myself onto the mule's saddle. Laehn took off into the grass, the mule following unbidden. I turned back to see them follow us in a single file, their horses picking their way through the grass.

For about ten minutes we blindly followed Laehn as he veered left and right, a driver with a severe GPS problem and a nagging map enthusiast in the passenger seat. Eventually he raised his hand signaling to stop, somewhere deep in the high seas of grass.

Laehn slid off his horse and let go of the reins. As it trotted aimlessly away, he started to walk, eyes on the ground, more or less in the general direction of where the Castle loomed, miles away. He raised his gaze to stare into the distance, turned to look the other way, and then crouched, examining the dirt.

I slid off my saddle and patted the mule. It snorted, shook its mane and snorted again, this time from the other end. Behind us, the others dismounted and hit the ground with heavy thuds, a battalion of marines ready to storm the target.

I wished.

"Here," Laehn called. I jogged over as he took off, bent double in pursuit of the invisible trail in the middle of grass that didn't look any different from any other grass in the meadow. The men followed, breathing heavily, the grass crunching and the ground pounding under their heavy boots. As unsure and anxious as I was, those footsteps reassured me.

The entrance had been tiny, almost invisible when I'd turned to look at it the last time, the night we had escaped from the Capital. It hadn't been anymore more than a hole in the ground, a jagged circle in the ground in the middle of nowhere just wide enough for us to slip through comfortably.

Getting the mule out then hadn't been easy, and as much as I wanted it with us, we couldn't bring it along for obvious reasons: a long time in an enclosed space, first and foremost, given its natural instincts would be, in a word, disastrous.

I swept my eyes over the field.

"Are you sure this is the place?" I called.

Laehn didn't reply; he kept searching. As he poked here and prodded there, cold fear gripped me. Somehow, I hadn't thought about getting here and not finding the passage. We had to call it off, pull the army back before they got hurt.

I opened my mouth.

"Found it!" Laehn announced.

It was with mixed feelings that I ran to where he squatted in the grass; relief that we'd found the hole and despair that we'd still have to go on with the plan. Not a very good combination at the best of times, and as I reached him and looked down into the hole, the sense of foreboding grew.

"We didn't bring any light with us, did we?" I asked.

"We didn't have any the last time we were through," Laehn reminded me.

"Exactly, and we had to walk through the dark,"

"We are wasting time," one of the men barked.

Laehn looked at me, looked down into the hold, and then dropped feet first.

Something nudged my shoulder, and I turned to find myself nose to muzzle with a long, white face. The mule snorted, dripping saliva down onto my arm.

"Hey," I said, standing up, "Thanks for everything, bud."

I put my arm around its head and stepped back, allowing the men to take their time jumping in after Laehn.

"You look after yourself, okay?" I said, "Stay… stinky."

The mule tooted.

"That's the spirit," I said. I took a last, good whiff, barely held in my lunch, prepared for the jump.

"Alan!" Laehn called, his voice impatient. I cursed under my breath, gave the mule a final pat and jumped in after him.

I landed on my knees, and the clang of metal echoed up and down the tunnel. I stood and blinked in the semi darkness as the memories began to return, and none of them very pleasant.

I reached out and touched cold stone. The last I'd been here, I had been angry, upset and confused, fresh after Kernine's words, the ones that had forced Bass to tell me the true story.

It seemed so, so very long ago.

The men stood silent, and I picked my way around them to struggle to the front. In the dim light, I saw Laehn take the coil of rope off his belt, loop it once around his waist and tie it down. His hand moved towards me, and I saw he was holding out the rest of the coil.

"Why do we need this?" I asked, "I thought it was a straight line?"

"It is," Laehn replied, "But we're going to be running."

"You have got to be kidding me," I said, aghast, "We're blind in here!"

"Loop it around your arm and pass it along," Laehn said, irritably.

It had impossibly just gotten worse. I looped the rope around my arm and handed it to the guy behind me. Laehn irascibly tapped his foot as the rope went all the way to the back, and when the last guy finally called he was ready, he turned to face the darkness ahead.

"Go," he said, and just like that, I was running along behind him, my hand stretched out in front of me like a demented idiot.

Being inside a claustrophobic underground tunnel when you've been on the verge of a panic attack for the last three days was an atrocious enough idea on its own; being forced to run through the said tunnel in pitch blackness, blindly following a rope tugging on your forearm?

Anyone stupid enough to do that deserved to have their face bashed into the wall. Of course, it's exactly what I received… and more times than I'd care to admit. And as an added bonus, I also slammed sideways into them at full tilt and even tripped and fell spectacularly. Thrice.

With each impact, the sound of metal on stone rang out through the passage and refused to leave until they had shamed me repeatedly. What was worse was no one else made any sound. It was just me who had to be the fool down there.

After what seemed like an eternity painful to both my body and my pride, the rope finally went slack, and I slowed to a stop, bumping into Laehn invisible in the middle of the darkness.

"What is it?" I demanded, my voice an echo.

"We're at the end," Laehn echoed back, "I need help in lifting the stone."

"How can you tell?" I asked, pressing against the wall to allow two the men to squeeze past me. I felt more than I saw as they climbed up against the slope of the wall, searching for the opening.

"There's an outline," Laehn said, and I saw it: a faint rectangle of light, the lines narrow and weak. The men braced their shoulders against the stone cover.

"On three," one whispered.

They heaved, and dim-yet-blinding light pooled in as the stone scraped aside.

Laehn held up his hand and put a finger to his lips. He jumped, grabbed the edge of the hole and lifted himself up slowly. He poked his head out, did a quick swivel and then hoisted himself up and out into the open.

He leaned down and held out his hand. I took it, and one of the men gave me a heave from below. I scrambled out and looked around.

The streets were empty; there wasn't a guard in sight. Somehow, impossibly, we had done it. We were in the city. Out there, beyond the walls, our army was gathering to attack.

From here on in, the only way was forward.

Chapter 14

The sky was beginning to change color as we ran. Laehn's timing was perfect; by the time we'd reach the Castle's inner wall, Ajold and Elrik would have already begun the assault.

As always, Laehn led the way. I was right behind him, flitting from building to building, keeping to the shadows and away from the lights. The men followed behind us, not as agile as I'd have hoped, but still fast enough to not fall behind.

My boots echoed on the stone no matter how much I tried to quieten them. Every tiny noise was amplified, bouncing off the walls and across the vacant streets. It was like the setting for a medieval zombie apocalypse; windows shut, doors locked bolted, and no one in sight.

It was all empty. Eerily empty.

"Where is everyone?" I whispered, catching up to Laehn as he paused around a corner.

"Inside their homes," he replied. "Mugatu would have them under curfew."

"Then where are the guards?" I asked.

He looked at me and nodded.

"I wonder the same."

He skipped across the street and leaned against the wall. I made to follow, but he held up his hand, the other one drifting to his belt.

A heartbeat later, I heard the noise: boots echoing off the street, two pairs, walking slowly. I crouched and saw them approach down the street adjacent to ours. They spoke in low whispers, and then broke into fits of giddy laughter.

A bottle glinted in the waning light.

They walked past the corner behind which Laehn hid, continuing down the street past me. They didn't see me, and I breathed, counting the seconds till they'd gone.

A flash of steel caught my eye, and I turned to see Laehn sprinting toward their retreating backs, his dagger drawn.

They were the enemy; they would have done the same to us. But my mind was screaming, my head was spinning. They were unarmed, drunk and in no condition to fight, and whatever the consequences, I couldn't let Laehn kill them.

"No!" I exclaimed.

The guards turned at the sound of my voice, but it was too late. Laehn plunged the blade into the first one's chest. Barely pausing, he threw himself into a midair spin, momentum yanking the blade out of the first one's chest and slashing it against the other's throat.

He turned to glare at me as their bodies fell.

"You didn't have to do that!" I snarled, "They didn't see us!"

His eyes grew cold.

"They would have been alive and behind us," he said. "And I could not afford the distraction."

"They did not need to die," I snapped.

"I'm an assassin," he replied, eyes flashing. "Killing is what I do. Don't interrupt me again."

I scowled, but he didn't pay me any attention; in a smooth movement he'd bent down, swiped his blade dry on the guard's tunic, and was up and running again.

There wasn't anything I could do but follow him.

We were on one of the main streets, and I could see the top of the inner wall not too far off. Within the wall was the courtyard through which I'd entered the Castle the last time. That was where we had to go, and from within those walls, we had to somehow get into the Castle.

So close, my mind said, *it can't be this easy, now, can it?*

I crouched in the shadow and watched Laehn sprint across the street and into a smaller alley. I glanced behind to see the five men, each one behind some bit of cover that was virtually useless at masking their bulk.

I steeled myself, and then lunged across the street.

A loud crack startled me, making me stumble against the stone and lose my balance. It had been the jarring snap of a crossbow nut.

As I fell, I heard a wrenching cry of pain cut short and trail to a gurgle. I landed on my knees, at the same moment as the painful thud behind me.

Heart pounding, I spun around to see one of the men lying flat on his face, arms sickeningly splayed out. The fletching of a bolt protruded from his back.

He wasn't moving.

"NO!" one of the others cried.

Movement caught my eye, and I saw a soldier on a rooftop, bending to reload his crossbow. He caught my eyes, and I saw the message in them and in his triumphant grin.

You're next.

His eyes shifted and widened. He awkwardly tried to move to cover, but a bow hummed behind me. Moments later, he pitched forward and fell off the roof, an arrow through one eye. The bile rose in my throat as he landed nauseatingly in a clash of metal.

I looked away as Laehn lowered his bow, his nostrils flared. There was anger in his eyes; he knew he'd slipped up.

I picked myself up and hurried to where the others had pulled their fellow against the wall. I recognized him as one of the two who had swords in the group. The other sword owner turned a tear strained face to me as I knelt down by them.

"How is he?" Laehn demanded.

The guy with the staff put a finger against the fallen man's throat. Looking away from us, he shook his head.

Laehn swore and turned to the sun. The sky had grown dark, and not too far away I could hear the roar of voices rise.

"It has begun," he said, "We MUST make our move!"

The bugle sounded; the last time I'd heard it, I'd been in the chamber deep in the Castle where my armor was. Then, the sound had been muffled and dim, but out here, it was much, much louder. It faded; and then seconds later it blew again.

The sword holder bared his teeth at Laehn.

"I'm not going to leave my brother here!" he snarled, "Not for you, or the thrice damned Champion!"

I made up my mind.

"Take him and leave," I said, interrupting Laehn's threat.

"What?" Laehn demanded, scowling at me.

"You heard me," I snapped, "Take him and go. Now."

The others looked at me blankly, and their companion on the ground just nodded.

"Victory to you, Champion," he muttered. The others helped him to his feet and to pick up brother's body. Alone, he began to shuffle the way we had come, one slow step at a time.

"We're down two men instead of one," Laehn said. He was angry, angrier than I'd probably ever have seen him. I'd rarely seen Laehn's temper flare, but now he was livid.

"We lost him the moment his brother died," I said. "You think he'd have survived the rest of the night in that state?"

"He would have been the most vengeful of us," Laehn snarled. "I know these men better than you ever would, Alan. I grew up with them, and I knew either brother would have done all he could have to take his revenge had the other fallen. We'd have been better off for it."

"You used them," I shook my head, "Like you used the others outside. Like you're using me, right here, right now."

I clenched my jaw. He didn't reply; he didn't have to.

The bugles had faded, but now came the sounds of yells and jeers, both from within the walls and outside. We didn't have time to argue.

We kept running, and the high walls came closer. Laehn turned a corner and beckoned.

I joined him and peered around.

At the top of the street was an arch, two stout wooden gates standing wide open on either side. Beyond the arch, I caught a glimpse of the familiar courtyard, with soldiers running in frenzy all over the place. Somehow, they seemed far too concerned over a mob of angry villagers swatting at the stone walls with spades and hoes.

We could have just run right through the arch and into the courtyard, if it wasn't for the slight complication of the six men between the gates. They formed a line facing towards us, only parting to let other soldiers from inside the city through into the courtyard.

"Is that the only way in?" I whispered.

Laehn nodded.

"What do we do?" I demanded, "Disguise ourselves as…?"

He ignored me, and lightly sprinted to the opposite side of the street. He looked at the men still following us and nodded.

My heart began to pound as I looked down at my belt. The razor-thing hung off it on my right, and the light sword in its scabbard on my left. It wasn't even a decision; I drew the sword.

Without warning, something boomed out beyond the wall. Laehn raised his head, and the guards at the arch jerked in surprise. The sound repeated, a deep, echoing wooden blow. And then again, this time escorted by creak and a groan of wood.

The battering ram. Impossibly, they'd survived long enough to haul it all the way up to the Gates. Now, they were using it like their lives depended on it.

They weren't wrong.

It boomed a fourth time, and I heard the distinct sound of splintering wood. Three of the soldiers at the arch turned to look into the courtyard; distracted, the others looked away from our general direction as well.

"Now!" Laehn barked.

If there ever was the perfect distraction, it was this. I lunged, my boots slamming the ground. I hurled myself out of the shadows and into the light, where they could see me.

It didn't feel real.

I was running up the street, out in the open, Laehn sprinting in front of me. The soldiers turned. Eyes wide as they saw me, they drew their weapons. They may have not been prepared, but they were ready.

I didn't know if the other three were behind me; my world shrank to all I could see through the slits in my visor. All I heard was the pounding, my heart booming in my ears, the thrill that was rising, leading the charge.

All I knew was I was afraid.

The cold handle was in my fingers, and the sword's weight dragged my arm down, like it always did. I felt the stone slap under my boots, hard and cold.

And all I could see was him.

His face nothing but a featureless metal visor, he braced himself, raised his sword and stood there, legs apart. He waited for me, and I obliged.

For those few seconds that lasted an eternity, there was nothing except him and me.

I was deaf. My heart pounded in my ears.

And then, all too soon, I was there, right in front of him, my nameless, faceless opponent. He stepped forward, and I swung.

It didn't matter I was miles off target. What mattered was that his sword met mine.

The shock travelled up my arms, and the resounding clash cleared my mind like the carpet had been yanked from under my feet.

And I was more alive than I'd ever been.

He slashed, and I parried out of sheer instinct. Drunk with the tiniest success, I was sloppy in the next parry, and his sword slid off mine and carried by his momentum, it slammed into my helmet.

Ears ringing, I managed to duck the next jab, and from nowhere, I threw a wild, vicious upward jab. Somehow, it connected with the base of his helmet, and he stumbled backwards, reeling. I saw my chance. I took a step forward, and I thrust.

I can't remember what exactly it was I felt as I watched him fall. I'd never taken a life before, and yet now I'd killed him in cold blood, never mind he'd been trying to carve my windpipe out in the first place. A father, a brother, a son, it didn't matter what he was.

I hadn't even hesitated.

And I didn't then. I pulled my sword out of him, and I'd already turned to the next before he'd even hit the ground.

The other three villagers were with us, roaring in frenzy as they lashed about with brute force. We'd made too much noise; even with the distraction and destruction the battering ram was doing to the Gate, more soldiers still managed to notice us.

We were running out of time. Laehn was everywhere, shooting, dodging, slashing, shooting some more. The villagers were going berserk, and I was alone, still at the arch.

There was a wild yell near my ear, and I impulsively dodged a wild swing.

Swords were clashing all around me, disorienting, throwing me off. The soldier swung again, and I sidestepped awkwardly. His mail gauntlet slammed into my helmet, and I staggered away, head spinning, dazed but recovering.

He was screaming, holding his hand to his chest in apparent agony; why, I didn't know, but I saw my chance and swung. My sword connected, and blood splashed up and through my visor, blinding my left eye.

I yelled, yanked my helmet off, viciously tore off a piece of my clothing and dabbed it to my eye. The fighting had stopped for now. With the helmet off and the wind fresh on my sweat soaked skin, the bloodlust passed and my vision cleared.

My hand started shaking, and I dropped the helmet. There were bodies at my feet, and I'd put two of them there. Blood was oozing out onto the stone, and the smell of sweat and death worked to bring me back to reality.

What were you thinking? my mind screamed, *You could have died!*

"I didn't," I whispered.

I turned away from the bodies and saw Laehn running along the wall, keeping to the shadow. He looked at me and spread his hands questioningly.

I jammed my helmet on, shoved my bloody sword into its scabbard and sprinted after him. The gray stone of the Castle rose high on my right, but Laehn kept hugging the boundary wall as he ran. He saw me stumble and crouched down to wait for me.

"Where are we going?" I wheezed. "The door's that way."

"Servants entrance," he replied. "Fewer guards."

I looked at the courtyard and watched the soldiers run around like ants on a toppled anthill. Laehn was right; there was no way we would have been able to go through the front door.

I grabbed his arm before he could move again.

"Once we're inside?" I demanded, "Then what?!"

He turned to me, but his eyes looked past me to the courtyard. It was with a horrifyingly cold chill that I realized the battering ram had stopped harassing the

Gate, and I couldn't remember when I had heard it last.

"Laehn."

"When we get inside, I will lead you to him," he snapped. "You will kill him. You will end this. *Trust* me."

He gripped me by the shoulder and pushed me in front of him. He forced me into a run, but he didn't have to; the soldiers were beginning to raise a hearty cheer that kept grew louder.

A few minutes later, Laehn grabbed my shoulder again and forced me to stop. He pointed at the Castle wall ahead, and in a fold of stone, I saw a small, closed door. The villagers who'd followed us were crouched on either side of it, and they were both streaked in blood.

Both.

There were only two of them. Not three.

"Where...?" I asked, but the sinking in my stomach threw up a spasm that choked the rest of my words. One of them glowered at me, slashes crisscrossing over his bare arms. A third of his staff had broken off, and the jagged tip was soaked in blood.

"Where do you *think* he is?" he snarled.

The other man avoided my eyes. He wasn't in any better shape, and blood dripped off the blade of his axe. I swallowed.

Laehn nodded at the door.

"Is it...?"

The man stood and rapped on it with his axe. When it didn't budge, he took a step behind and swung. The wood shuddered as the axe bit into it at the top and then again at the bottom, right where the bolts would have been. The other man leaned on one foot and threw his weight into a mighty kick. It connected, and door splintered at the edges, slamming open to hang limply off its weakened hinges.

"Go," Laehn said.

The drab, gray walls beyond the door were a far cry from what I'd seen of the rest of the Castle. There were no paintings, no fancy murals, and just plain old torches burning in brackets on the wall instead of the elaborate glass chandeliers.

Laehn was a shadow, always a dozen or so feet ahead of us, ducking into doorways and around corners. He led us into what looked like a large, mostly empty kitchen, and then out again down long passages.

We bumped into two soldiers, leaning against a wall and sharing from a bottle, their weapons undrawn. I didn't say a thing as Laehn did what he did best.

We kept going, and at the end of the passage stood a closed door. Laehn slowed down as he reached it, crouched, and put his ear to it. We caught up to him when he stood and cautiously pushed it open.

The first thing I noticed was the light. A glass chandelier was suspended high above us, throwing the first proper light I had seen since we'd entered the castle. It was a dining room, I realized, and the path we'd taken was the one the servants would have used to deliver the food from the kitchens. The room wasn't enormous, but it was large enough for me to see the King having his meals with his family here on a regular day.

The long wooden table and the high uncomfortable chairs were hidden under great shrouds of cloth, probably covers used in between meals. There was a fine film of dust on them, though, and I figured they hadn't been taken off ever since Mugatu took over.

There were more entrances other than the one we'd come through; a double door opposite us, and two single doors each on either side. All five were closed, and Laehn was already making his way towards the ones at the end of the room.

I looked up at the chandelier, glinting innocently above us. There had to have been dozens of little stands, an on each one a small candle. How they ever managed to light them and keep them lit was beyond me.

The others were already far ahead of me, midway down the room.

My eyes shifted from the chandelier to a glint against the wall. I realized there was a balcony running around above us. Sure, there was a second floor, and the ceiling here was definitely high enough. The balcony was absurd, though. It brought to mind the image of a man selling first class tickets to see the royal family dine.

The shine against the wall annoyed me, and I stopped walking to stare at it. I couldn't make it out; it was like a reflection of the chandelier's light off a mirror, the kind of trick you play on cats when you're bored and there's something reflective handy.

But there wasn't anything there for the light to bounce off, I thought, unless…

The patch of light moved.

My heart jumped off a springboard and rocketed to my throat.

"Ambush!" I yelled.

My voice broke the spell.

A dozen archers rose up from behind the balcony railing, crossbows at their shoulders, all pointed at me. At the very same instant, the four doors along the sides slammed open, and more poured in.

We'd been fools.

The crossbows snapped, and I spun around by instinct and ducked. Nanoseconds later, six bolts shattered against my towel.

I stood up again and faced the utter mayhem in front of me.

Soldiers screamed, running full tilt with spears lowered. The crossbowmen on the balcony cursed as they struggled to reload. The villagers bellowed, laying about the soldiers near them, throwing blood and gore over the fine carpets and clean walls.

Laehn was a demon. He ran, stabbed, jumped onto the table and drew his bow. He fired, spun around, fired again. One by one, the archers fell, but before he could shoot down the last two, a soldier threw himself over the table at his knees and knocked him to the floor.

Then, they came at me. As I grabbed the sticky handle and drew my sword, everything I'd learned from Laehn and Ajold, all the moves and the stances Elrik had drummed into me, the entirety of my fighting technique jumped ship like they'd seen the icebergs approaching.

There was no style, no finesse. I screamed, swung, slashed, and repeated.

It was luck, and it was intimidation. Kernine had died, and thanks to the deserters on the Hill that day they'd have known it was I who killed him. With the first few lucky swings that put down the reckless spear chargers, I'd accidentally cemented fear into them.

The soldiers who came at me now were scared. Fear was good, it made them hesitate.

None of this passed through my head at the time though, if you're wondering. No, those solders were expecting fancy footwork, and all I gave them was brain dead screaming and slashing.

My fear? Gone

My qualms about killing? Gone.

My nausea at the blood I was spilling, the gore I was spreading?

It's amazing how much adrenaline can change the way you look at things.

After all the anticipation, after all the fear and the pain, I was finally there, swinging my dripping sword, doing what they had brought me here to do.

But it wasn't glorious, it certainly wasn't beautiful. It was ugly, and it was sickening. I lost myself in the rage, the rush and the adrenaline, and they kept coming. They just kept coming.

I took a blow to the head. I wasn't sure how, where or when; all I knew was that I was on the floor. My ears rang, my head throbbed and I was myself again. My eyes opened, and I saw the soldier almost on top of me, sword raised. Before he could swing it down and cleave me in half, I lunged. My sword plunged through his ribs.

He stumbled away, dropped his own sword and fell over, yanking the handle out of my hand and taking mine with him.

I stood up slowly.

The room was splattered in blood, and the doors were open and still more men poured in. Laehn and the staff guy were at the only closed door on the other end of the room. The other villager was lunging about with his axe halfway between me and them. As I watched, the last crossbowman still alive on the balcony aimed his weapon.

The axe wielder bellowed as the bolt plunged into his arm. He reached up and yanked it out in a spurt of blood. He used it to stab at a soldier who got too close, and then threw it at another, missing spectacularly. Blood streaming down his arm, he didn't slow down, not even as a trio of pike men surrounded him.

"Laehn!" I roared, "Laehn!"

Laehn couldn't hear me. He was at the closed door, shooting down the men in the other doorways and trying to stem the flow. He didn't see his friend halfway down the room, moments from being skewered by the men around him.

As they raised their spears together, I grabbed my sword and tried to yank it out of my latest victim's corpse. No matter how hard I tugged, it didn't budge; it was lodged hard I his ribcage.

"LAEHN" I roared, but it was too late. Together, the pikemen thrust.

Three spears stabbed into and through him from three different sides; they raised him up, thrashing and writhing, a horribly grotesque trophy. I watched helplessly as that villager jerked in agony, screaming in heart wrenching agony. I watched, helpless, as he died right in front of me.

It was my fault. I had killed him.

"NO!" I roared.

I let go of the useless sword and ran at them, bare handed as I was. It was a strange thought I had as they as they turned to face me, spear tips dripping with the blood of the man they had killed, blood that was on my hands, not theirs.

Before this night, the only lives I'd taken had belonged to roaches, spiders and rats in our apartment that turned Mona into a puddle of tears. But in the last hour lone, I'd lost count of how many men I'd killed. I'd never known them before I'd attacked them, and I hadn't even seen most of their faces when I struck them down.

Just as I'd never known the villagers who came with us, nor the man who now lay dead on the floor, his body in a growing pool of his own blood. I'd killed him, too. It was on my order he'd been here tonight.

And yet his death was making me run at his killers, wanting revenge. What made him any different from any other soldier I'd slain by my own hands since this evening? He'd died following orders, just like them.

I don't even know what I'm talking about. The thought buzzed and faded before it could make its point, leaving me standing bare handed in front of three soldiers holding dripping spear points levelled at my midsection.

On my belt still hung the Armament bonded razor; as lucky as I had been with the sword, I was still more than likely to slice my own arm off with that thing as much as anyone else's.

There was nothing for it now, though. I reached down, but before I could grab it, the three soldiers jolted and fell forward, one after another.

There were arrows in their backs. Of course. Laehn glowered at me from the other end of the room, a new arrow already nocked.

I swallowed, skirted the villager's body, jumped over the soldiers' ones and ran to Laehn and the last man still standing.

"Help him get the door open!" Laehn roared. Behind him, the villager was slamming his shoulder against the double doors, the wood creaking with every impact. It didn't seem to be doing any good, and he knew it.

I moved to join him, and something heavy scraped against the side of my helmet, showering my left shoulder in sparks. A spearhead stabbed into the wooden door, the haft quivering ominously.

I didn't waste time looking to see who'd thrown it. Together, the villager and I threw ourselves at the door, and it finally gave way on the third time.

We fell heavily into a hallway beyond the chamber. The villager pushed himself to his knees.

"Laehn!" he bellowed.

Laehn fired off a shot, and then raced to join us. He and the villager grabbed at the doors, and I yanked down the spear before they slammed it shut.

"We need to barricade it," the villager panted.

I jammed the spear in between the handles, and stepped away from the doors. There was a moment of silence, and then the doors buckled. The spear held, but the soldiers slammed again, and the haft creaked.

We didn't need to speak. We ran.

Pictures and ornaments flashed past us as we went, down one hallway after another, hopelessly lost. Laehn finally ushered us into a small empty room and pushed us away from the doorway. I fell on my knees, lungs burning. The rush was over, and I was having trouble breathing.

"Alan!" Laehn snapped.

"They were waiting for us," I wheezed. "They knew we were here."

"They did not," Laehn snapped, "Mugatu made a lucky guess. He never could have known it, but he was smart enough to…"

"What's the point?!" I demanded. "He knows now. He *knows*!"

"We have come this far," Laehn said. He reached into his quiver and paused.

"What?" I demanded.

Wordlessly, he tipped it over, and five arrows slid out.

"Is that all?"

"I have my dagger," he replied, quietly.

It was too late to back out. I knew it now. The army had failed. We were trapped inside the Castle with no way out.

We'd lost. Already.

We had nothing to lose, though, and nothing else to do. It was a strange feeling in me as I jogged alongside them, down one hallway after another. When soldiers saw us, we fought. I picked up a fallen sword and we ran some more.

I didn't care right then. It had all been for nothing, and if I died around the next corner, it seemed appropriate. All these months and hours of toil… nothing seemed worth it anymore.

Again, they jumped out at us; a spear head came at my face, but somehow it missed, grazing the side of my helmet in a shower of sparks. The soldier holding it was out of balance, trying not to fall over. I lunged, and my sword tore through the armor at his chest and slid in between his ribs.

I turned around. Two more were dead, and Laehn was bending over to yank his arrows back out of their flesh. On the floor, slumped against the wall, was the last thing I wanted to see. My chest heaving, I turned away.

Laehn and I were alone.

We didn't jog anymore. There was no need for hurry, and so the hallways were wide and empty as we walked. Behind us I could hear the sounds of boots echoing off the walls. There were voices, and they were following us.

We couldn't run anymore. There was no point in running, and I was exhausted. Laehn didn't need to tell me it was over; he didn't have to. Weapons out but lowered, we just walked.

"Down the hall," Laehn said, "Turn to your right. You'll see the doors to the throne room."

I recognized the pictures on the wall and the statue in the alcove we just passed. I'd been down this same hallway once before. Then, I'd been distracted by the beauty and the colors. Now, it all mocked me with its bright cheerfulness.

"Why the throne room?" I asked, dully. I didn't really care what he said; the silence was boring into me, and I needed him to say something, to hear anything other than the jangle of metal and the screaming in my ears.

"He will be there," he replied, "Now he knows you are within the walls. He will go where you can find him."

I cocked my ear at the distorted voices ringing off the walls.

"How can you be sure?" I asked.

He didn't reply. Jaw set, he kept walking, eyes on the wall ahead.

"They're coming," I said.

He reached in his quiver, drew out his last five arrows and looked at them, each of their tips used and bloody. He turned around and facing the end of the hall.

"Come on," I said, tiredly.

He didn't reply. Slowly, he nocked an arrow to the string and straightened his shoulders.

"Laehn," I said.

My tired brain turned over. *Something is wrong,* it told me, *really, really wrong.*

"Laehn," I said, "Come on. We have to go."

"Go," he replied.

"Not without you."

He didn't acknowledge me. Like the statue a few feet away, he stood still, eyes on the door at the far end of the hall.

My stomach free fell to my knees.

"Don't do this, Laehn," I said, my voice cracking, "This isn't the time for a stupid heroic sacrifice. I need you."

"Yes," he said, "You need me. *Here*. This is as far as I go."

"What do you mean?!"

Finally, he looked at me and smiled.

"The Law will always uphold itself," he said. "You will face your Tyrant alone. And you will win."

"You're not going to sacrifice yourself, Laehn."

He turned away from me.

"Bass knew he would never survive this journey," he said, "I knew I would not, either."

"Damn you, Laehn!" I snarled, "You promised you'd be with me to the end! You promised you'd help me fight him!"

Laehn smiled again.

"And that, my Champion, is what I'm doing now."

There was no arguing with him. As I stumbled back, heart in my throat, I saw it now. I would die in the throne room. He would die here.

I closed my eyes, turned and walked away from him. The voices and the footsteps grew louder, and I didn't look back. I didn't want to.

I turned the corner, and the familiarity punched me like a fist to the gut. I'd drunk in its beauty the first time I'd walked down this hallway; I'd looked at each and every painting, at all the lines and colors on the wall. Now they watched me, untouched like it had been yesterday and nothing had happened in between.

So familiar, and yet so different, it all came to me as I walked down the hallway. The memories flowed, shifting around me, spiriting my exhausted mind from the pain and the fear and throwing me into the past. Laehn walked behind me, apart from the rest of us, as always. Ajold, pompous and loud, his red trimmed armor gleaming as he led the way up the hall.

And I saw Bass, limping along just in front of me, stabbing Tom into the carpet as he complained about the beauty hurting his eyes.

I blinked, and they were gone. I was alone in that hallway.

My eyes fell on the two familiar large doors, shut tight. They loomed up, harshly staring down on me as I approached them. Beyond them sat my destiny, as clichéd as it sounded.

The reason I was brought here, the cause of all the pain, suffering and heartbreak... behind them I'd finally face Mugatu, and from there, what would happen would happen.

The months of training, pain and agony... it would all end here.

And then…

And then I saw the tapestry. The large, floor to ceiling painting of random color, lines and indistinct shapes, the one Ajold had disregarded and I had forgotten all about. I looked at it again, and sure enough, the shapes began to move.

I had not imagined it after all.

The colors and shapes shifting, changing, and merging, they called to me as they had the first time I had walked these halls.

Mugatu had probably been waiting all this time to meet me. He could wait a little longer.

I walked up to the tapestry and ran my eyes over it.

Last time, the pictures had moved with every step I had taken. I'd been distracted then, and I'd imagined it to be a trick of the light. But now, as I stood still and watched, they moved for me.

I can't remember all what it was I saw there; the pictures were many, and they were fast. Lines moved, colors blurred, shapes merged, and through it all, I stood and watched.

Images from the past, from the present, from the future; and as soon as I understood one, at the moment I comprehended its meaning, it changed. As it went, it took with it my memory, all it had told me, replaced by the next image. The cycle repeated.

I didn't understand why; and it told me I didn't have to understand. I was a small part in a much bigger picture, I realized; what happened today would only be another stitch in the fabric of all that was.

Some pretty deep stuff.

The images came and went, gave and took, until finally, a picture came into focus, one that stayed. It was a face, the face of the Champion; it was the face of all Champions.

And it wasn't just one face. It... they... were many. Even as the eyes looked down at me, the features were ever shifting, ever moving, the color and the landscapes behind it blurring and running into each other.

The eyes glared down at me, blazing gold, green, blue, and black. They judged me, sensing my weakness, despising it.

It was the epitome of the madness that this whole journey had been. I was standing in front of a moving painting, and the painting did not like me.

The eyes softened, and mouths smiled. The lips parted to speak, and I blinked.

Just as fast and as sudden as it had begun, it was over. The faces, the eyes, the images... nothing. In front of me was nothing but a blank tapestry, random lines and squiggles.

I looked up at it, hoping for them to come back, knowing as I did how I was probably crazy.

But they were gone, and their work was done. I believed.

I turned around, and the doors loomed up in front of me, menacingly hiding the unknown behind them.

My heart boomed.

I dropped the bloodstained, unbalanced sword, clenched my fists and breathed in. I closed my eyes, bowed my head and stepped forward.

Chapter 15

The doors scraped against the ground. The echoing screech of protest reverberated down my spine, and my fingers bit into the wood. I didn't know what it was I'd been hoping was behind the doors, but whatever it might have been, a sea of swords, spears and blue trimmed armor was definitely at the bottom of the list.

Soldiers. They were packed in there, armor, weapons and all. Most wore helms, their expressions concealed, but even of the faces which were bare I couldn't tell what they might have been thinking.

It had been a trap from the start, and we had all fallen for it, walked into it like a bunch of idiots without a clue… which was exactly what we were.

There was nothing else to do. I let go of the doors and walked into the throne room. It creaked behind me and I kept going, the horrible sense of déjà vu growing stronger with each echoing step I took. It was all the same; the same colors, the lights… and yet it wasn't.

Laehn and Bass weren't escorting me like they always had. Ajold wasn't leading the way with his pompous strides and wildly swinging arms. And most importantly, the enormous throne room wasn't empty. The soldiers parted as I approached, clearing a lane for me to the thrones on the other end, their spears levelled at me. All eyes were on me as I strode, blood dripping off my hands, staining my armor and my soul.

They watched me, faces blank. They shuffled as I passed, the spears brought down and their tips shoved almost to my face.

I ignored them, looking past the spear points and the polished armor, my eyes on the man lounging completely at ease on the golden throne, the one I'd last seen Zaahis on. But where the King had looked drawn and exhausted with worry, the man sitting there looked fine, gleaming in that specific brand of gloating freshness only pure triumph can give you.

"Finally," Mugatu called, his voice echoing off the high walls, a tone akin to calling out to a wandering friend who's not quite right in the head. "Here I was, starting to think you'd gotten lost. I was about to send someone out to go look for you."

Laughter rippled through the room.

I didn't reply; I ignored them and kept walking. The doors closed behind me with an echoing boom of finality. I didn't react, but I could have done without another reminder of how there was no going back.

"And so you ended here," Mugatu's grin grew wider. "Alone and friendless. As I knew you would."

I walked. I'd been afraid that morning. I'd been afraid when we'd fought. I'd been terrified when I stood over the bodies of the men I had killed.

I wasn't afraid anymore.

I reached the base of his throne and clenched my fists, letting the blood drip on the royal carpet.

"That's not going to be easy to get out, you know," Mugatu observed.

My visor raised, I looked up and glared at him, the man who had done all this to me and now sat there gloating. I was mad enough to climb those steps and punch the smirk off him, and the only thing keeping me in check were the spears still within jabbing reach.

It had been one bad choice after another that had led me here. I didn't need to make one more to hand the win over to him that easily.

He was bald, I saw, and the eyes that looked down at me were thin and, well, cruel. A thin, white scar ran across his wide forehead, like he'd lost an argument with a whip, and I loved the whip all the more for it.

He was in full armor; black and gold, purple cape over his shoulders, it was much more sinister than mine. At the end of throne's right armrest sat his helmet, the visor turned to me. Like the rest of it, the helmet was jet black, and had golden veins running through it.

It was beautiful in a creepy and very unsettling way.

"Bass should have been here," Mugatu sighed, pulling my attention away from his visor. "It's a shame. He will be missed."

"How do you know-?" I demanded, then stopped.

"How do I know Bass died on the Hill?" he finished. He chuckled and shook his head. "Oh, dear Alan. I've been waiting too long for this."

My fists tightened.

"Never really thought it possible for that man to die," he said, idly tracing one of the patterns on the arm of the throne. "It would have been fun keeping him around in chains, hearing him complaining. I'd have hung that stick of his just out of reach, you know. It would have been so much fun. I had *plans*, you know. And then you went and got him killed."

His eyes snapped to me, and for the first time, the mocking glee was gone.

"Him and my lieutenant," he said quietly. "I underestimated you."

I stared at him, unblinking.

"They tell me you killed him yourself," he continued, turning his attention back to the pattern on the arm. "That you were a warrior like they had never seen."

I heard a breath of air pass behind me, and the soldiers shuffled uncomfortably.

"And here I look at you, but the word 'warrior' doesn't really seem to match," he said. He leaned forward. "Tell me, Alan, Champion. Were they true?"

I swallowed.

"Come down here and find out for yourself," I snapped. Rather, I tried to snap, but my voice came out higher pitched than I'd intended, and ended more on a whine.

Mugatu leaned comfortable and smiled.

"Where are my manners. I haven't even introduced myself properly," he stood and make a mockery of a bow to me.

"I know who you are," I snapped, my fingers itching to wipe the smirk off that face.

"Oh, do you?" he looked down at me and grinned, baring yellowed teeth. "Call me Frank. Frank Lee Morris, that's what I was back home. You might have heard of me, if you're into history. Which year are you from, anyway?"

"None of your business," I said, and this time, my voice came out marginally better.

"Now that's just rude," he frowned. "You're saying you don't know who I am?"

He slammed his fist on the armrest, and the soldiers collectively flinched.

"Sorry, sorry," he raised a hand at me in apology, passed it over his forehead and sighed. "It's just annoying, Alan. After all the work I put into it, no one even knows what we did."

I frowned, but curiosity got the better of me.

"What did you do?" I demanded.

"Only broke out of Alcatraz," he replied. "Something no one ever did before, might I add. Well, me and those numbskull Anglins, but they probably drowned and died when the portal opened, so let's forget about them."

"Alcatraz island?" I demanded, "You were a criminal?"

He shrugged.

"Narcotics, a little bank robbing here and there. They gave me a life sentence."

He broke off into laughter.

I couldn't believe what I was hearing.

"How were you a Champion?!" I demanded, aghast.

"Eduud Summons the one who can defeat the blah, blah, blah," he sighed and waved a hand. "Doesn't matter who we were over there as long as we do what we're supposed to here. And I did," he grinned. "I played the game, helped them out, became the hero and mentor they thought I was. But why stop there? If you have the means to get to the top… why not go for it?"

I didn't reply. Still reeling, I didn't know what to say.

"Don't get me wrong, I like my name," he rubbed his chin thoughtfully. "Frank. Still doesn't have that… that *thrill* a Mugatu gives you, though. *Mugatu* brings fear to mind, and power. Now *there's* an inspired name."

He leaned and spread his arms.

"And look at me now," he laughed. "All it takes is a little ambition and a little smarts and you can rule the world."

He looked down at me.

I bared my teeth.

"Are we going to fight or are you just going to keep sitting there and talking?" I snapped.

The soldiers shifted.

Mugatu… Frank… threw back his head and laughed again. He was in a pretty good mood, and you couldn't really blame him. I'd walked right into his trap like the fool I was, after all.

He wiped his eyes and shook his head.

"Kid, I like you," he said. "You're the brave, foolish sort, aren't you? You're no coward, I give you that. You murdered all those poor people to get here, and there you are, with the balls to stand there like that in front of me. I like you. But see, I have to admit, I have it pretty good now. But… I mean, come on. After all the trouble it took getting here, I'm not about to let go if it that easily. You know what I mean."

He smiled. I scowled.

"But to stay the King indefinitely, I'm going to have to make a few sacrifices. You might probably know that saying: you can't make an omelet without breaking those eggs."

"Before we begin, though," he said, arranging himself comfortably on the throne, "You should know I have a slight problem on my hands."

"Me," I spat.

He shrugged, "Well, yes and no. Let me tell you a story, Champion, and when I'm done, you'll understand everything."

"Spare me the monologue," I said.

I guess in the face of death, fear just doesn't have what it takes anymore.

"Come, now," Frank tutted. "A monologue is quite due. I have you in the palm of my hand, and you don't even realize it. How else would you feel the real despair you're supposed to, unless you know how exactly you came to be standing on your own there, at my feet?"

"Then get it over with," I snapped.

"See, everyone forgot a few simple rules that were set down a long time ago," he said, ignoring me. "They go on about the Laws, the Laws, the goddamn Laws, but they forgot one of the most important ones there is."

I scowled.

"When the first Tyrant rose, and the First Champion was Summoned to do battle with him, it was all haywire," Frank shrugged. "And I suppose The Lawmakers were making it up as they went along. Quite understandable, really. Then, someone realized that after the Choice was granted, the powers couldn't be taken back unless the Champion decided to go home. And, of course, it was another Law that stated you couldn't send him home unless he willingly decided he'd had enough here."

He rolled his eyes.

"Much like I did so very recently, the Lawmakers saw how it was just a step for a Champion to throw down the King and become a Tyrant himself. He had the power to do that, after all; just look at me," he grinned, and then his expression soured. "The Lawmakers, of course, had to meddle in the whole thing."

He sighed and shook his head.

"See, the Law states that all Tyrants would have Champions Summoned to battle them. But a Tyrant who used to be a former Champion… in this instance, me… would have quite a bit of an advantage over a new, untested Champion… this being, of course, you… freshly Summoned to defeat me. You wouldn't know the first thing about the tourist locations, who's who in the world, that sort of thing. Following me so far?"

I scowled, but I didn't reply. There was something to what he was saying. I had to hear it.

"Good," he smiled charmingly. "So, the Lawmakers did what they do best: they wrote another Law. If a former Champion goes bad, like yours truly, and when Eduud does what he does and Summons a new Champion, as always happens… the new Law stated that the Tyrant can NOT harm the Champion… *till he has Chosen.*"

He stopped and scowled, the first sign of any real anger he'd shown. I stopped breathing.

"You see why you're still alive, boy?" he yelled. *"You didn't make the damn Choice!* The one thing, the

ONE THING that could have gone wrong, and you went and did it!!"

He slammed both fists against the throne, the clang echoing like a gunshot. His helmet teetered on the edge of the armrest, but didn't fall.

His anger washed over the hall like a tidal wave. His soldiers cringed, and even I turned away involuntarily.

Frank Morris closed his eyes and inhaled slowly.

"The fact you didn't Choose," he said, visibly trying to keep his voice even. "It helped you more than it did me. How's that for irony, eh? You're standing there, in front of me, as calm as you please. All I need to do is just step down to you and I can finish it…. but *I cannot touch you.*"

His fist clenched, he made to pound it on the throne again, only he managed to control himself. Teeth grinding in frustration, he continued.

"As long as they are bound to me or follow my orders, even my men can't hurt you if they tried. You, Alan, are invulnerable right now. Go ahead, enjoy it."

The men around us murmured and shifted slightly. My hand drifted to my belt. The only weapon I had on me was the one my razor had turned into, and I brushed my fingers over its handle

"Here I am, sitting on the throne, in plain view," he said. He spread his arms, the hate in his eyes enough to set me on fire. "Come on, take your shot. I can't hurt you. No one here can."

I curled my fingers on the weapon's handle.

The scowl returned.

"The moment your blade touches me, boy," he said, "The moment it *touches* me… that's all I'll need. Touch me, and you void the Law. I will be free to skewer you where you stand and leave your body for the crows. So, Champion, come on up."

He smiled.

"If you think you can kill me with the first strike… you're welcome to try. It's the only strike you will get."

He gestured at me to approach him, but I didn't move. My knuckles were white on the haft of the razor, and my body was trembling.

For a long moment, there was silence. The room was hushed, and all eyes were on me.

I didn't move.

Finally, Mugatu sighed.

"Shame," he said, resting against the arm, allowing the electricity to seep away, "I was rather hoping you'd have been man enough to do it. I could have ended this whole thing much sooner. Still, though, all roads lead here."

"Are you done?" I demanded.

"No, not quite," he admitted. "Think about it from my point of view. I can't kill you, not by my own accord, and I can't have you running around, either. Not too good for my health, and frankly, being a ruler wouldn't be as fun if I always had the thought of you still plotting against me, nagging like those kind of thoughts do."

He stood and put his hands behind his back, like he was about to pace thoughtfully, "If you had Chosen one of the three, that damn law wouldn't have held anymore, and I could have wiped you off at any time I pleased."

He looked down at me.

"I couldn't harm you, I couldn't take you by force… so annoying," he shook his head, "So the only way I could deal with you was if I could get you to come and stand there in front of me of your own free will."

A cold hand clutched at my heart.

"You predicted this?"

He laughed out loud again, reveling at the display of power he was putting on.

"'Predicted'?" he echoed. "Dear boy, the only reason you're standing there alone is because I wanted you to. Every move you have made, everything you have done, is because I desired it."

My breath caught in my throat.

"You lie," I hissed.

He shrugged, "Suit yourself."

A loud scrape from behind me interrupted him, the sound echoing down the room and inducing a murmur in the men. Everyone began to turn, and when Frank's eyes flickered to the door as well, I followed suit.

Laehn stood there, a hand on each door, his bow still clenched tight in his hands. He gave the soldiers a contemptuous look as they raised their spears, then glanced at me and up at Frank.

Hope soared in me. As he let go of the doors and took a step forward, the soldiers stamped and stabbed their spears at him, blocking his path. At any moment, I knew he'd break into his frenzy, and when he did, I was ready to take my stab at Frank while he was distracted

"Let him pass," Frank called.

The soldiers looked at each other and then stepped aside. They parted the way they had for me, with their spears still out and pointed at his face. Laehn ignored them and began to walk towards me, ignoring the soldiers who took nervous steps back as he approached them.

The doors slammed shut.

Confused, I watched him come down.

Why isn't he attacking them? my mind screamed.

Then I remembered; five bloody arrows were all he had. Using them up on the soldiers wouldn't serve any purpose. He was coming to cut the head off the snake.

I turned to Frank, grinning savagely, but what I wasn't expecting was for him to be looking so pleased. It didn't matter. Any moment now, I knew Laehn would fire, and on his signal I needed to attack. I prepared myself, watching in my mind as I ran up those steps and plunged my blade into Frank's neck, the one place I had a chance of killing him with the first blow.

Frank sat down easily and raised a leg to rest his foot on his other knee. He looked past me, watching as Laehn approached.

"Well timed, archer," he called. "Conversation was just about swinging over to you."

Laehn was right by us. I stared at him, waiting for him to catch my eye so I could show him I was ready to do what needed to be done. He ignored me, but I still bent my knees as he drew up, and counted the moments till he reached me.

He drew up to me, and walked a few steps ahead.

And then he knelt and placed his bow on the ground in front of Frank.

"I have done as you commanded," he said. "My tasks are complete, Sire."

Standing there, looking at that picture, I felt a bucket of ice water pour down on me. My world turned upside down.

"You...?" I whispered.

To his credit, he had the shame to ignore me.

"I TRUSTED YOU!" I roared, "I BELIEVED YOU!"

"That's usually what a spy is supposed to do, you know," Frank said, "Make their targets believe them, trust them, that kind of thing. He really came highly recommended, and I must say, after these results..."

I drew my weapon and slammed the end on my chest. The blade sprang out, and I probably would have decapitated Laehn on the spot; or tried to. It was Laehn, after all.

But before I did more, a collective stamp of boots resonated through the chamber. I paused, blade raised, and looked over my shoulder at the forest of spears aimed at my back.

I began to shake. My arms couldn't hold the Weapon up any longer, and I let them drop and stumbled away, my chest heaving with a sob.

Still on one knee, with his head still bowed, Laehn did not move.

"Don't be too hard on yourself," Frank said, condescending. "It's not your fault. I'm just too good."

He grinned at me, but I was still glaring at Laehn. I didn't know what to say.

What could I say?

"When I found out that you hadn't Chosen, well, I was furious," Frank admitted, "I always plan for everything, but I hadn't planned on you being a total incompetent fool. Which is probably where the word foolproof came from, I suppose, when even the antics of people like you are taken into account. I figured that even if I traipsed off across the Realm to find you, there was squat I could do if I did. So, I needed you to come here."

He gestured.

"The only way you would ever do that is if you managed to get your armor and bond your Weapon with the Armament. Only then would you be arrogant enough to think you were ready to face me. But I'm not a very patient person at the best of time," he shrugged, "One of my few weaknesses. I needed you here fast. And that's where Bass comes in."

"Bass was a traitor, too?" I whispered.

On the ground, Laehn closed his eyes and Frank laughed out loud in delight.

"Oh, you really did a number on him, didn't you," he guffawed. "Broke him hard enough to even doubt the great honorable Bass's integrity. No, boy, Bass would never have turned traitor. Ever. Took his duties far too seriously, and as a result was so, so easy to manipulate."

"You killed all the other Champions," I said softly, "But kept him alive, just so he would lead me to you."

"As he would have put it: Aye," Frank chuckled, and then shook his head with a sigh. "Oh, you fool. You had to go and get him killed, hadn't you? I was waiting to see his face when he found out I'd used him the same way I'd used everyone else."

I glared again at Laehn, head still bowed, eyes still closed.

"You needed to get your armor before Bass would even contemplate an assault on the Hill," Mugatu continued, "And so I delayed my attack for as long as I possibly could. You were so inconsiderately slow, weren't you?"

"If you wanted me to get the Armament, why did you have Kernine ambush us there?" I demanded.

"Because it had to be convincing," Frank threw up his hands in disbelief, "Come on, even you could have guessed that."

"But Kernine..." I said, "He hurt me. And you said..."

"You thought he did." Frank corrected. "You just hurt yourself. You wouldn't have bled, even if he'd swung his axe at you. At the time, you'd have probably thought it was the armor protecting you, which it would have."

"But he tried to stop me from getting to the Armament," I said, "And he..."

"A ruse," he waved a hand. "To fool Bass, not you. You'd have believed anything, as gullible as you are. But then he was overenthusiastic."

He sighed, "So hard to find good help these days. You're the exception, Laehn. And I never managed to thank you for that pigeon you sent me the night before your little rebel alliance marched."

He grinned at my reaction, savoring the pain he was driving through me with every word.

"Speaking of which," he examined his fingernails, "Your little diversion should have been dealt with by now."

"All the men Laehn killed..." I spat. "All of them, all yours. Is this how little you care for your followers, that you'd have them as expendable bait?"

I heard the soldiers shift uncomfortably behind me.

Frank sneered down at me.

"Men?" he scoffed, "Groveling cowards, the lot of them."

This time, a definite murmur ran down the room.

"Of course," he said, looking around at them. "They know what would happen if they fail me. Loyalty can be bought, Alan. Fear… take it from me, when you earn fear, there is nothing you can't do."

The murmurs stopped.

"Of course, I had to have them killed," Frank shrugged. "As thick as you are, I couldn't risk you becoming suspicious as to why Laehn never dropped bodies. And Bass would never believe it. So I had to have Laehn be convincing."

"You're a sadist."

"Why, thank you," Frank adjusted himself on the seat. "You're probably wondering why Laehn would do that to you, I supposed. Rest assured, he had noble intentions. He was smart enough to realize I would win, so he offered his services in exchange for his family's protection. A fair trade, you must admit. After all, he has already lost so much to this never ending Champion and Tyrant war."

My hands were still shaking. I balled them into fists, but it did nothing to help.

"Look," he said. "We could go on talking till dinner, but I have a realm to run, so let's cut to the chase, shall we?"

"Gladly," I snarled.

He spread his hands.

"It seems like we're at a stalemate," he observed. "I can't hurt you, and you're too cowardly to hurt me. All I can do is to make you Choose, and you probably wouldn't do it if I asked nicely, now would you?"

I glowered and he shrugged.

"Thought as much. It doesn't matter. This is my chess game, boy. And this is where I make the last move."

He grinned, sending a shudder down my spine.

"Bring forth the prisoners!" Mugatu called.

The doors behind the thrones creaked open, and two soldiers marched in, King Zaahis' arms locked in theirs. His hands were bound within an inch of snapping his wrists off; he was bloody and bruised, filthy hair matted over his face, and his feet dragged as they hauled him up to the thrones.

My heart leaped to my throat as they held him dangling between them, a broken shadow of the man I had last seen. He raised his head and looked at me, and under the dirty tangled locks, his eyes gleamed as bright as ever.

The man still had faith, but seeing him there like that sucked out the last of mine.

Frank stuck out his lip and nodded in mock sympathy.

"Dirty thing, war," he said. "People get hurt all the time. It's a shame, Zaahis; I quite liked you. But, well, you were the unlucky bit of royalty keeping the seat of my throne warm when I was ready to claim it."

The King's gaze flickered to Laehn, still kneeling a few paces away from me, and his eyes dulled. He looked at me, and his lips contorted into what he probably hoped was a reassuring smile, which unfortunately came off as a painful grimace.

So caught up was I with the King that I hadn't noticed the soldiers bring in their other prisoner, and the moment my eyes landed on him, my stomach free fell.

It was Eduud.

None of them dared touch him, and he glided along silently in the middle of the four uneasy men escorting him. He reached the King's side and stopped, his face hidden in the depths of the green cowl.

"So good of you to join us, Great One," Frank said, a slice of respect served with the mocking overtones of his voice.

Eduud did not acknowledge him; the cowl turned and focused on me. He hadn't changed since I had first seen him months ago. Hope flared in me again, bright warm hope. Eduud could save us, I realized. All it would take was one portal...

"You probably wonder why he doesn't leave," Frank interrupted, cleaving through my faith, "He's a prisoner. But to his Laws, not to me."

He chuckled. "Gotta love the loopholes, eh? He's nothing more than a machine, and all he can do is what he's been told to do. Shame, really. He's quite legally a prisoner of war, and the Law states he is mine unless I explicitly set him free. And between you and me… why would I ever do that?"

He threw back his head and guffawed.

"You won't win, Frank," I said.

Whatever prompted me to say that, I don't know; yes, it was so incredibly cheesy, and yes, it was so incredibly embarrassing. The words were out of my mouth, and there was no taking them back.

"I already have," Frank grinned triumphantly. He stood up and pointed at me.

"You, Champion, have a Choice to make," he said. "Eduud is here to see to that. Don't bother planning on leaving here unarmed by deciding not to Choose. If you don't, I'll just kill the wretch you see before you, and non-violently escort you down to your own personal dungeon cell. I'm not really sure if you dying of starvation amounts to us harming you, but it would be interesting to find out, wouldn't it?"

He gestured to Eduud.

"And if you Choose, it will end sooner. The Law wouldn't hold anymore, and I could kill you myself and be done with it. I give you the choice as to the means of your defeat. Let them not say I was not generous to my enemies."

This was it then. All this time, pain, heartbreak, the loss and the training… for it to end here, like this. After all of it, he had still won. Either way, he won.

"To be quite honest," Frank said, leaning down as if to see me better, "I would like to apologize to you."

He leaned back again and began to idly trace one of the patterns on the throne's arm.

"I never had anything personal against you," he continued, "You were unlucky enough to be the one he Summoned. It's all his fault, really."

He nodded at Eduud, who still stood unmoving, cowl still fixed on me.

"Don't get me wrong, I'm still going to kill you," Frank laughed. "But just so we're clear. If Bass or any of the others you were with didn't apologize to you before, let me do it for them. From one Champion to another, I'm sorry you had to be dragged into this."

He looked down into my eyes, and for the first time, the gloating triumph wasn't there on his face. He really was sorry, and I could see beyond a doubt that he meant it.

It didn't change anything, though, so I scowled up at him.

Frank shrugged and leaned back.

"Well, you would have been waiting long for this," he said, "So go on ahead: Choose!"

I looked up at him, then at the King.

Time slowed down.

Horror chilled my heart.

The Choice that I'd been denied, the one I never thought I'd get… I was being given it now.

I would have the Powers that had been denied me.

But Frank had them as well. And if this would end in one on one combat as the Law dictated, whatever I chose would either kill me or save me… depending on what *he* had Chosen in the first place.

In all the time I've been here, and after everything I had learned about him, I had never thought about asking Bass what Mugatu's Choice had been. He sat there on the throne, lording over us, and what I picked could be very well be his downfall… or my own.

I'd never bothered to ask before, and I might have to pay for it now.

I looked at Eduud, who stood there watching me, and at Laehn, still bowed down next to me.

Strength, Wisdom, or Skill.

Rock, Paper, or Scissor.

I breathed.

It was that perfect moment of clarity; there wasn't a sound in the throne room, and my thoughts were clear. The fate of the realm, the lives of the King and myself, all hope of returning home to Mona… it had all boiled down either Frank or I winning this rock, paper and scissors battle.

"Choose!" Frank bellowed.

My brain screamed into overdrive.

Frank didn't look buffed enough to have Chosen Strength. It would have had to be Skill or Wisdom, my mind worked out. Paper or Scissors.

I had to Choose.

Rock, Paper or Scissors.

"CHOOSE!" he roared.

The soldiers bellowed together, and banged their spears on the ground.

Scissors, Paper, or Rock.

Paper, Rock, Scissors.

The spears banged again, and this time the men began to chant.

"Choose!" they insisted, "Choose!"

Eduud watched me silently, that damn cowl so still, I felt like ripping it to shreds.

The King's eyes never left mine. He stared, eyes boring into my soul.

"Choose!"

Thud.

"Choose!"

Frank drew his sword, the metal glinting evilly in the torchlight. He climbed down the steps in time to the chanting, and walked to the King.

"Choose!"

Thud.

"CHOOSE."

Rock, Paper, Scissors.

I was going crazy.

Frank grinned, and yanked a handful of the Zaahis' hair, forcing his chin up and exposing his throat.

"CHOOSE!" the soldiers roared, "CHOOSE!"

Frank tutted and shook his head. He held the blade against the King's throat, and prepared to make the slash.

"HOLD IT!" I yelled, "I'll choose!"

It worked. The soldiers went quiet, and silence, blissful silence returned. Out of the corner of my eye, I saw Laehn turn to look at me, but I fixed my eyes on Mugatu's.

Frank raised an eyebrow.

"Oh. And?"

I ran my tongue over my cracked lips.

"I Choose," I said, the three choices cannonballing inside my head, "I choose…"

Frank rolled his eyes, and his hand moved.

I was out of time. I had to say something. I had to…

"SCISSORS!"

Chapter 16

Frank lowered his sword, his face the dictionary definition of the word confusion.

"What?" he demanded.

I was hyperventilating. The pressure in me was seeping out, and it took with it the memory of the last few seconds. Caught up in the moment, I'd chosen at random, and now completely forgotten what I had picked.

"What, what?" I demanded.

Frank let go of the King's hair, letting Zaahis' head fall heavily onto his chest. Frank looked down at me in incredulity.

"Did you…" he shook his head, as if trying to clear it, "Did you say *scissors*?"

THANK YOU.

"Scissors, yeah," I said, feeling the beginnings of a ramble coming on, "Rock, paper and scissors. I chose scissors."

Frank looked at me like I'd taken off my armor and was now doing the chicken dance at his feet.

"Scissors?" he echoed, "For real?"

Zaahis slowly raised his head and locked eyes with me, misunderstanding in abundance there. And

Laehn, still on the ground, was slowly shaking his head, probably rolling his eyes as well.

"Skill," I clarified, "I Choose Skill."

The tension returned like someone had flicked a switch. The soldiers murmured and shifted, and Frank frowned.

"Interesting choice," he said.

Zaahis still looked at me, but I couldn't tell what he was trying to say; goosebumps were rising on my arms, and I had the feeling that I had made a terrible mistake.

Eduud glided towards me and stretched out his hand.

"Do you, Champion, Choose the Skill of Blades?" he boomed.

Frank watched me as he climbed up the stairs. If I'd Chosen wrong, he would have been delighted; but that wasn't glee on his face. Nor was it defeat.

It was annoyance.

Either I'd done something right or something wrong. There was no way of knowing which, so I licked my lips again and swallowed.

"Aye," I whispered.

Eduud stretched out his arm, and my right hand lifted up and yanked me forward its own accord. I skidded across the stone toward him, and my palm touched his; and that's when I was zapped by a million volts.

The pain was incredible, far worse than when the Armament had bonded with my razor. My teeth were locked shut, and my throat spasmed, my agonized scream never making it past puberty.

And then it was over, and our hands separated.

I fell in a heap, landing hard on my knees with a clang that echoed through the silent room.

"It's been centuries," Frank said softly, "I've forgotten how that felt for me,"

He sat back in the throne and glared at me as Eduud glided to where he had been standing.

I shakily climbed to my feet. My body was tingling, my teeth buzzing, the hair on my arms and legs standing on end. The soldiers watched me warily, and I distinctly heard the nearest one's gulp echo out of his armor. Laehn had moved away from me, and now stood in front of the closest line of soldiers, watching me keenly.

The tingle grew stronger in my fingers and they began to burn. Somehow, I knew what they wanted; I grabbed at the thing my razor had become, and I pulled it out of its sheath for the first time that night.

My arms moved by themselves. I stretched, twisted, and the blade sprung out. My feet shifted and my knees bent, and just like that, I was in some sort of battle stance, blade out and ready.

Confidence pooled up in me, flowing out of my arms and into every cell in my body. I felt fresh, cool, ready. Bass had chosen Skill. This was what he must have felt like, every day.

No wonder he had been able to move like he did; there was a wide smile on my face as I looked around at the soldiers, counting them, dismissing them. I could take them, my mind told me conversationally, and this time, I *knew* it. I could. I could take out every single man there till I was the only one standing.

I had the power.

"Enjoying it?"

I looked up at Frank, lounging in the throne, and I bared a feral grin at him.

"Yeah, it can be a bit intoxicating at the start," he agreed, "You'll get accustomed to it… or not."

He raised his hand.

I heard stamping feet and the snapping of wood. I spun around to face the soldiers as the ones in the front holding spears, took a step back and allowed the row behind them to step forward.

The men in this row held crossbows; and as one, they raised them up and pointed them at me.

I really, really hated crossbows.

A unified thrum and click echoed off the walls.

Of all the mistakes I'd made… this was the one that cinched it. I'd thought he would fight me, like he was supposed to. I'd been a fool.

"Well, finally," Frank sighed in relief, "No matter how good you know your plan is, there's always that bit of tension at the back of your mind till it's done. I tell you, I hadn't been this worked up over strategy since we broke out of Alcatraz. And that one took two years to plot, mind you."

I snarled up at him, my arms buzzing. I hungered to lash out and draw blood. It was in me, the energy, begging to be released.

"It all ends here," he said, "I planned your every move. Everything you did, you did because I wanted you to. Isn't your fault, kid, you were doomed the moment Eduud picked you to get Summoned. And now, I end this, for both of us."

He raised his hand, and the crossbowmen straightened.

I tensed myself to run, dodge, somehow survive… but then I realized it wouldn't be enough. There were too many bows; and there was Laehn. As skilled as I had become, I still doubted if I could take him on.

I bowed my head.

"It'll look pretty nice, now won't it," I said quietly.

With his hand still raised, Frank looked down on me and smiled.

"What was that?"

"You claim to have accomplished so much," I said, raising my head to glare at him, "Gaining all that power, fooling them all, manipulated me, everyone, into doing what you wanted. Tricked me into thinking I had friends."

"Yes, if there's a point you're trying to make, please get to it before I kill you,"

"But you won't kill me," I said, "Your men will. Not you."

I don't know what I wanted to say. I was doomed, dead where I stood. But if there was one thing I could have tugged at, it was his ego, and if that was the last thing I did, so be it.

Frank looked at me for a second before he threw back his head and laughed.

His mirth echoed off the walls, an evil, resonating sound that made even his own men fidget in their armor.

"This is precious," he gasped, wiping away a tear. "You're actually trying to talk me into fighting you. Even if that would have accomplished ANYTHING."

He shook his head and chuckled.

"How dumb do you think I am, boy? I twitch my finger, and you're a pincushion," he said, "That ridiculous towel of yours may be bullet proof, but it isn't large enough to cover all of you. Tell me, why would I bother trying to come down there to kill you myself, when you'd be dead in the time it would take me to pick my nose?"

"Because you're a coward," I snarled.

He spread his hands.

"So be it. I have the power I need. I am where I am now, and I'd rather not take any risks. I'm perfectly comfortable with having them kill you."

He grinned.

"Anything else?"

The energy vibrating inside spoke up, telling me I could take him, and all the guards in that room. I didn't ask it to, but my mind was already calculating angles of attack, points of intersection, ways to jump and deflect the incoming blows it predicted.

I was like a computer on fire. I was frustrated.

And all that energy and the frustration were making me angry.

"Are you SCARED?!" I roared.

The soldiers looked at each other, and for the first time, I could sense real, tangible doubt in them. Some of them darted quick glances at Frank, still smirking on the throne.

"Well, this had been fun," he said, "Goodbye, Champion."

He gestured.

I braced myself for the clicks and the impact of bolts which would skewer me like an overused pincushion.

They never came.

I opened my eyes as Frank's face hardened. He jerked his hand again, much more violently. Still nothing happened.

I cautiously turned my head to look at the soldiers. The crossbows were still trained on me, but their faces... all eyes were on him.

"SHOOT HIM DOWN!" Frank bellowed.

No one moved. My words, desperate as they had been, may have failed on him, but they'd worked on his men. And as I understood that, the energy started to build up in me again. I was like a hyperactive kid on chocolate. I was the roadrunner on caffeine.

I was a Champion who'd just Chosen.

Frank's face grew red. He rose to his feet and pointed at me.

"SHOOT," he roared, "HIM. DOWN!"

"They don't want to shoot me, Frank," I said, grinning, "They don't want to do your job for you."

"I WILL BURN YOU TREASONOUS COWARDS ALIVE!" he roared, spraying spittle, "EVERY LAST ONE OF YOU!"

I spun my weapon; it was magic. As I did, I let out a manic laugh that echoed off the walls, filling the room. I terrified myself, but I wasn't me. I was something more.

"They want to see if you're really powerful enough to defeat me," I yelled, "Come on, Frank. Let's give them a show, shall we?"

Shaking in unbridled fury, Frank stood there at the top of the stairs looking like a volcano on the verge of exploding. His eyes fixed on me, and the hate I saw in them would have laid me down at his feet, begging for mercy.

The old me.

Mugatu's eyes cooled. He calmed down, and flexed his fingers slowly.

"A show is what you want, is it?" he asked softly, "I shall do my best."

He took his helmet and lowered it over his head. His hand drifted down to his sword, and he made to step down.

Only he didn't. He jumped.

He soared, a gleam of black and gold metal and a twisting of a cape.

And then he landed right in front of me, on one knee, sword pointed out to one side, eyes burning at me through the open visor.

My arms moved, my feet adjusted, pulling me away and setting me up in a battle stance, but inside my armor, I was very suddenly freaking out. The soldiers were backing up around us, clearing a ring of space. Frank Morris stood up slowly, and for the first time I saw how big he really was. His armor was a third larger than mine, and he was three feet taller than I was. He wasn't as big as Kernine had been, but he was far, far more menacing.

And that was saying something.

"My Weapon went back to being a wooden paddle when the next Champion was Summoned," he said conversationally, "So I had this made. It serves its purpose well enough."

I eyed the broad, curved blade, and looked into those hate filled eyes.

"Why would you Choose Skill, I wonder," he said, "You did not know what it was that I had Chosen, I know. Maybe you would have tried to deduce it and picked accordingly? Maybe you thought

I needed Wisdom, of Pages no less, to do what I have done?"

He stepped forward, and his visor slammed shut. I looked into the black and gold helmet and saw myself reflected there, small and weak.

"You think you can win because you chose Skill?" he demanded, "You've felt the power for all of five minutes, and now you think you can take ME?"

I didn't have time to reply. He lunged, and my blade jumped to block. He didn't pause; he moved again, and I replied. He advanced, swinging and slashing, and I backed away, my arms parrying his blade before it reached. My visor clanged shut over my face, reducing all I could see to what was visible through the slits. It was like I was watching someone else playing a first person sword game in fast forward; I hadn't a clue what was happening.

Without warning, without a clue of respite, it was over. He stood a few paces away and I was on one knee, panting.

"I didn't need wisdom," he snarled, walking towards me again, "They told me back home I had an IQ of a hundred and thirty three. Not that I needed them to tell ME how smart I was."

He slashed again, and I parried. He changed his angle and thrust before I could react. The tip of his blade brushed past my neck. I thought he'd missed… then I felt the pain and warm blood trickle down my neck.

"Surprised?" he snarled, "You should be. Skill of Blades was what I Chose, too."

He pulled and swung again. It was a good thing that my arms didn't need me to tell them what to do now, because my brain wasn't in any shape to take command.

Of all what had happened that night, this was the last straw. I'd messed up again. No matter how hard I tried, I always messed up.

What was the point to trying, then?

He spun stabbed, slashed, and my arms moved, trying to hold my ground. Mugatu spun and kicked me, sending me through the air to land and slide across the stone floor on my butt.

"You have lost already, Alan," Mugatu snarled. There was no trace of the glee I'd heard when I'd first seen him. This was pure wrath, pure loathing.

"I made my Choice CENTURIES ago!" he roared.

I leaped to my feet as he ran at me again. The sword arced towards my head, and I bent over backwards to watch it pass inches over my visor.

"You will NEVER defeat me!" he yelled.

I jumped up and straight into the path of a clenched, mailed fist.

Disoriented and deafened, I was on the ground again, ears ringing and my head feeling like it had intercepted a baseball bat in mid swing. I braced myself for the next blow to finish me off, but Mugatu looked like he was drawing it out, enjoying himself.

"Stay down, boy," he snarled. I opened my eyes as he paced around me, the sword pointed at my chest. My fear was gone. All I knew was the pain, just pain everywhere.

"Finish it," I said, "Just get it over with."

"Did Bass ever mention your eyes, boy?" he demanded, still pacing, "Did he ever talk about what they meant, why Eduud needed to Summon people from far away to defeat the Tyrants here?"

He laughed and shook his head.

"Of course he didn't," he said. "If he had, you wouldn't be here."

I was starting to have enough of his voice. I pushed myself to my feet, but he roared and slammed me down again. I landed on my face, my jaw and nose bashing against the inside of the helmet. Blood dribbled down my chin as I raised my head again.

"I said STAY DOWN!" he bellowed.

He didn't have to; I hadn't any more strength to stand again, even if I'd wanted to. For now, he looked like he wanted to gloat, and I was fine with it. I needed a few seconds to catch my breath.

The person I'd been before the Choice would have never survived till now. I was stronger, faster... just enough to keep going a little more.

"The reason why they need Champions, boy," Mugatu said, "Is because of their *eyes*."

I closed my eyes and laid my head down, letting my pain wash over me, slowing my breathing as I prepared. I followed him with my ears as he walked around me, his footsteps echoing.

"Oh, the secrets and the lies they try and keep from us," he said, "About the Laws, about everything. It took me all that time to figure them out for myself. Some of them I had to ask Eduud directly, others... well, let's say I did a lot of travelling."

He paused somewhere beyond my head.

"Our eyes," he breathed. "It's what we've seen. What we have witnessed. It's *that* what makes us more powerful than the Tyrants we had to throw down. *That's* why they bring us here, Alan."

I slowly pushed myself up by one elbow, wincing as the pain stabbed. He was looking into the distance, the sword held at his side.

"I have seen pain," he said, clenching his free fist. "I have seen suffering. I have seen the cruelty behind the uniform and the badge. The anguish and torture of fathers separated from their families... for life."

He took two steps towards me and kicked out. His mailed boot connected with my helmet, and I saw stars. The world faded into focus, and I realized my hand was empty. I'd dropped the Weapon.

"Eduud did what he had to," Mugatu said. "Bringing a Champion to defeat me. It was what I had expected. But you? You RUNT?"

He kicked again, this time at my gut. My armor absorbed most of the force, but I still skidded backwards a foot, my armor shrieking on the stone.

"HOW DARE you think you can defeat ME?" he roared. "You call ME a coward in front of these pathetic mewling whelps?? TAKE A GOOD LOOK AT WHERE YOU ARE NOW!"

He stamped on my leg, and I couldn't keep myself from giving him the satisfaction of hearing me scream. I blinked away the tears of pain and watched him walk away again.

"What is it you've seen, Alan?" he asked, back to me. "What do your eyes have behind them that's more powerful than what's behind mine?

Pain lanced through me. I forced myself up on an elbow again, my left shin throbbing. He'd know that I was trying to sit up again, but this time he let me.

"What have you seen, Champion?" he asked softly.

I gasped in a pained breath, and then I saw her. I saw her eyes, her hair, her smile.

I saw what I was fighting for. WHO I was fighting for. And it was all I needed to reignite the spark, grasp my Weapon and push myself to my feet for more.

"WELL?" Mugatu thundered, turning to face me as I stood shaking, blade pointed at him.

"I've seen love," I whispered. "I've seen goodness. And I've seen hope."

He walked towards me, and even though I couldn't see it, I knew he was leering.

"'Love'?" he sneered. "'Hope'? I expected nothing more."

He swung, and I managed to dodge it.

"I have seen life," I panted. "And I have seen death. I have seen peace and I have seen pain."

Some of that pain lanced through my chest, forcing me back on one knee.

"Yes, do go on," Frank waved an arm.

"Whatever happens now," I wheezed. "Whoever wins... it doesn't matter. We're all... a small part of... the bigger picture. A... a stitch in the *fabric* of reality..."

Frank sighed audibly, and hung his head ruefully. Without warning, he took a step toward me and swung. This time, I was too slow to duck. The sword slammed into my helmet, and I heard it crack at my ear. The strength in that blow should have thrown me to the floor, but it didn't.

Impossibly, I was still standing.

Mugatu took a step back and raised his visor. He was smiling.

"Finally," he said. "I was getting bored."

My helmet dangled uselessly off one side, so I reached up and took it off. My reflection flashed over the reflective steel. My nose looked as broken as it felt, and the savage cut on my lower lip spilled blood over my chin.

But... my eyes.

They had changed. My eyes were glowing bright gold.

I felt strength rush through me, golden power, if that made sense. This wasn't my Skill... this was something else. I dropped the useless helmet and clenched my fingers into a quivering fist.

"What is happening to me?" I whispered.

Mugatu grinned savagely.

"Things just became a little more interesting," he said. His visor slammed shut again, but not before I saw his eyes burn, just the way mine had. But his weren't gold; they were black, an abyss of hatred, lust and fury.

He bellowed and came at me, sword raised. With each step he took, I saw darkness seep out of him, an aura of terror and rage that made him somehow loom bigger and more menacing than he already did.

But it didn't matter. Whatever it was I was feeling, it had taken away my pain and my exhaustion. Quivering energy fed into me, and somehow, I tapped into it. My Weapon spun in my hands and I waited for him to reach me.

Waited.

Time slowed as he swung, and my blade rose up to meet his. The jar from the impact ran down my arm, reverberating around us, a deafening sound that resonated through the Throne room.

Time sped up.

I'd thought we had been fighting before, but that had been nothing. *Now* we fought, blades whirling, bodies spinning, blurs as we danced around each other.

Oh, man. Did we fight.

If I thought it had been energy feeding into me from before, then this… this was something else. A golden halo shone around me, shielding me, almost, from the impact of his swings. A corona of rancid darkness cloaked him and his armor, a black hole that sucked away a part of me every time I came close.

I could not keep track of what we did, how I struck or how he stabbed. All I knew was that we danced across the room, at some point in the middle of it all I was vaguely aware of the soldiers backing away in terror.

My fingers twitched on their own, my arms and legs moving before I could even think of what to do. Our blades kept meeting over and over again, and no matter how hard he swung, no matter how much I countered, we kept at it as the minutes flew by. Never tiring, ducking and weaving like I'd only imagined I could in dreams, we kept at it.

And then I was lucid again. I felt the power was wearing off, the reservoir of energy beginning to deplete. I was slowing down, and he knew it, felt it, and pressed the attack. I ducked under his blade and swung straight up. The edge of my blade caught him under the jaw, and knocked him backwards.

It was the first blow I'd landed that had taken him off his feet. I moved to finish it, but my foot spasmed, and I fell on my knee with a stifled cry. The pain had returned.

He sat up, his helmet broken. With an oath, he tore it off and threw it away, revealing the gleaming black eyes that were as bright as they had been when I'd seen them last.

"Lucky blow," he grinned, "You're losing your conviction, Champion."

He was on his feet and at me. He slashed and I ducked, and then bashed my handle against his nose before he could jerk away.

He bellowed in rage and swung at me, but my feet had already taken me out of harm's way. He stood there, glowering at me with blood dripping down over his lips, as evil a sight as I'd ever see.

"Not yet," I said.

He started coming at me, and I started backing away again. His eyes still burned deep black, and he wasn't tiring. My arms, on the other hand were like lead, and my thighs were shaking so badly I could barely stand up. Beads of perspiration dripped into my eyes, blinding me, and I didn't see when the flat of his blade caught me right in the face.

The impact threw me a couple of feet and slammed me hard onto my back. He loomed over me and swung at my throat. I parried, but the angle was all wrong. The top of his blade slid off mine and pried through the armor at my inner forearm to tear a narrow gash along the inside. Red hot pain made me drop the razor with a howl.

"So much for all that, then," he gloated, leaning down to look into my eyes, panting slightly. "A final show, final effort, and yet at the end, for nothing. I'd have spared you this pain, this humiliation, if you'd allowed the archers to take you."

I reached out to grasp my Weapon, but he punched me in the face. It felt like a brick colliding with my nose, and I almost passed out. When I came to, he had his weight pressed on me, his knee crushing my chest.

"Was it worth it, Champion?" he sneered, "Was it worth this pain?"

It was over. The golden elixir was gone. I was down, and I wasn't getting up again. He knew it; they all knew it. I wanted to say something cool right then. I mean, if you're going to die, might as well go out like a badass and not be remembered as the guy who cried to his death.

I opened my mouth, but all what came out was a wheeze, some spittle and the taste of copper.

"Pitiful," he sneered. "I feel it beneath me to even kill you myself. But it wouldn't become the history books, now would it?"

The soldiers were silent. I felt their eyes on me, my limbs trembling, my chest spasming as it clawed for breath. I tried to look brave as he bent over me in triumph, but as hard as I tried, I couldn't keep the tear from leaking out the corner of my eye.

At that, he leaned back and laughed.

"I'll be kind," he said, "and make this fast."

He raised his sword.

"THUS," he bellowed, "THE LAST CHAMPION DIES!"

I heard a whine. And another. And another.

Three arrows hit him in quick succession, literally milliseconds apart. The first two pierced his arm, and the third plunged right through his wrist, forcing him to let go of the sword.

The heavy weapon clashed deafeningly on the stone by my head as he lifted his knee off me and stumbled away in shock and pain. A fourth arrow took him straight through the thigh, forcing him down onto a knee, and the last one plunged into his side, just under his arm.

Still on my back, I heaved in a pain wracked gasp of breath and turned my head.

Five arrows were all Laehn had. I saw the look on his face as he spread his arms and held out his bow; it was an expression that in all the time I'd spent with him, I'd never seen before.

It was one of peace.

The soldiers were all around him, and yet his dagger was still in his belt. It was déjà vu as three spears thrust from behind, their points stabbing out through his chest.

His face spasmed, and his bright blue eyes met mine. In that last instant, I watched, helpless, as the light went out. If he'd spoken, I wouldn't have heard.

But he didn't have to. His words were in my head, playing like they were stuck on repeat.

"I have been with you since the start of your Quest."

"I promise you this, Alan; I will be with you at its end."

And then the spears were yanked out of him. He jerked, and then he fell. The bow clattered against the stone, the sound weirdly deafening in the silence.

"I will be with you at its end."

Laehn was gone.

*   *   *

Somehow, the energy was back. It coursed through me, pushing me up onto my feet, reaching my blazing hand out to grasp the Weapon. It was not more than adrenaline, and I knew I had hardly a minute before it wore off.

A minute was all I needed.

Mugatu still knelt down, blood seeped through the fingers he pressed against the wound on his chest. As I limped toward him, he used his left hand to break off the arrow in his thigh, dropping the shaft onto the other four he'd removed.

He looked up at me and I saw the black glow gone, his eyes brown once more. He bared his teeth at me as I swung, but even in pain, he wouldn't be denied. He ducked, pushed me away, and lunged for his sword. Grabbing it in his left hand, he parried my next swing, then struggled to his feet and jabbed at me. The blade pierced through the metal at my shoulder, slashing through skin. I cried out as blood flowed down the front of my armor and hesitated.

Right hand clenched to his chest, Frank began to rain blows on me, throwing me back one step at a time. He'd slowed down, and his left arm wasn't as sure as his right; and yet when he stabbed low again, I wasn't quick enough to move or parry. His sword cut into and through the armor under my arm and slid into my side.

It was red hot agony.

"Is THIS all your hope can do?!" he bellowed. "Is THIS all?"

A savage grin of triumph and pain on his eyes, he drew to stab again. This time I spun, pain and grief and rage giving me momentum, and I yelled as I lunged with every iota of strength I could summon.

I couldn't see where the blade hit him, but I felt impact on the handle, the crushing of metal and the jarring of bone. My arms worked on their own, shoving and thrusting, pushing it deeper into him, as deep as it could go.

I looked up into Frank's face, inches in front of mine.

"I don't believe in hope," I snarled. "I AM their hope."

His eyes widened, teeth bared with blood and spittle running down his chin.

Time stood still.

His expression changed; the grin turned into a scowl, then a contortion of fear. The eyes, still wide, morphed from fury to terror, and I felt warm, sticky blood run down the Weapon's handle and onto my hands.

His sword clattered against the stone. Frank Lee Morris choked out a swear, and more blood dribbled out of his mouth. His arms rose up and landed heavily on my shoulders, but try as he might, his fingers couldn't close.

I couldn't stand it any longer. The pain stabbed in my shoulder where his hand rested, and the cut in my side drove a white hot dagger into me. I yelled and heaved, and his hands slid off. His eyes were dull as I yanked on the Weapon with all the strength I had left, and he slid off the blade, falling in a disgusting crumple of arms, legs and armor.

My hand was shaking; my fingers couldn't hold onto the weapon any longer. I let it go, and the clang it made as it bounced on the ground echoed with severe finality.

I looked over at the soldiers, and there was fear in their eyes as they dropped their weapons.

"Thus passeth a Champion," Eduud boomed, his voice like thunder amid the clangs of metal on stone, "And cometh a new Age."

It was over.

Chapter 17

All around me, the soldiers were dropping to their knees, the clangs reverberating among the fading echoes of Eduud's announcement. The guards holding King Zaahis now let go of his arms and knelt before me like the others.

I looked around at them and cast a final glance at the sprawled heap behind me. The blood was pooling under what remained of the Champion who would have been a Tyrant.

He never should have done it, my mind whispered. *You did what you had to do.*

Before I could think up a reply, a spasm ran through me.

The last of my golden adrenaline had gone, taking with it the anesthesia that had kept me standing all this time. I was done.

My legs crumpled, and I fell.

Lying on the ground, I felt every ache and pain in my body with excruciating detail, as if all the cuts and bruises on my body had been pissed off at being ignored and were now taking it on me and didn't believe in a queueing system.

I was in agony.

I felt the ground tremor as people moved around me, and voices, indistinct and annoying, buzzing in my ear. I wanted them to shut up so I could fall asleep in peace, but I couldn't find the strength to speak.

I felt the warm tickle as blood ran down my neck, and a stab in my side with every breath among every other ache. I was bleeding out on the stone.

I was dying, just the way Bass had died.

Laehn had died, too. It was fitting this way.

It was fitting how we all died together.

And then I wasn't dying anymore.

I opened my eyes, and King Zaahis' bruised face hovered into view. Crouching over me, he grinned as I blinked, and reached down to give my shoulder a hearty shake. I prepared to wince, and then realized it didn't hurt. In fact, nothing hurt anymore.

"What happened to me?" I asked.

Zaahis helped me sit up, and that's when I noticed Eduud looming up over me, a greenish yellow glow fading away from his hands.

"Thou art healed," he proclaimed. "Thy sacrifices saved thine people, thus the Law remaineth upheld."

"Please tell me it's all over now," I moaned.

Zaahis gave me the best grimacing smile he could manage through his broken teeth.

"It's all over now."

He stood up and helped to my feet. My dizziness and fatigue gone, I looked down at the bloodstained armor I wore. The rips, rents and gashes were all there, but underneath, my skin was whole again. For a heart stopping moment, I remembered the last person I'd heard about who Eduud had healed. I needed a mirror.

I raised my arm and frantically searched the reflection on the metal brace for signs of long blonde hair or new pointy ears where they had no business to be. After a moment of suspense where my heart did one of the free falls it had grown so proficient in over the last few months, my face winked at me.

I heaved a sigh of relief. My nose wasn't broken any more, and the blood had been wiped away from my chin, but the face that looked at me was my own, and my hair was as brown as it ever had been. And my eyes weren't glowing anymore, as I'd figured.

"All hail the Champion!" a soldier yelled.

There was a scrabbling of metal against stone, and the soldiers yelled out in unison.

Hypocrites, the lot of them. I couldn't stand the sight of their faces; the recent memories came flooding back like from out behind a busted dam. I turned away from them, wishing I could block out their cheers.

I needed something to focus on, take my mind off them. Something…

"Laehn?" I said, my heart clenching.

Zaahis' eyes dulled, and he bowed his head.

"He died a hero," he replied, sorrowfully, "He gave his last to protect you. He had a change of heart, and it cost him…"

"No," I said, turning away from him, "It wasn't a change of heart."

"Excuse me?"

"Don't you see?" I demanded, "This was his plan. All along. He fooled every one of us."

Zaahis shook his head, confused. The cheers were starting to thankfully die down, and the closest soldiers were edging in, trying to hear what we were saying. I paid them no heed.

"Laehn knew that I couldn't take Frank alone, that probably no Champion Eduud Summoned probably could. But he couldn't do anything on his own, either, because Frank was too smart, and too powerful. He had to fool him into trusting him, and strike when he least expected it."

"Where are you pulling all this out from?" Zaahis asked. "Are you sure you're feeling alright?"

"The tapestry spoke to me, Zaahis," I said. "I saw things. I know."

His face cleared.

"So it's true, then," he muttered, "The tales of the…"

"Look, none of it matters now," I interrupted. "Laehn is dead. Just as Bass is dead. And Ajold and the rest of the people who fought of me, the people I tricked into killing themselves, they're probably all dead too."

My voice echoed up and down the silent room. The old me would have cringed and tried to hid behind the nearest cover. Who I was now did not give a mule's flatulence what they thought.

"My Lords, if I may," one of the soldiers scooted forward on his knees, head bowed, "We received reports from the Wall. Many died, but it is a fact that someone in the Champion's armor was seen leading survivors in a retreat once the ram was set on fire."

I gave him a look, and he started to tremble.

"And Elrik?" I demanded, "Laehn's brother?"

"Lord… Mugatu had specific instructions to not harm him," the man replied, eyes fixed on the stone in front of him, "He was to live, to honor the deal made with his brother. L-Laehn."

I nodded, acid rising up in my throat. It was done, then. The time was now.

"I think you have a promise to keep to me," I said softly.

Zaahis looked at me, and nodded.

"Indeed."

I turned to Eduud, my legs beginning to tremble again.

"I can leave now, right?" I demanded, "I can go home, to where you kidnapped me from?"

"If thou wisheth to return, I shall hasten thee to thy end," he replied.

I felt like sinking to the ground and crying, but I kept a grip on my emotions. I was too angry, too upset and too conflicted to know which emotion I wanted to show.

I was finally going home. It was all what mattered.

"I'd stay to say goodbye to Elrik and Ajold first," I said, my voice cracking. "But Mona's been waiting for me long enough. Tell them for me, Zaahis. And thank them for all they did to help."

He didn't nod and promise me he would, like he should have done. Instead, Zaahis looked down at me, his eyes wide in confusion.

"Mona?" he echoed.

"My wife," I said. "She's all alone at the apartment, and she's been alone ever since I..."

I trailed off as a look came over Zaahis' bruised and beaten face. It was shock and... and a cold hand clutched at my heart when I realized it was sorrow. His expression sent a knife through me far more painful than any blade I'd taken that night, a pain greater than all the ache and agony Mugatu had ever inflicted on me.

"Zaahis," I said, my voice quiet and trembling, "Zaahis, what is it?"

He took a step away from me, shaking his head.

"They didn't tell you," he whispered, "Of course you don't know."

My heart in my throat, I reached out and grabbed him by the shoulders.

"What didn't they tell me?" I demanded, "WHAT DON'T I KNOW?"

"Calm down, Alan," he said, his emaciated frame trembling under my fingers, "Just… calm down."

Unwillingly, I let go of him, and he took a step away from me.

"What didn't they tell me?" I demanded, struggling to keep my voice even, "That I can't go home yet? There's something more I have to do?"

"You *can* go home," he said, raising a hand, "It's… it may not be the home you once knew."

My heart was beating loud, fast, a drum in my ears. After all I'd done, after everything we'd gone through to get here… *this couldn't be happening.*

"What," I whispered, "Do you mean?"

Zaahis closed his eyes.

"I don't know how to explain," he said, weak and weary, "Bass always did this part when…"

"BASS ISN'T HERE NOW!" I bellowed, grabbing him by the collar. "WHAT DIDN'T THEY TELL ME?"

"As far as I know it," Zaahis said, speaking slowly as if trying to calm me, "The way time moves here and the way it does there isn't always the same. From what he told me, Bass was Summoned only a hundred and fifty or so years in your time before Mugatu was. But here, by our reckoning, seven centuries passed between them."

I listened, but I wasn't understanding.

"There were Champions who were taken from your future, too," Zaahis continued. "But they came here in our past. I don't know why…"

"What," I demanded, "does that have to do with me?"

Zaahis shook his head.

"Just because you were summoned a few months ago by our estimate," he said, "doesn't mean that the same time has passed back where you came from. If Eduud sends you home, it could be a year since you left, or a decade, or even more. And it could even be the reverse… you could land back in your past. We don't know why; it just is."

He swallowed.

"I'm sorry, Alan," he said, reaching out a hand to me. "But your wife… chances are she wouldn't have even been born… or worse, she would have died a long time…"

He didn't finish because I punched him in the face.

Already weak, he fell over. He tried to stand up, but I wasn't done yet. Standing over him, I drew my fist and punched again, and then again. The cuts on his face opened once again, his royal blood dripping onto the royal tiles. I didn't let up. I kept punching. I was screaming, too; a wordless cry of pain and rage and a whole lot of other things I couldn't keep track of as all the feelings in me poured out in that moment and manifested themselves repeatedly against the King's nose.

I felt hands on my shoulders, dragging me away. I grabbed one and twisted it savagely till I heard something crack, spun around and broke the soldier's nose. More came at me, trying to calm me; I wanted them to come. I wanted to hit something, feel the impact under my fists.

My Skill was still with me, and I threw them off as they came, and out of the corner of my eye I saw the King sit up and cradle his broken nose. My Weapon winked at me, forgotten on the floor. I ran, picked it up and spun around.

The soldiers receded at once, pale with fear. I wasn't interested in them, or in the King.

It was Eduud I wanted.

I roared and ran at him, blade high. No one was foolish enough to interfere, and he hovered there, not even bothering to move as I closed the distance between us like a stampeding bull.

I swung at him, but the blade passed right through his robes, coming out on the other side like he was no more than mist. I howled and swung again. Nothing happened.

"Think not that thou art the first to strike me," Eduud said. His voice wasn't accusing, or even angry. He was just stating a fact. To him, it was all this was. Fact.

I dropped the Weapon and sank onto my knees. I was spent. There was nothing in me anymore, nothing I could fight for. I wanted to curl up in a ball and let it all go away, for them to ignore me. But even that was denied me.

"I can't imagine what you're going through now," Zaahis said thickly, his hands pressed against his nose as he limped up to me again. "I never knew you had a wife."

"It was all a lie," I moaned. "You used me. You took her, you took my life from me, you led me on… you *lied*. All along. Have you no shame?"

I looked up at Eduud. "I lost her the moment you brought me here. And I'm not the only one you did this to. You bring Champions here all the time, ripping them from their families and their lives. And for what? To fight your battles for you?"

"The Law will be obeyed," Eduud replied.

"Have you no heart?" I whispered.

"Guardian of the Law, I am," he said. "The Law I serveth, and nothing more."

Frank had been right, I realized. Eduud was nothing more than a machine, programmed to do what it was supposed to and nothing more than that.

I choked on a sob.

"I'm sorry, Alan," Zaahis said again. "I truly am."

I hung my head and let the hot tears flow.

"How do you know?" I whispered. "How do you know they don't go back to when they come from?"

"Tis the Law," Eduud replied.

"WHY?" I roared, "WHY would you DO that?!"

"I offer thee thy Second Choice, Champion," Eduud boomed. "Return to thine home, to times unknown. Or remain, and beith a Mentor for Champions for the trials that layeth ahead."

I glared at him through blurred eyes.

"So *there's* why they didn't go back," I whispered. "The ones who stayed. You took what they had. You made it so they couldn't help but stay, because they had nothing to return to."

"You're the last Champion," Zaahis said, slowly. "Another Tyrant *will* rise. Be it ten years from now or a century, we will need another Champion to face him. That Champion will need a Mentor, Alan."

I stood slowly, my fists clenched.

"And help you do to others what you did to me?" I demanded.

"What's done is done," he said. "And as much as it pains me to say this, Alan… there is nothing for you where you came from. Here, you are a hero. You will be honored, and you will live for centuries. Your time back home was over the moment you were brought here, my friend."

"Keep talking," I swore, "And I swear you won't stand up again by the time I'm done with you."

It wasn't a vacant threat, and we both knew it. Zaahis backed away, hands raised.

"You *used* me," I spat. "You used me to do what you were too cowardly to do yourselves."

"It's the Law…" Zaahis insisted.

"Your Laws are just *shackles* you've made to bolt yourself to the wall!" I exclaimed, my voice breaking, "You said *only* the Champion could have killed Frank. I didn't kill him, Zaahis. *Laehn* did. *Laehn* shot the arrows and ended his life. If he hadn't, I would have died. Explain THAT."

"He *helped…*"

"Your Laws are redundant!" I roared. "Fight your OWN battles! Deal with your OWN problems! Leave ME and my people OUT of it!"

I stabbed my finger at Eduud.

"Send me back," I snarled, "I've done what you wanted me to do. Now keep the promise Bass made me - if you have the honor to do such a thing. Send me back. NOW!"

"She's DEAD, Alan," Zaahis exclaimed. "She's GONE. There's NOTHING for you to go back to."

"I'll try my luck, then!" I yelled. "I'll try HOPING. Now SEND. ME. HOME, or so help me, I will slaughter you where you stand along with everyone else in here!"

"You don't mean it," Zaahis whispered, aghast.

I bent and picked up the Weapon. It glinted in my hands, and Zaahis swallowed.

"Try me," I said.

Eduud didn't respond at first. Just as I was about to shout again, he glided past me, a cold, heartless wraith of a creature. The soldiers shuffled away, clearing a wider space around the three of us, frightened and yet curious to see what would happen next.

They didn't care, either way. Like sheep, they took what came, and it was enough for them.

Eduud stopped twenty feet away and slowly turned to face us. He raised his hands, and his green robes began to glow. The halo brightened, a bright, blinding yellow light that poured out of him in waves. A marble sized ball of the same light began to pulse in the center of the space between us.

It grew larger as I stared, throbbed, and then exploded into blinding, shifting color. A sharp sting of ozone made my eyes water, and when the light dimmed, there was a three foot long ring of pulsating, sparking light on the floor, the colors spinning and shifting as we watched.

"You do not have to do this," Zaahis spoke up again. "Alan… we need you."

I ignored him. The Weapon still in my hands, I strode forward. Wind whipped up from within the inside of the portal, blowing my hair back and making my towel flap.

"Do YOU, Champion…" Eduud began, but I didn't wait for him to finish.

I stepped into the circle of light, the blinding colors forcing me to screw my eyes shut as I did. My foot sank through nothingness where the ground should have been.

I closed my eyes and gave into the light.

And I fell.

Epilogue

"You sure you want to do this?"

He smiled.

"Yeah," he said, "I am."

She pressed her lips together and nodded. He loved it when she did that, especially since it only ever happened when he was about to do something that would worry her.

"And you're sure you don't want me to pick you up?" she insisted.

He reached for her hand and squeezed it.

"I'm sure."

She squeezed back, and her eyes followed him as he opened the door and stepped out. He looked at her again as he turned to close the door, both arms on the wheel, her pink hair pulled into a ponytail just the way she knew he liked it.

"Hey, I'll be fine," he said, "Get going."

"Call you tonight," she said.

"Love you," he replied.

She blew him a kiss, and he stepped away as the window silently rolled up. She pulled out of the parking space, and he watched as the car spun around. She honked once, and he raised his arm in reply before she drove away.

The car disappeared round the corner down the street, and once it had gone, he turned to the rusted metal gates. They, along with the wrought iron fence that went with them had become all too familiar over the recent years.

Jaw clenched, he slung his backpack over his shoulder and pushed the gates open.

The graveyard was a quiet place at the best of times. Very few people came here, if at all; these days, the living didn't seem to want all that much to do with the dead.

It was a winding route he had to take, past gravestones both old and new. The first few trips down the path had been confusing, but over time he had grown used to it, his feet taking him where he had to go without him having to think about it too much.

As he passed, he read out the names on the tombstones, a habit he'd grown accustomed to. A fresh stone caught his eye, a new grave he knew he hadn't seen two weeks ago when he was here last. He paused in respect before continuing on.

He'd rarely seen people here, other than the random mourners who popped up less than occasionally. He hadn't been expecting to see anyone that day, though, so it was a surprise when he turned the corner past the old oak tree and saw the man the seated on the flat, wooden block.

The stranger couldn't have been older than thirty, and yet from this distance, the dirty, graying black beard and the knotted, tangled hair falling over his stooped shoulders aged him considerably. A faded old baseball cap was jammed over his head, the peeling peak throwing a shadow over his face. The faded jacket hanging off him was coated with grime, and the ripped jeans looked like they hadn't been through the washer in weeks.

It was as if he was trying to advertise just how homeless he was, sitting forlorn there, eyes on the gravestone. It didn't look like he was reading; rather, the stranger had the countenance of a man staring into the distance, nothing but memories keeping him company.

The watcher shrugged his shoulders and walked up to the stranger, who heard his footsteps and turned his head. What bit of face was visible over the matted beard was creased and drawn, as if it had been deprived of a week's worth of much needed sleep. It showed in the dull brown eyes, sunk as they were into their sockets.

This was the kind of hobo mothers tell their kids to run away from, the man thought wryly. There didn't seem to be too much danger of this one having the energy to run him through with a knife, though, so he kept walking.

"Hey," he said, not wanting to be rude.

"Hello," the stranger replied. His eyes ran up and down in appraisal.

The former nodded at the tombstone, "You knew her?"

The latter followed his gaze back to it.

"Once," he admitted, his voice calling to mind gravel on a blackboard, "A long, long time ago."

The other bent down and rolled a sizable rock towards the grave, and positioned it so it faced the stranger on the opposite side of the mound. He sat down and slung the bag off.

"You're new," he said, for want of conversation, "I can't say I remember seeing you around here."

The stranger gave him a slow nod.

"I'm from… out of town, you could say."

"When did you get back?"

He drew in a labored breath and blew it out in a sigh.

"A week ago," he replied, "I suppose."

The other ran a thumb lightly over the bag's strap, slightly annoyed. Company was the last thing he'd been expecting, and the unforeseen guest didn't seem to be interested in leaving any time soon.

"Was she anyone to you?" he asked, breaking the silence.

The stranger didn't reply for a while. The other pondered whether or not to pose the question again, but just as he opened his mouth, the stranger sighed.

"We were close… a long time ago," he said, "We… parted ways. Didn't know that…"

He broke off.

The other raised an eyebrow.

"She never mentioned..." he began, but then seemed to think better of it. He shrugged, and then pulled the bag onto his lap and unzipped it.

The flowers were a bit crushed, he noticed ruefully, but still fresh enough. He carefully reached past it and pulled out the cardboard box, then set the bag on the ground.

The stranger's eyes shifted to him as he opened it, the aroma of chocolate icing too hard to ignore. The younger man looked into the small box and paused, considering. A moment later, he shrugged again and held out the box.

The stranger looked at the two slices of chocolate cake inside, and then up at the other, reasonably confused.

"Go on," he said, "Have one."

Carefully, hesitantly, the stranger selected a piece, and the younger man took the other, crumpled up the box and shoved it into the bag.

"Thank you," the stranger said, his voice quiet.

The other smiled and took a bite.

The two ate in silence. After a couple of minutes, the younger man reached into the bag again and pulled out a bottle. He popped the cap open, drank a mouthful, and held it out to the stranger, who hesitated once more before accepting.

"You do this... often?" he asked, puzzled, "Share your food and drink with random people in the middle of a graveyard?"

"It's my birthday," the other replied, gesturing at the cake, "And, well, she and I always used to have chocolate cake, and we've never missed a birthday since."

He jerked his head at the tombstone. The stranger ran his eyes over him again, then nodded.

"Your mother?"

The man smiled sadly and nodded.

"And this?" the stranger asked, shaking the bottle.

The other chuckled mirthlessly.

"That… well, that began three years ago," he said, "The first time I… the first time I did this here. You're actually sitting in my spot, by the way."

The stranger's eyes widened, and he made to stand up.

"No, wait. It's okay," the man said, raising his hand, "It's fine."

The stranger sat down again and looked at the bottle. He sighed and raised it up, letting the drink flow without the bottle touching his lips.

He handed it back, and the other took another gulp.

"What do you do with the extra piece if there's no one else around?"

The other shrugged, "I leave it on the stone."

The stranger nodded.

"Usually, I talk a bit to her. You know. Tell her what's going on with me since I visited last. Call it stupid sentiment, like everyone else…"

"No, no," the stranger sighed. "I understand."

He looked down at the tombstone for the umpteenth time.

"How… how did she…?"

His voice cracked, and he trailed off.

The other leaned forward and looked at the stone, toying with the bottle in his hands.

"Long time coming, to be honest," he said. "She was always depressed. Had to do with Dad leaving before I was born, mostly…"

He sighed.

The stranger licked his lips before speaking.

"I'm sorry,"

He shrugged. "Wasn't anyone's fault but his. Grandma used to blame him for running away and leaving us, but Ma would never hear of it. She was convinced he'd been kidnapped or something. Neither of them ever told me the story."

The stranger hung his head, his eyes closed.

"She tried her· best," the other continued. "I wasn't an easy kid to raise, I'll admit. Especially for a single mother. But she was and always will be amazing."

He smiled, shook his head and sighed, "Damn, I miss her."

"Aye," the stranger said softly.

They passed the bottle around again.

"Grandma hated him for leaving," the younger man chuckled.

The stranger watched him as he took another swig. "And you?" he asked, "How do you feel about him?"

"I dunno," the man replied, "I mean, where has the guy been for the last twenty years? Alright, so he left, but why didn't he even bother to visit, or... or write?"

He clenched his fist and closed his eyes. Wordlessly, he held out the bottle, and the stranger accepted it after a pause.

"Do you suppose he's still out there?" he asked, the bottle shaking slightly in his grasp.

The man shrugged.

"Maybe. Who knows?" he sighed, "I'm doing okay. I have a job, a girl, plans to make it through college. Ma gave me everything she couldn't get for herself. If he'd only been there, though..."

They fell into silence. The man glanced at the stranger.

"So," he said, "Do you have a name?"

The stranger coughed.

"Al," he replied after a long pause.

"Like... Alan?"

He paused some more before he spoke.

"Yes," he said, "Something like that."

"Good to meet you, Al,"

"And you," he said.

The younger man took the bottle and drained the last out of it. He stowed it inside the bag, then dusted his hands and looked up at the darkening sky.

It was getting late, and he had already spent more time than he had intended to.

He reached into the bag for the last time and pulled out the bouquet. Straightening some of the flowers, he stood and then knelt before the foot of the gravestone.

He read the epitaph again, like he always did, every time

Ramona Peggy Daele
Loving mother and wife.
1969 - 2011

Al's sunken eyes followed him as he laid the bouquet down at the base of the tombstone and bowed his head. Minutes passed in silence until he stood again, brushed his knees, and slung the backpack over his shoulder in one smooth movement, as if anxious to leave this place

"It's getting late," he said, turning to Al. "I have to get going."

Al nodded. "Thank you for the cake."

"A pleasure," he replied. He hesitated for second, and then extended his hand.

The stranger reached out, his own hand trembling. They gripped for a few seconds, and then let go, the younger man trying not to react to the feel of grime on his palm. He nodded again, and then walked away.

He'd gone a few paces down before he heard Al cough behind him and the wooden block scrape on the stone pavement. He stopped and turned around.

Al was standing, hands in his pockets, a strange expression on his face.

"I... I didn't wish you," he called, and cleared his throat. "Ha...happy birthday. ... Son."

The younger man flashed him a grin. "Thanks, Al. See you around."

A smile lit Al's face up, instantly casting decades off the grimy, crinkled face.

"See you around," he said, his chin quivering. He slowly turned and walked away down the path. The younger man stood and watched him go, brushing his hand against the side of his jeans as the stranger finally disappeared around the bend.

He looked back up at the sky, and then kept walking.